Praise for *Matadora*
"Readers, like those tens of thousands that used to fill bullfighting arenas from South America to the Iberian Peninsula, will find themselves absolutely unable to look away. This searing, sensual novel is an adventure not to be missed."
— *The Globe and Mail*

"Luna must be counted among the most vital and alluring of Canada's literary heroines. She simply enthralls."
— *National Post*

Praise for *Smoke*
"Ruth is so full of vitality, so drawn to so many things simultaneously, so alive, reading her is always likely to be more of a D.H. Lawrence rollercoaster than a Virginia Woolf Ferris wheel. Ruth is utterly compelling."
— *The Globe and Mail*

Praise for *Ten Good Seconds of Silence*
"Elizabeth Ruth's prose bursts with colour and metaphor."
— Camilla Gibb, author of *The Relatives*

SEMI-
DETACHED

Elizabeth Ruth

Cormorant Books

 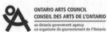

We acknowledge financial support for our publishing activities: the Government
of Canada, through the Canada Book Fund and The Canada Council for the Arts;
the Government of Ontario, through the Ontario Arts Council, Ontario Creates,
and the Ontario Book Publishing Tax Credit. We acknowledge additional funding
provided by the Government of Ontario and the Ontario Arts Council to address
the adverse effects of the novel coronavirus pandemic.

LIBRARY AND ARCHIVES CANADA CATALOGUING IN PUBLICATION

Title: Semi-detached : a novel / Elizabeth Ruth.
Names: Ruth, Elizabeth, author.
Identifiers: Canadiana (print) 20230215769 | Canadiana (ebook) 20230215874 |
ISBN 9781770867130 (softcover) | ISBN 9781770867147 (HTML)
Classification: LCC PS8585.U847 S46 2023 | DDC C813/.6—dc23

United States Library of Congress Control Number: 2023934983

Cover design: Shannon Olliffe
Interior text design: Marijke Friesen
Manufactured by Houghton Boston in Saskatoon,
Saskatchewan in July, 2023.

Printed using paper from a responsible and sustainable resource,
including a mix of virgin fibres and recycled materials.

Printed and bound in Canada.

CORMORANT BOOKS INC.
260 ISHPADINAA (SPADINA) AVENUE, SUITE 502,
TKARONTO (TORONTO), ON M5T 2E4

www.cormorantbooks.com

For CC, ERC, SO
&
my dearest, Violet.

And, for the homeless youth of Toronto.
Someone somewhere believes in you.

Having one foot in one world, and the other in the real one. For me, endings are never really endings ...
— Carol Shields, interview with Barbara Ellen in *The Guardian*, April 28, 2002

December 20, 2013
7:44 a.m.

IN AN ORDINARY city, full of extraordinary moments, a girl stands outside the Brickyard Bistro, at the intersection of Gerrard and Greenwood, cradling a puppy inside an oversized white coat. Her eyes are closed. A howling wind swirls, unwrapping her from a snowy cocoon, delivering her from one storm into another. She sucks in a wintry chill but feels no air enter her lungs. She opens her eyes. A beguiling white powder spreads out in all directions, and she scans around for anything familiar. There is nothing, no storefronts, not the curve of road nor the slant of light cutting across rooftops. Not even the air tastes as it should. Panic pushes through her ice-kissed veins. The last thing she remembers she'd been running through the whiteout. And after that? She looks to the sky, God's most reliable witness, but a foggy veil offers no comfort. She hugs the puppy closer. The wind stills, silence descends, and in that space between life and death where time collapses, and anything is possible, she steps out onto the deserted, glistening road. Before she knows it, she has crossed.

THE STORM WAS swift and brilliant, and it hardened the city to a new fate. Ice coated hydro wires and the treetops, painting a brittle glass sky. Frozen crystals glittered and crackled underfoot. Every slick surface shone a cold sterling, every home and school and office tower sparkled in the morning light.

Carlaw was a river of glass. When Laura pressed on the gas pedal, her back end skidded out, and she had to pump the brake to stop. Remarkably, her Beemer wasn't the only car on the road. A slow-moving chain had formed behind her — two grey sedans, a black SUV, and a tiny blue-and-white two-seater. Together they stuttered south. She marvelled as drops of cold, clear water fell, tears against her windshield. Was it a sign? She'd been waiting for something to drop into her life and break it open. It wasn't that she didn't love Cat. She did. But love can be a vacant house, empty for a long time before anyone notices.

At Gerrard the streetcar tracks looked treacherous. Not wanting to risk an accident, she pulled up to the restaurant across from the small dog park. It wouldn't be far on foot, at the most a ten-minute walk to the east.

She stepped cautiously and by the time she'd crossed Jones, she was making her way through a white flurry, covered in a shroud of snow. An old woman, hunched and paralyzed on one side of her body, was trying to drag her bundle buggy along the road. Empty bottles clinked and crashed. An orange tabby darted out from between two parked cars, and back again.

Rounding the corner at Condor, Laura spotted the house. A charming white wood frame with green trim, this was a home her artsy clients would covet. Located in the centre of the city, close to public transit, it was neither a cookie-cutter semi nor one of the glorified hallways people called condominiums. From outside, number two was innocuous and gave no hint of having been vacant for six months. The snowy façade was reassuring, something about the way the glass in the old front windows caught the light in waves. The windows were eyes, peering out while at the same time taking her in. She made her way up the walk when she heard a voice.

"What are you doing here?"

Laura spun around. The question was so faint and far away she almost wasn't sure she'd heard it. A figure came into view. A girl bundled into a vintage coat — winter white — with an ivory velvet collar and four large gold buttons up the front. Her face was pale, alarmingly so. She had a slight frame but carried herself with confidence. *How old was she? Sixteen, seventeen maybe?* Her skin gave off a translucent sheen, as if she were bloodless or malnourished. Laura couldn't pull her gaze away.

"Well?" the girl pressed. The corners of her mouth curled upward when she spoke, not a smile exactly, an invitation.

"This place is going on the market," said Laura. "I'm the agent."

"Where is the woman who lives here?"

Laura shrugged, avoiding an answer. Something was sniffing the ground at her feet. A puppy. "Is that your dog?" she asked, taking a step back.

The girl bent down and lifted the Scottish terrier into her arms. "We've been out here a while." Her tone was matter of fact, her expression neutral. Laura noted the green of her eyes and a string of star tattoos cascading down the side of her face. "Does your family know you're skipping school?"

The girl tugged an army surplus bag higher up on one shoulder and tucked the puppy into the front of her coat. "I have no family," she said.

Laura was about to contradict her. Everyone had a family, although she knew that wasn't the case. There were overseas orphanages filled with unclaimed babies, local children apprehended by social services. Her best friend, Beth, worked at a shelter and had shared story after story of kids whose families had kicked them out of the house or driven them out with years of violence. Some of them ended up working the streets. Was this girl one of them? "Do you have a name?" Laura asked.

"I changed it. You can call me Astrid."

Astrid. The name was sharp, jagged. It suggested stars and swords and spears and courage, someone who could take care of herself. But could she, really?

"I'm Laura," she said.

"Invite me in, Laura."

She squinted to find the girl's eyes. Maybe she was a meth addict? Lots of kids on the street used. What if Astrid mugged her? She could have thug friends waiting around the corner. "I can't do that," Laura said, climbing the front steps.

"You could if you wanted to."

Laura's chest tightened, guilt pressing down on her, a heavy wet wool blanket. The temperature hadn't yet dropped low enough for emergency warming centres to have opened. "Can I call someone for you? A friend, maybe?"

Astrid stepped forward. "I bet the owner would let us in."

Laura fumbled in her bag with frozen fingers, slipped her key into the lock. The owner was in a stroke-induced coma, which was why the Office of the Public Guardian and Trustee had hired her to deal with the house. There was no outstanding mortgage, no will or next of kin, and the property taxes were long overdue. "Sorry I can't be more help," she said, pressing the front door open and ducking inside. She locked the door quickly, shutting out winter, along with the girl and the puppy.

Relieved to be safely indoors, Laura unzipped her black parka and felt the furnace inside her chest ignite. Ten years in residential real estate and she'd not lost the sense of anticipation upon first entering a house. A front door was a threshold to a new, undiscovered world, the small and secret intimacies people wall up over a lifetime. She removed her wet boots and set them by the door. "Hello?" she called out. "Anybody here?" Nothing except the howl of wind pressing in around the door frame at her back.

Every house makes a first impression and it's not about paint colour or artwork hanging on the walls; a house has a soul, a personality. From outside, with blue-white snow as backdrop, the property had seemed tranquil, ordinary. Inside it was melancholic. One foot down and she was flooded with a palpable mix of regret and longing. She stepped into the small living room and the smell of cigarette smoke hit her. The hardwood beneath her socked feet was warped and worn to the nails. She drew the plain cotton curtains expecting to find Astrid gone, yet there she was, in the front yard, watching the house. The puppy spun circles around her legs. Just then, Astrid lifted her hand to wave and Laura waved too, before she thought to stop herself. She backed away from the window and let the curtains fall once more. Don't engage, she thought, they'll leave eventually.

The living room wallpaper was a muted blue with pink-and-white water lilies and grey cranes. A collapsible puzzle table stood in front of a faux fireplace with a peacock fan grate. Laura ran her palm along the arm of the couch and noticed a bit of cat hair. Nothing a lint roller couldn't take care of. The green slipcover matched the upholstered chair and the fringed shade on the lamp that stood behind it. Beside the chair was a magazine rack holding a dusty copy of the *Toronto Star Weekly* and a 1944 edition of the Canadian Bowling Association handbook. A pastoral oil painting hung over the fireplace and on the mantel sat a deck of playing cards and

two board games, one with an intriguing title, The Merry Game of
Fibber McGee and the Wistful Vista Mystery. The other was a time-
worn edition of Monopoly. An open phonograph stood against one
wall. Laura moved closer and found a 78 of Frank Sinatra's "I'll Be
Seeing You" on the turntable.

Wow. Someone had wanted to cling to the past! It was as if
she'd stepped into a time capsule, and decades had not advanced.
She pulled a pen and a small red notebook from her bag and began
jotting down details for the estate sale and to use later in preparing
feature sheets for the listing:

> Dining room, standard for the time.
> A Duncan Phyfe table. (Reproduction?)
> Four lyre back chairs. Need reupholstering.
> Small buffet and china cabinet.

A wooden tea cart stood near the entrance to the kitchen. On
it, a Brown Betty and two white bone china cups and saucers, their
rims decorated with gold. Only one of the flared cups bore the stain
of black tea marking its centre. Laura lifted it to her nose, sniffed.
Earl Grey and English lavender. Her mom's favourite. Marilyn used
to say a good cup of tea could fix most of life's problems. All at
once Laura felt a rush of ambivalence about how she'd handled the
girl with the dog. What if Astrid really needed help? She fiddled
with the chain of her mom's necklace, worrying the Star of David
pendant between her thumb and forefinger. When had she become
so wary and mistrustful of other people? They'll be fine, she told
herself. She was just overthinking it.

Wax flower arrangements coated in dust … cobwebs and dead
flies in the windowsill … stacks of newsprint piled beneath the
window … a French copper chandelier. She wrote that down. Some
clients enjoyed a vintage touch. She'd seen one like it in the Paris

hotel where she and Cat had stayed on their honeymoon. From their balcony in Montmartre, they'd had a clear view of Sacré-Cœur. How it had gleamed, a white beacon of hope under the new moon; she'd felt anything was possible back then. *Sacred Hearts*, she thought, adding to the translation. She'd expected to feel that way forever.

The kitchen was large; it held an old icebox, a full-sized refrigerator, and a gleaming modern electric stove. The robin's egg blue paper that covered the wainscotting was worn and peeling and needed to be removed; the entire space would have to be painted. Laura tapped her pen on the countertop. Improvements could easily snowball: a clean paint job would make the tired cupboard doors look as though they need replacing. The countertop would stand out. At the most, she'd pay for a coat of paint and some staging. The real question was, what type of buyer would appreciate this home? She corrected herself: in many ways a house chooses its inhabitants, not the other way around. A good agent knows that.

She climbed the staircase to the second floor and for some strange reason felt she was trespassing, as if by going upstairs she was breaking an invisible seal. What if the homeowner woke from her coma to learn her home had already sold? Was it ethical to list while an owner was still alive? Her contact at the Trustee's office had told her the coma was irreversible, and funds from the sale of the house would be put toward the owner's debts. Whatever was left would go to the government. She doodled an *S* in her notebook and added two vertical lines, a dollar sign. Sad as it was to think about the situation, it was time to sell. If a realtor was going to be paid to represent the house, that might as well be her.

Three black-and-white photographs hung along the ascending wall — a wedding party, with the bride in a Juliet cap veil and the groom in his World War I service dress, and an oval frame with a posed shot of a new mother holding an infant in a christening gown, the stern-looking face of the mother staring out at her, almost reproachfully. Laura stiffened. At forty, was she still young enough, healthy enough, deserving enough to be somebody's mother?

The last picture was of workers posing in overalls in front of a sign that read: Armstrong Brick Work. She scribbled in her notebook. The area stretching between Leslieville and the Pocket had a rich history that buyers might find interesting; much of it centred on brickmaking and wartime victory gardens. Given that it was winter, she'd need a good strategy for selling this place. Better not hold offers to a particular date, she thought. That way she could list at a higher price.

On the second-floor landing there hung a large black-and-white photograph of a women's five-pin bowling team, the Toronto City Majors. The back row of girls stood hip to hip with their arms slung loosely across each other's shoulders, the front row kneeling with bowling bags in front of them — bobby soxers who looked no older than twenty-five. Each girl appeared to be jubilant, triumphant. Laura lingered on their faces for signs of what, she did not know. A clue as to how to be happy? Evidence that happiness had ever been possible.

She felt a warm, buzzing sensation as her fingers met the dusty wood of the frame. She traced the outline of one girl's bright eyes with her finger. When she was not much older, her mother had been diagnosed with early-onset Alzheimer's; they didn't know how rapidly the disease would progress and Laura hadn't yet given up her internship cataloguing artefacts at the ROM. Now, years later, her mother was gone, and *tick-tock, tick-tock*, she was still trying in vain to get pregnant. Don't be so sentimental, she thought, withdrawing her hand.

In the bathroom, she jotted notes on the original claw-foot tub with its worn enamel. That would need to be reglazed. The white toilet and sink were stained yellow. The towels were frayed. She peeked into the small bedroom and then entered the larger master suite. On the floor, in one corner, sat two bowling ball cases, one made of tan leather and the other white with red piping. The leather was cracked with age, like an old woman's face. There were no closets. A large dresser with a dozen drawers lined one wall. On top sat a mantel clock. She ran her palm across the top of its smooth, curved surface, came away with a handful of dust. Sneezed.

She'd viewed hundreds, maybe thousands of properties before today and none of them had managed to preserve, in such detail and dust, the lives that had once been so vital there; she felt as if the owner could walk through the front door at any moment. Laura shivered at the thought, but she could hear no creaking floors, no shallow breath. She was definitely alone and yet, curiously, she didn't feel that way.

In the dresser she found folded collared shirts and pants, neckties and handkerchiefs, socks and underwear. In a small drawer sat two black ring boxes. The first was empty. Just the white satin cushion where a ring should've been. When she pried open the top of the second box, she found a rose gold wedding band. Her chest tightened. She plucked the ring out of the box and gooseflesh prickled up her arm. Holding it to the white light of the window, she squinted to make out the inscription: "Annie and Eddie. December 1944." The ring was smooth and cool to the touch. It gave off a slightly pinkish-purple hue. She clasped her hand around it and craned her neck in the direction of the hall and the bowling team. Which one of you did this belong to?

Suddenly she was tired, bone-weary, the sort of exhaustion that comes on in a flash after exposure to the cold or a profound loss. The decrepit three-quarter spool bed looked oddly inviting. Instead, she threw herself into the tufted mustard yellow chair beside it. A glider. The arms were threadbare, the springs, useless. She rocked backwards, sank deeper into the cushion's uneasy embrace, and felt her body mould to the shape of the person who'd last sat there.

1944

EDNA FERGUSON WAS rocking, hard and fast, back and forth like a mechanical toy. What had just happened? She glanced at the man lying dead at the foot of her bed, one side of his head smashed in, blood pooling around him like a crimson cloak. What was she going to do now? Her body was a tremor, her hands clenched to fists. The room stank of whiskey. It was hard to catch a breath. *Focus*, she thought. *You need a plan.* Footsteps raced past her, down the stairs, and through the first floor of the house. Out the bedroom window a dark sky churned, and sleet soaked the pane of glass. The electric lights of a lit Christmas tree twinkled through the neighbour's window. Downstairs, the front door opened and slammed shut. She stopped rocking. "Annie," she whispered. "Annie, come back!"

LAURA WOKE IN the rocking chair groggy and disoriented, with a crick in her neck. She gave her head a good shake. It had been years since she'd had such a vivid dream. She peered across the room; of course there was no dead body, no blood anywhere. How long had she been asleep? She checked her watch and it had stopped, as if time had become irrelevant, a thing that could be halted, reversed, something that could cease to exist, and if not for the insistent buzzing of her smart phone, she might've never woken. Cat was calling. She didn't pick up.

Outside, the crisp air was polished to silver as it rolled down into her lungs. Lights adorned the houses and shrubs, setting the neighbourhood aglow in red and green and gold, the tacky, joyful radiance of Christmas. She placed the house key in the lockbox and set off for her car, eyes trained on a power line overhead. A soft blue moon was already pushing through the clouds and she felt its diffuse light on her face. Her phone rang again and this time she answered. Cat sounded frantic. "Where the hell are you?! I've been calling for hours!" Laura had missed their anniversary date. They'd agreed on a late lunch together and the beef locro Cat had prepared now sat cold in a soup tureen.

"Shit." Laura tripped over a snowbank stepping into the road where there was more traction. "I'm sorry," she said. "I fell asleep at the Condor house."

"Jesus." Cat's Argentine accent, barely noticeable anymore, was more pronounced over the phone.

"I'm on my way now," she said.

11

"That's it? Just, sorry and I'll be home soon? I was getting ready to call the fucking police! Jesus!" Cat repeated, and then she hung up.

Laura hung up, with a sinking feeling in her stomach. How had she slept through their anniversary? Her mother would've called that a bad omen, and maybe it was. The cool metal of the rose gold band she'd pinched from the house was nudging up against her own ring. She admired her left hand, the shiny 18-karat talisman that Cat had confidently pushed over her knuckle ten years ago in front of the officiant and their loved ones; the ring's magic had lain in its covenant with the future. Now she removed it and admired her hand with only the rose gold band on her finger. *It suits me*, she thought, stacking the rings once more.

She passed a stately red-brick home with a wooden toboggan on the front porch. A cyclist in reflective riding gear and a Santa hat pedaled slowly past her through dirty white sludge, panting with the effort. An suv ripped down the seam of road leaving tire tracks, parallel white zippers, in its wake.

Laura felt the muscles in her neck and shoulders tense. It had been five years of fertility treatments, less than a month since Cat had told her she wanted them to stop trying, two weeks since she'd gone against Cat's wishes and secretly started a new cycle of gonadotropin injections. So what? Cat may have given up, but as long as there was the slightest chance, the faintest hope, even a thread of love, she'd hold on to that.

She set off trudging through two feet of snow as the white stuff came down in pellets and left sharp pinpricks on her hot cheeks. She decided to leave her car where she'd parked it and head straight home on foot. How long would this storm last? She and Cat had booked a ten-day stay in Buenos Aires for after the holidays. Would their flight be cancelled? What if flying interfered with her cycle? She should probably rebook.

"Laura, hey!" She looked up and Toby, a former client and member of her book club, was standing in the driveway of a four-bedroom Edwardian. She was struggling to collapse a lime green stroller and lift it into the hatch of her minivan.

A small sound escaped Laura's lips. They hadn't seen each other since Toby had had the baby. Laura reached for the stroller's base to help.

"Here, let me."

"Isn't this surreal?"

The van, advertising Toby's florist business, was parked with its sliding door ajar. Laura glanced inside. An infant was strapped into a car seat beside a diaper bag and a small blue suitcase. Laura's chest tightened. She stared at the child swaddled in a sheepskin bunting bag. A moony little face peeked out, eyes blinking.

"That's Jackson. He's six weeks old today."

Laura tucked her gloved hands under her armpits for warmth. I bet it happened by accident, she thought spitefully, and it all rushed up again, like the dangerous, unseen bulk of an iceberg: the incredible debt she and Cat had accumulated paying for donor sperm and IVF, the trips they might've taken instead. She thought of the other undiscovered dreams, secondary for so long, that had never had a chance to materialize. "Congratulations," she said. "He's adorable."

"Thanks," said Toby. "Our pipes burst so we're going over to my parents'."

Laura's eyes followed the curve of the road, leading away from a cutting desolation. There'd been too many missed opportunities, stunted and miswoven cells, futures undone. Too many babies not yet wished into being. The hundred-year-old Norway spruce fronting the property seemed too weighted down with ice. What had once been solid, straight, and sturdy was now bent to the point of breaking.

Ravina Crescent was the most charming street in the neighbourhood, even more so at this time of the year. McCeckran Real Estate had developed the area in the 1920s and tried to sell it as the "Rosedale of the East." It had worked. The rich flocked there, until 1935 when Harper's Dump went in where the brickyards had been.

"Hey, remember that wasted space under my staircase?" Toby adjusted her son in his car seat. "I've turned it into a meditation spot."

Laura forced a smile. Meditation and massage, hot yoga and the weekly mani-pedi, these were the latest panaceas for the restless middle-class mother. Lately, it seemed so many of the other white women in the neighbourhood were spending money to "get grounded," "be mindful," or "slow the pace of life." She couldn't help thinking it was ironic that people who already had so much would indulge themselves further. Was she any different? If it hadn't been for her infertility, she too might've become another privileged "wife" with a nanny. Toby was one of them now — designer stroller, inflated lifestyle, big mortgage. Next thing, she'd be renovating her kitchen.

"I'm glad you're happy with the house," Laura said, feeling a twinge of guilt for being so judgemental. There was nothing new about trying to buy happiness. She knew from experience; she and Cat had spent $50,000 on sperm from a cryobank, $75,000 on fertility hormones, cycle monitoring, and IVF and had nothing to show for any of it. She should've started trying to conceive years earlier. She should've noticed when Cat stopped making regular eye contact.

"Nice running into you," she said.

"See you at next book club."

Laura's phone buzzed — a text from the office about a package of business cards she'd been waiting for. She nodded and waved goodbye to Toby, knowing what she'd already known; love was made brittle by the kind of pressure her relationship had been under, even the most passionate love. It cracks, fissures, vanishes into a cool mist.

EDDIE ROLLED THE man's body in a thick tarp she'd grabbed from the basement and heaved him down the staircase. Gravity helped with the weight, but once she'd hauled him across the dining room, into the kitchen, and out the back door, her muscles were aching and ready to give. Gale-force winds sent snowdrifts across the yard, obscuring visibility. Her clothes were wet; she was as soaked with sweat as she ever got pulling bricks out of the fiery kilns at work. There was no stopping, though. The shock had worn off.

She propped the body against her Dodge pickup and struggled to hoist it onto the floor of the truck. A driving wind knocked her back twice, then finally it was in. She moved with purpose, automatically, like someone else was making the decisions. It was her, hard as it was to believe. Twenty-five-year-old Edna Ferguson, originally of Hamilton. Daughter of Walter and Margaret, sister of Henry. Brick maker, puzzler, and two-time Regional Champion for the Toronto Women's Bowling League. Average in every way.

What would her parents think if they saw her now? Henry? He'd never been known to back down from a fight, if a fight was required, but he wouldn't defend her in this. And yet, until today, she'd not once regretted moving to the big city or bucking tradition. She'd woken each morning happy enough, was in love for the first time. The future seemed to have cracked open with radio reports that Allied forces were making gains overseas. Hitler had left his headquarters in Rastenburg for Berlin. French troops had liberated Strasbourg. At breakfast just this morning, the *Toronto Daily Star* headline declared, "Whole City Stopped As If By Giant Hand." Now, mere hours later, she was disposing of a body. Eddie reckoned that the hand descending upon the city, smothering it in ice, was the hand of God that had carried Annie away and would soon be coming after her soul.

Blood had soaked through the tarp and stained the snow purplish pink, a detail she wouldn't notice until sun-up. When the body was locked in the back of the pickup, she returned to the house and used a dozen rags, all of her towels, and the tin of turpentine she kept in a root beer crate to scour all traces of blood. She worked backwards, from the kitchen door through the dining room and hallway to the staircase, then up to the second floor. When she was certain she'd left no evidence, she turned her attention to the weapon.

Lifting the five-pin ball up before her face, she examined it for splatters of blood she may have missed, or a bit of flesh? The stinging stink of turpentine lined her nostrils and her throat and made her gag. She turned the wooden ball in her hand as if to reveal the future, to reveal where Annie was. Her stomach lurched. How could a single day contain both the greatest pleasure and the deadliest pain? Her hands were raw from the chemical eating away at her skin, but the bowling ball was clean, polished to a fine shine. She hadn't missed a thing. She set it back into the tan case, beside its mate, and zipped the case closed.

HEAD DOWN, LAURA moved deftly for home, eyes on the ice underfoot. Waning light draped Jones Avenue in a glittering luminescence. Silver, sonic silver, argent, plate, sterling. What was the precise colour of visible light? If she knew that maybe she'd know other things too, like whether she would get pregnant again or whether Cat would forgive her for starting another round of IVF? Ghost white, seashell, old lace, bone. It fell somewhere in the middle of the electromagnetic spectrum, didn't it? Combining all colours. White light was a mask for a rainbow, a wish not yet granted, a cloud covering God's eye. It was there and yet not there.

"You can't sell that house."

Laura turned and there was Astrid, with the little black dog, a few feet behind. "Are you following me?" She saw the contrast between the girl's icy skin and the dark stamp of her tattoos. Her teeth were chattering, and she was shivering. So was the puppy.

"No," said Astrid.

What had Beth told her about most shelters? No pets allowed; kids who wanted beds had to abandon their dogs and cats and ferrets or relinquish them to animal services. Many were unwilling to do so, preferring instead to keep their tiny chosen families intact, despite extreme weather, hunger, or the dangers on the street. With one hand, Astrid buttoned her coat higher to warm the puppy and Laura felt her heart squeeze. There was nothing and no one in her life for whom she'd make such a sacrifice. "Just so you know," she said. "I don't carry any cash on me."

"Who says I need money?!"

At close range, the snow came down slowly, in a benign, even descent to the ground; but across the street, in front of the housing project, it lashed through the glow of a street light.

"What then?"

"I already told you, we need inside that house."

"Listen, I don't know what you're thinking. You can't squat there."

Astrid burst out laughing. She stroked the puppy's head. "Pretty sure you couldn't stop me. I may only be eighteen, but I know that much."

Eighteen? Laura breathed in sharp needles of air. She seemed younger than that. Should Laura threaten to call the police? And tell them what? That a teenager was stalking her? She walked on, waiting for some noise to break the tension. There was no bhangra or folkhop blaring from the housing project windows, not even the tonal bell of the nearby public school. All she heard was the cacophony of boots crunching snow, her own hurried breath, and the pop and snap of branches breaking. "Do you hear that?" she said.

The wind rose and a comforting chime came from every direction, a fork sounding a note on a champagne flute. It was the music of a thousand tinkling icicles suspended from tree branches. "Ice," said Astrid, lingering on the word. She pronounced it slowly, a dull, deadening tone of nostalgia cutting into her voice. Laura pulled the collar of her parka up higher as a screaming fire truck barrelled around the corner. The dog, spooked by the piercing sound, leapt from the girl's coat and shot off.

"Buddy!" Astrid flew after him. She was swift, even with the ice underfoot and the army surplus bag bouncing up and down on her back. She slid across the pavement, her boots making a smooth, quick sound on the ice.

Laura rushed after them. She caught up to Astrid in the next block, east of Pape. Someone had dumped a pail of rotten food out onto the street, and it had frozen to the ground. The dog sniffed it out and was noisily pawing at the scraps when Astrid grabbed him by the scruff. She shoved him into her coat. "I thought he was done for," she said. She sounded distressed, fragile. "I couldn't bear for us to be apart."

Laura bent over to catch her breath. "How long ... have you ... had him?"

"Since the storm began."

Laura was going to say that wasn't very long, only a couple of days, there might be another owner somewhere in the city desperate to reunite with the dog, but she stopped short. The relief in Astrid's voice was apparent, and Laura couldn't bring herself to suggest that Buddy didn't belong to her. After all, how do we know when something or someone is meant to be ours? Hadn't she always known motherhood was for her? "Buddy's a good name," she said, reaching out and scratching the puppy's chin, where his goatee was growing. "It suits him."

Astrid flinched, took a step backwards. "Don't! I didn't say you could." She lifted one leg to show the combat boots she was wearing. "See these stompers," she said. "Steel toes. Also, I have a knife in my back pocket. You don't want to mess with me."

Laura raised her hands. "Whoa, you're the one who followed me. I'm not looking for any trouble here."

"Liar," said Astrid. She knew human nature. "Everybody's looking out for himself."

Laura watched her remove one wool mitten and stroke the top of her dog's head. She'd been fucked over; anyone could see that. But Laura wasn't to blame. Beneath the weighty, undulating sky, it was dark though not black, glowing too, and in that strange silvery darkness their strained silence was amplified. The shelter where Beth worked, Nellie's, wasn't that much farther, she thought, just tucked off Broadview. She could insist on accompanying the girl there, hand her off to the staff. Maybe Beth would even be on shift. "I have someplace to be," she said. "Could I help you find a shelter?"

Astrid blinked, wide-eyed. "Too late for that." She was bundled under the thrift store coat, half of her ghostly face concealed by its upturned velvet collar. She sounded dazed and tough, and there was also vulnerability about her, a kind of raw need Laura associated with children or travellers in a foreign land. She couldn't very well leave the girl and her dog outside alone again, now that she was sure Astrid was homeless.

"Where will you go, then?"

Astrid shrugged. Behind her, a beam of yellow light pressed through cloud cover, framing her in a golden halo. Her mouth suddenly showed the faint stain of red. *Was that lipstick?*

"Really, it's not safe to stay out," said Laura.

Just then, a small bird with a grey throat and breast and a yellow beak flitted between two leafless trees. "Look," said Astrid, sounding gleeful.

"A sparrow?"

"Something familiar." She turned and, carrying Buddy, started back in the direction from which she'd come. Within a few seconds they had both disappeared into the snow.

EDDIE RACED HER Dodge into the vacant lot at Cherry Beach and skidded to a stop, facing Lake Ontario. Sleet pelted through the amber glow of the truck's headlights. She tried to scan the shore and couldn't see more than a few feet in any direction. No one and nothing else was out there, save the relentless wind and God's wrath falling all around her. That very morning, the mayor, unable to get to City Hall, had made a radio broadcast appealing for people to stay home. Eddie switched off the engine. Moonlight now, a dim reminder in the distance of a faint and fading life. She pushed the driver's side door into the wind and stepped out in her brother's old shearling-lined wool coat. The twenty-below temperature slammed into her. The snow around her boots was a foot thick, and she crunched lower. She couldn't see the lifeguard cabin on the beach. There were no cormorants flying overhead.

Annie must've found someplace to hide, she told herself, snuck into a neighbour's basement, taken shelter in the back seat of an abandoned car? She'd return. Eddie needed to believe it. She'd even left the house unlocked, in case Annie made her way back while she was gone. But as she opened the back of the truck and heaved out Annie's father, she knew in the chilled marrow of her bones what she couldn't allow herself to admit: gone was gone, and there was to be no returning. Not for Annie. Not for her. Not for this sorry son of a bitch she was dragging across the frozen pebbles of the beach.

She should've driven straight to the police and not tampered with evidence, reported the crime because by midday, suspicions would already be raised. Armstrong's lodge brothers would be asking questions; that was for sure. If any of the neighbours had noticed, they might wonder about her taking the truck out so late. With gasoline on ration, she didn't usually drive unless for work. How could she have explained? What could she have said that would bring understanding or clemency? Walking backwards, stumbling, because her muscles were exhausted past usefulness, she was running on automatic when she hauled that rolled-up tarp to the water's edge and dropped it. Went back to the truck for bricks.

Two in each gloved hand, back and forth she carried small red gravestones to the lip of the lake and set about shoving them under the tarp, in and around the man's body. She used to be proud of the strength and power in her hands, how they could fill a kiln full of bricks as fast as any man, stand all day in front of those coal-fired ovens, at 1800 degrees Fahrenheit, in the heat of the summer sun. These were the same hands that had dug out clay, extracted shale from deep deposits using a steam shovel. With them, she'd blasted dynamite, layering into the quarry, and dumped the shale into dinky cars to haul up to the yard in cables. Brickwork was tough, physical labour. How many would do the trick now? she wondered. Fifty? Sixty? Each standard Armstrong brick weighed five pounds, she knew, miniature rectangles of sand and clay. She worked faster, her hands numb even in the thick gloves. As she shoved the cold bricks against the dead man's skin, remorse and contrition churned inside her — and hardened in her heart. "Take back this man," she heard herself say, under a fog of breath. "His kind has no place here." She might as well have been speaking of herself by then. She turned her head to the side and vomited.

After the bricks had been placed, nearly one hundred of them, and the Inglis pistol stuffed down into the rolled-up tarp, Eddie reinforced it with a heavy rope. She left the flashlight on the passenger seat and grabbed her snow shovel from the back of the truck.

With the shovel tucked up under one arm, she kicked and slid the man out onto the frozen lake. Ice underfoot was solid, a good two feet, she figured, but once she'd gotten a few yards out, she felt it thin; there was some measure of give beneath her boots, maybe air pressing up, which suggested moving water.

Carefully, and without being able to see a foot in front of her, or behind, Eddie lay face down on the frail ice in her coat, spread her arms and legs to distribute her weight, making it less likely she'd fall through. With the shovel, she now pushed the dead man out ahead of herself, keeping him at least a yard off. She wouldn't have minded going under, except for the uncertainty of Annie, and what might need taking care of next. The moon was obscured and no starlight illuminated the sky; the night was obsidian, as black as the dead man's heart. Eddie swam through that darkness feeling her way on her stomach, listening to her tight, rasping breath in the sharp air, to the scrape of the shovel slapping the bumpy ice.

The wind swirled snow into tornadoes across the surface of the lake, and Eddie felt the temperature drop. Her toes had gone numb, even in woollen socks. Her cheeks burned with cold. Ice had formed on her eyelashes and eyebrows. And then she heard it — a low gurgle in the distance, a slow didgeridoo. She waited, motionless, not sure if she'd imagined it or perhaps let it out of her body, and then, there it was again, louder, closer, coming from under the surface of ice, moaning. Eddie could feel vibrations against her rib cage. Pockets of air pressing up from the depths, spreading into this sad lament. Or was it ice splitting apart in another region of the lake, the sound an echo of separation?

She closed her eyes and with one final heave shoved the dead man as far away as she could, out into what had to be deep enough, and, as if a great gaping mouth had opened, there came a crack like a bullwhip. Ice split, then a slosh of water as the man's body was swallowed. She waited to be next, braced for frigid water, motionless, her heart a jackhammer. But the lake was sated. She was still there a minute later when she opened her eyes and the dirge returned; the lake's frozen wail was full of rage, this time sounding like a man's voice.

LAURA STOOD AT her kitchen island watching Cat place a Tupperware container of cold beef locro into their refrigerator. "I'm so sorry," she said. "We can still celebrate. How about Netflix and some popcorn?"

"Not really in the mood anymore," said Cat.

"We haven't even had a chance to talk about my new fertility counsellor," she said. She should confess about going to the clinic, but the timing wasn't right, and, anyway, why bring it up at all until they called her in for the embryo transfer. She reached out and ran her fingers through Cat's thick, wavy hair. "I was hoping you'd come to a session with me?"

Cat shook her head, a wordless gesture that might've seemed dismissive to someone who didn't know her as well; really, she was trying to hold anger and frustration at bay. "We've been over this already."

"I know, I know, therapy's not your thing. The counsellor thinks we should at least consider adoption."

Cat turned to open the fridge door. "You know I wouldn't feel the same way about an adopted kid."

Laura withdrew her hand. "That's a terrible thing to say!"

"Is it? I'm just being honest." Cat moved a carton of organic eggs to the top shelf to make room on the bottom for a block of cane sugar she used to sweeten her coffee. "I wanted us to have a baby together. It's complicated enough being two women. I can't see adding more parents to the mix."

Laura felt her heart begin to freeze, then harden. Cat had claimed biology didn't matter, that family was whomever you chose to love.

That's what marriage was, after all, chosen family. "We'd be the parents," she said.

"You heard them at the info night. They encourage contact with birth families."

"So we'll specify a closed adoption."

Cat shut the refrigerator door. "And what about the kid? What if they eventually want to know where they came from? Doesn't it ever bug you that you don't know anything about your dad?"

"Not really," said Laura. He was some guy her mom had been out with a couple of times, not an artist, or anyone Marilyn could get serious about. To Laura he felt like part of someone else's life, not hers.

"Well, it would bother me," said Cat.

Laura slid up onto a stool. She did sometimes wish for an extended family, especially now that her mom was gone. Being the only child of an only child, whose parents had long ago died, was a slight branch on a thin family tree. "How is adoption different than the anonymous sperm we're using?" she said.

"*Were* using. Past tense. We've moved on, remember?"

A red heat spread up Laura's neck and face. "You're being so closed-minded."

Cat turned to load the pots and pans into the dishwasher. "C'mon, ticking all those boxes on the forms felt weird. Could we handle a child who'd been sexually abused? Were we open to becoming an interracial family? Did we feel okay about a child whose birth mother was schizophrenic? What about an older child? A sibling group? Jesus, it shouldn't be like choosing pizza toppings."

"There are so many kids who need a family, Cat. And I don't see how it's any different than selecting our donor from a cryobank. We made the same kinds of decisions when we considered donors' cultural backgrounds and education levels. I remember us spending a long time discussing psychological profiles. Nobody knows how their kid'll turn out. That's part of the deal. Beth already said she'd help if there were special needs. She knows all the available resources in the city."

"Oh, well, in that case."

Blood rushed to Laura's temples. She heard a whooshing sound, her strong pulse, in one ear. International adoption had been closed to them because they were a same-sex couple. China was even closed to single women now that they'd caught on to lesbians applying as singles; she'd looked into that. And how likely was it that a birth mother in a private scenario would choose them over a straight couple? If Cat wouldn't even consider a public adoption through the Children's Aid Society or Jewish Child and Family Services, then going ahead and using their last embryo truly would be Laura's only chance to become a mother.

"What if we switched?" she tried. "You've never wanted to carry, but you could. For us. I mean, benefit of having two uteruses in one marriage, right?"

"Laura."

"Just think about it again. Please?"

Cat closed the dishwasher and locked it. "We both know you won't be satisfied unless it's you. Besides, they don't make butch maternity wear."

"You're making jokes?"

Cat stood with her lower back against the dishwasher, her thumbs hooked into the pockets of her jeans. "I know it's hard giving up on the dream, *pero* it doesn't have to be all bad. We'll have more opportunity for travel now. I wouldn't mind getting to Argentina more than once a year. I think it might help to look at things differently, see the positive side. We'll be child free, that's all, not childless. It'll have to be enough."

Enough?

What was she talking about? There was never enough love. Or time. Laura could practically hear the minutes, hours, years ticking by. She and Marilyn had been each other's best companions. Partners in crime, her mom had called them. "So, I should just stop wanting this, it's that easy?"

Cat's dark eyes softened; she was sympathetic but weary and worn out by repeated disappointment. "We need to accept reality," she said. "Holding on is driving us apart."

"I know that!" snapped Laura. But maybe she could experience the mother-child bond again, from the other side.

Cat ran water at the sink, squeezed dish soap onto her hands and rinsed. "I can't help feeling this has something to do with your mom's death, Laura." Laura made no attempt to disagree, so Cat continued. "I don't want us to waste any more money on this."

Laura swallowed hard. Time was the most valuable commodity there was. Not money, not real estate. Time, the very thing her mom had been robbed of.

Tick, tick, tick.

Out the kitchen window, snow began to fall, flakes that took the shape of puzzle pieces. Laura moved off the stool to gain a closer look. That was when she saw the outline of a face on the glass, in condensation. She caught her breath. "Astrid?"

Cat finished drying her hands on a tea towel. "What did you say?"

The outline was already blurring, the snowflakes unremarkable now.

"Nothing," she said.

THIS STORM, THE worst in Toronto's history, had swept in from the Gulf of Mexico and immobilized the entire city. Bread and milk deliveries ceased. All businesses and schools were closed. A streetcar trolley had overturned, trapping passengers. In total, twenty-one inches would fall and nine people would be reported dead.

After the body was sunk, Eddie headed back to her neighbourhood to begin a foot search for Annie. *I will find you*, she thought, cutting the engine and coasting down her street with the headlights off. She parked a few houses away from home and climbed out into a strong wind that jerked the door open, throwing her off balance. She was knocked to the icy ground with a muffled thud. Her knees took the impact, sending sharp pains up both legs. The flashlight she'd been holding slipped from her hand and skidded into a snowbank. She caught her breath, then struggled up onto both feet only to be felled again.

"Who's there?!"

She hadn't noticed her neighbour loading an ice saw and tongs into the back of his truck. At this time of year, when the ice was at its thickest, he'd be going to harvest from Ashbridges Bay. Eddie tasted bile and felt she might pass out from fear of discovery. Should she stay down low and hope he hadn't seen that it was her? Even if he hadn't recognized the Dodge pull up, he'd be wondering who was poking around in the dark on such a night, and why. "It's only me, Mr. Doyle," she said, standing.

"Miss Ferguson?" He took a few steps closer, squinted. Moonlight caught the metal of the chisel he held in a gloved hand. "What brings you out at this ungodly hour?"

Shivering, heart thumping — *breathe, breathe* — her pulse in her frozen fingertips now, as blood flowed away from her heart into her limbs. Eddie wiped snow from her coat, acting as though it was the most natural thing in the world to be out. "Sorry for giving you a start," she said. "I've just now been to Hamilton and back. My mother's ailing, and I'm afraid I haven't slept. Dropped my keys getting out of the truck." She jangled them in the dark to make the lie sound reasonable.

"You sure are a queer one," he said, shaking his head in disbelief.

He might've only meant that she was odd, but he might've meant more. Other neighbours must've wondered about her too, Eddie thought, what with her living alone and working where she did. Doyle was a gruff, tough man with fixed ideas. He was also a good neighbour, and she was in no position to argue. "The pit opens in a few hours," she said, fishing the flashlight out of the snowbank and pretending to head for home.

"You must've used all your gasoline making that trip," he said. He was still shaking his head when he climbed up onto the driver's seat of his own truck and slammed the door. Seconds later, he fishtailed down their street and skidded around the corner. Eddie let her shoulders drop with some measure of relief, but not enough. Not nearly enough. A cold wind blew, starting a ground blizzard. Fallen snow spiralled up into the night air, fine as dust. It glistened by the light of the moon. She felt it on her burning cheeks, and it scorched her lungs, making her cough. Her knees ached.

After the rumble of Doyle's engine had faded, Eddie pressed on through the blizzard, searching for Annie down one street after the other, calling out; in vicious argument, the storm raged. The black sky flashed yellow sheets of lightning, a rare thunder-snow, rumbling low and menacing. Still, she was undaunted. It was the season for miracles, and she had to believe.

She shone her flashlight into every darkened door in the neigh-bourhood, including the entrance to the United Church and the local dance hall, where Loyal Orange Lodge No. 67 met, and Annie's father was Deputy Master. Along with the other LOLs in Canada, it had been turned into a recruiting office to assist the war effort. Nobody was there. She peered behind every letter box, around each tree and snow-covered shrub. No sign of Annie. Across Jones, she ran through Goel Tzedec, the old Jewish cemetery, praying to any God who would listen.

As the pink light of dawn rose over the city, glossing ice and snow with the illusion of warmth, Eddie saw her own breath. A stillness enveloped the streets, like the pause her body made between breaths; that brief, involuntary loneliness that left her feeling she might be the last living creature on Earth, untethered to time or space or to anyone. *Lord have mercy on my soul*, she thought.

Men and women began to emerge from their homes, bears slip-ping from cozy dens. They looked in on elderly neighbours and inspected their properties for damage. They stood in their front yards bonding over the experience of the storm. "Hope my roof don't cave from the weight of it," one man said, as Eddie passed. "I ain't never seen nothing like it."

Eddie kept her head bowed, eyes cast down, no longer entitled to be part of this community. She didn't belong to the wider world anymore, or to this day, or any day coming. *Thou shall not....* Her head began to pound, and a pain spiked behind her eyes, but she'd keep going, on fumes if she had to.

Soon, workers were heading out for their morning shifts at the nearby Wrigley and Colgate factories and at Reliable Toy, where they made plastic bullets, bayonet covers, and toy soldiers. They carried packed lunches in tin boxes. Eddie wasn't hungry or thirsty; or, if she was, she couldn't feel those things because she could barely feel her body. Too many hours out in the cold, too much panic and fear.

She covered ground between Pape and Greenwood, Dundas and Danforth, frostbite setting into her toes and fingertips. It was the guilt that pained her. In a matter of hours, she'd become less human, a bag of bones, a waste of skin. She was a lesser person with a diminished spirit, and it seemed now that no matter the effort she made, Annie was lost. "Annie!" she hollered, not caring who heard. "Annie, come back!" But the storm was indifferent and only the name returned on the howling wind.

An hour later, exhausted, numb, with no voice left and the flashlight dying in her hand, Eddie dropped to her knees on the streetcar track in the middle of Gerrard, ice below, a relentless white closing down from above, and she wept.

THE MORNING SKY glowed burnt orange through the stained-glass windows of the Flying Pony coffee house on Gerrard. Laura sat, sipping an eggnog nutmeg latté with her back to the black brick wall and her clients facing her, anxiously. They were a couple of long-time renters from the west end who wanted to get into the market, so were wading into that predictable sales peak right before Christmas. With less competition in winter, they hoped to avoid bidding wars; though she'd warned them it wasn't necessarily going to be the case, and there would be few homes to choose from in their price range, at the bottom of the market. They'd been to see friends on Craven, an alley street running north through the India Bazaar, and learned the neighbour was about to list. Now they wanted to put in a bully bid.

"Are you sure?" she asked. The place was a tarpaper shack. Built at the turn of the century with cardboard walls held together with kindling, and newspaper for insulation. Originally, the house would've belonged to a worker's family, maybe one of the men who blasted dynamite or dug clay in the brick pits. "Why don't I arrange a viewing first?"

"There's on-site parking," said the husband. "And a bit of a backyard."

"I understand, but it's better to buy right in the first place."

The wife was picking apart her croissant, leaving a small hill of buttery flakes on the table. "We'd know our neighbours there," she said.

Laura scrolled through her address book and logged into Stratus with her ID and PIN. "Okay, I work for you." She used her fob key to input an authentication number. They're going to regret it, she thought. The reality of sinking money into a fixer-upper, the exorbitant cost of baseboard heating, termites eating away at the back porch. Such surprises bring stress, and stress on a relationship quickly strips the home ownership dream of its illusion. "I'm just checking to see what the previous owner paid," she said, clicking into GeoWarehouse. "Okay, here it is." She turned her phone screen around for them to read. "That was nine years ago. It'll go for twice that now."

"What are we waiting for?"

The wife sounded desperate, Laura thought, vulnerable to debt; buying into a new life was a thrilling ride and it was hard to jump off. She opened a document for them to sign. If they were determined to try for this "divorce house," who was she to stop them?

Ten minutes later she'd called in to register an offer of $559,900 — $25,000 less than the value of the adjacent house, which had sold in the spring, and $100,000 over her clients' original upper limit. No conditions. Peter Kaminski, the selling agent, was gloating through his phone. She could practically hear the cheap grin as she hung up. "Expect them to sign back," she said.

"We can't go any higher," said the husband.

"Honey, I don't want to lose this one."

Laura bit her lip to stop herself from speaking. There are worse losses, she thought. Invisible ones. Losses that force a higher price than any bidding war. Never mind the financial expense, houses exact an emotional toll. Childbirths and deaths, job promotions and bankruptcies, first kisses and heartbreak — the major events new owners experience and those that went on before they ever got there, all of these settle over them like an invisible shroud, and before they know it, their lives have become something they no longer recognize. Marriage can be that too, she thought, any marriage, a repository of memories that just won't go away, and even the most committed lovers can discover too late that they've made a mistake. Homeowners aren't the only ones who suffer from buyer's remorse.

Laura brought up the calculator function on her phone. "Just so you know," she said, tapping in a few numbers. "Going up another couple grand will only add fifty bucks a month to your payments." She watched the woman behind the counter crank the radio, and heard the announcer say that a second wave of freezing rain was about to hit the city. Officials were warning of power outages and traffic pileups, the need for the homeless to seek shelter indoors. She glanced outside, wondering what had happened to Astrid and Buddy, and right then a petite figure in an oversized white coat with gold buttons passed in front of the picture window. Laura craned her neck, but the wind picked up, sending snow flying. "Why don't you two stay and discuss," she said, standing. "I'll call as soon as I hear anything." She grabbed her parka, hat, gloves, and bag, and rushed for the door.

HOME HAD DISAPPEARED the year Annie's mother left and with it went faith in love. That's what happens when you lose the one who means the most. Why believe in things you cannot touch or taste or smell? Why trust in that which will only desert you? Sitting at her vanity in a blue liquid satin dressing gown, in the bedroom her mother had painted in Annie's favourite colour — emerald green — she could scarcely recall the woman's face or hold on to the musical sound of her voice. She tried to conjure soothing lullabies, even a gentle scolding. From out of the vanity drawer, she lifted a black-and-white photograph. She studied it and then forced herself to stare into the mirror and concentrate on her own features, to find similarities — the particular green of their eyes, the arcs of their dark brows, and their long, thick lashes. Over time, the woman who had been her mother had blurred and faded and now all Annie had left as proof of that relationship was the photograph.

"Give it to me." Her father's baritone startled her from the doorway. He'd been to a pub with some other Orangemen, and she hadn't expected him back for a few more hours. "You hear?" He stank of pipe tobacco and whiskey. The Protestant brotherhood was cloaked in the sauce as much as in secrecy.

Annie rose slowly from the covered bench. He'd destroy the photograph as he'd done with every other reminder she'd had. Tear it up or toss it into the fireplace. She'd never see her mother's face again. It wasn't much but it was all she had. "It's mine," she said, clutching it.

"Yours?" He stumbled into her room. "Who puts food on the table around here? What about those clothes on your back?" He careened and used the end of her waterfall dresser for balance. "I don't want that ugly mug in my house!" His pencil-thin moustache needed grooming. He held out an open palm, expectantly. "Now, what did I tell you?"

The walls seemed to have darkened in his presence, the coral pink curtains hung like meat in a butcher shop. He didn't want to see her mother's image, and yet she knew he was forced to look at it every day nonetheless, in her own eyes, her colouring, and he would try and beat it out of her whether or not she gave up the picture. She quickly stuffed it down the quilted ruffle collar of her dressing gown.

He lunged, and before she could dodge and weave around him, he grabbed her by one arm. His grip was firm, and he shook her. "She's dead to us! I've told you a thousand times."

"She's not dead, you drove her away!" Annie would run too, if there were some place to go. She'd run and never look back.

He raised his open hand to strike her, and she squirmed, resisting. As the blow landed, she managed to pull away and scuttle across the room. The photograph fell out onto the hardwood floor, but she retrieved it. He slumped down with his back against her dresser, muttering under his breath. Then his tears came on. Same sob story every time, Annie thought, disgusted.

"You're pitiful," she said, tightening the satin belt of her dressing gown. She felt like crying now too, and not because of the beating. She understood why her mother had run off, but why hadn't she taken Annie with her? Or come back to collect her?

A few minutes later he passed out, blotto, and Annie crept downstairs and outside into the front yard, to take in some air under the stars. Their five-bedroom house stood on the east side of Broadview, facing the Don Jail, another lonely prison. One day soon, maybe tomorrow, she'd have enough saved to buy a train ticket to anywhere, rent a room. Her coat hid her dressing gown. She pulled a head scarf down low over her face in case of a passerby and tied it under her chin. Her lip was split, and she tasted the metallic tang of blood. Tomorrow her Tangee lipstick would cover things. Her mouth smarted some, no more than any other time.

People said a girl without a roof over her head was as good as dead, but a roof and four brick walls didn't make for a home. Home was a sheltering sanctuary of love where prayers could be answered. You knew it when you had it and missed it every day that it was gone. Nothing could be worse than living here with him, she thought; the echo of loss ringing throughout the large, empty house, those lodge meetings that whipped him into an Imperial fervour, and the whiskey bottle. She scanned the manicured yard, with the cool night air soothing her sore face. Nearby, a night bird sang in a circular, tremulous rhythm, a whip-poor-will. There it was, camouflaged by mottled brown-and-grey feathers, perched on the hedge, its large round head cocked, eyes watching her in the dark with curiosity. "Hello pretty," she whispered. "Shouldn't you have flown south by now?"

She stepped around the side of the house where an expensive, double-firing technique had been used on the corner bricks. They were black and blue, the lining of the brick seeping colour, like shiny hunks of molten coal. By moonlight, it appeared that a thick, dark menace was holding the place together. She shivered. It was an ugly house, one that matched her father's character.

She kicked at the side of the house. Was this all fate had in store for her? *No*, she wouldn't accept that, she'd take matters into her own hands, bide her time, and keep pinching money whenever he left his billfold on the dining room table or dropped his pants at the foot of the bed. And there was the money she'd been siphoning at the pit each pay period. A scant amount from the safe, every chance she got. No one was the wiser. She turned to go back inside just as the first snow of the season began to fall, big, heavy swaths of it, snow falling like cotton batting, covering the house and the yard, and her footprints, as fast as she laid them.

WHEN LAURA STEPPED out of the coffee house, she was hit by a blast of arctic air that stung her face and made her teeth ache. Wind had blown large snowdrifts across the street and knocked over a row of industrial-sized garbage cans.

"Astrid?" She craned around. Once again there was no trace of the girl or her dog. Very few cars were on the road, even fewer pedestrians. The neighbourhood looked empty and void of colour. No, that wasn't accurate, she thought. The storm hadn't drained the city of colour, it had painted over the old colours — the fire hydrants and bus shelter ads — with muted hues of grey and white, pale pink and indigo. In fact, there were so many variations of white that it was dizzying.

"Boo!" said Astrid.

Laura spun around and there they were, in front of a sari shop window. "Okay, now I know you're following me," she said, marching up to the girl.

Astrid gestured to the Flying Pony with her chin. "You looked warm back there. I miss that feeling."

"I was trying to work."

Strands of silver ice, jewels, clung to the store's awning. Astrid gazed at a mannequin in the window wearing a fuchsia sari. "Get a load of that," she said. "Everything here is so different now. It's super." For a moment, Laura wished someone else were there. Cat or Beth. Beth would know what to do.

"Astrid, I don't know your story, but people must be looking for you."

She lifted Buddy from her coat, set him down. "Maybe I don't want to be found." It wasn't exactly a lie, and it wasn't the whole truth, either. She was back with a purpose. The rest was a blur.

"I don't buy that," said Laura. There was something peculiar about the girl. She evaded direct questions and when she did speak, she sounded odd, outdated. The way she moved? Evading gravity too. Laura pulled her hood down to shield her face from the biting wind and once more felt the weight of her conscience descending; she'd sounded callous just then, indifferent. It was not how she really felt. A streetcar turned at Coxwell, heading their way.

Astrid pointed at the rusty red rocket. "Is that a trolley?"

"Here." Laura rummaged through her bag for a pen. She tore a piece of paper out of her notebook. "This is my cell number." She scribbled fast. "If you change your mind and want some help with housing, just call. Okay?"

Astrid accepted the paper.

"I mean it," said Laura. "Call me any time."

She crossed the street carefully, throwing her weight forward to balance on the ice, and boarded the 506 streetcar heading west. From the aisle she watched them through the window, shrinking into the distance.

Instead of staying on all the way home, Laura found herself pulling the cord early. As she stepped out onto the road, ice cracked underfoot, a violent sound, breaking apart beneath her weight. *Ice.* What was the word in Spanish? Cat had used it last night on the phone, describing the storm to her father in Argentina. *Hielo.* That was it. *La ciudad ha sido sellada en el hielo.* The city has been sealed in ice.

The code on the lockbox at 2 Condor Avenue was easy to remember: 1973, her birth year. She stepped into the front hall thinking she should've brought Astrid here with her. What harm could there really have been? Even without a lit furnace, a drafty old house was still warmer than the street. She probably should've shown the place to her new clients too, and yet she had the curious and disconcerting sense that the house was hers, her secret. At least, until it was ready to be listed.

She sat on the old, dusty divan in the front window taking in the mournful feel of the place. How could a house feel so sad? A keen draft chilled the back of her neck. Needs double-pane windows, she thought, shivering.

She reached into the pocket of her parka for the notebook and pen but before she could finish writing, her eyelids grew heavy, and she was stretching out. Curled on her side, she fell into an impossibly deep sleep.

EDDIE PEELED OUT of her wet, bloodstained clothes and stepped into the claw-foot tub. At first, the water coming through the pipes was tepid, then it soon ran cold. She didn't move as the icy liquid poured out and, inch-by-inch, covered her skin. Gooseflesh rose all over her body, but she was already numb. Her fingers and toes were inflamed and discoloured from the beginnings of frostbite. She stared at her distorted reflection in the water, from the only place in the house where she didn't feel like a criminal. The face staring back had a familiar angular jawline, the same short black hair as hers, and yet it was a stranger's face wearing that hollowed out expression. She slammed her eyes shut. No matter how many times she replayed her relationship with Annie, looking for ways to make it come out differently, no matter how she rearranged the details or reconsidered her actions leading up to that fateful night, it all fell out the same, inevitable as death. Teeth chattering, she reached for a pumice stone and began to scrub, scraping the abrasive stone back and forth, then faster, furiously, until her body was bleeding and raw. She worked as diligently as she had removing evidence from the floors and walls of the house.

After, she changed into clean overalls and rolled her bloodied clothes into a heap. She stuffed them into a brown paper bag next to the bags containing all the bloody towels. In a few hours, when the pit opened, she would be the first to arrive and she would toss those bags into the ovens. Act like nothing had happened. Let it burn; let it all burn up, a hellfire.

LAURA YAWNED AWAKE on the divan in the small living room. She lay a minute longer as her dream faded, listening to the howl of the storm continuing to blanket the city. Something about the blizzard, she thought. She pulled the collar of her parka up around her neck, tried to remember. All that was left was a residue of feeling, an unspeakable sadness, and the sense that change was coming, that things would never be the same. Pushing up, she stretched both arms over her head. Was it the kind of change that would rattle her insides with nervous excitement or threaten her security? Outside the window, giant snowflakes drifted down in large, romantic gestures.

She was still thinking about Cat's comment, that pregnancy might be her way of coping with losing her mom. So what if it was? There was no single good reason to have a child. Cat had wanted a child to carry on her name. Was that a better reason than grief? Less selfish? Beth expected her children would tend her in old age, a dubious insurance policy if ever there was one, and a thought Laura found a bit disturbing, but people had children for all kinds of reasons, noble and ignoble: creating the illusion of immortality, to repair a marriage, because it was socially expected, or they feared being alone. Why not to heal a broken heart? Laura rubbed her hands together to warm her fingers. Was that really so wrong? If trying one last time meant going against Cat's wishes, that was a risk she was willing to take.

Laura stood. The collapsible table displayed an unfinished jigsaw puzzle of Paris; the Eiffel Tower in the background with the Seine and Notre-Dame Cathedral in the fore. *I need a real vacation,*

she thought, admiring the puzzle. An adventure. Not the predictable family visit she and Cat made to Argentina every year. She also
needed to start going to bed earlier; this was the second time she'd
fallen asleep on the job.

Glancing back into the front hall, she put herself in the place of
a prospective buyer entering this house. Did the hallway cause her
pulse to race or slow? Was there a quality of light coming through
the living room windows that gladdened the heart? Was there flow
through the home that allowed for the mind to also wander? Maybe the symmetry of the architecture made her feel secure? She was
adept at reading houses and would ultimately use this information
to help her close a deal.

Houses spoke clearly; the remnants of unresolved arguments
that lent an inexplicable, uneasy feeling inside a particular room,
the bygone passion of lovemaking that eventually bled an owner's
relationship dry. Laura heard and understood these things, the
hidden lives of houses. Good agents were part detective, part psy-
chologist, and part businessperson, driven by the satisfaction of
matching the right people to the right lives.

People, by contrast, were puzzling; there was so much more
room for misunderstanding. The subtleties of interpersonal commu-
nication and body language, needs inferred from gestures. She could
hardly read Cat anymore. Had she meant it when she'd insisted they
could be happy without children, or was Cat just telling her what
she thought Laura wanted to hear? Cat did that, offered an infuriat-
ing sort of dishonesty that could appear altruistic on the surface, but
which Laura knew was Cat's way of avoiding conflict.

Clients weren't much better in the honesty department. They
usually came to her with a "must-have" list, a fully renovated
kitchen or a finished basement or a claw-foot tub, claiming it was
all about resale value. There was almost always a personal reason
for the list — a needed retreat from an unhappy marriage or a desire

to impress the neighbours. Over the years, she'd learned to interpret what clients really wanted by listening to what they didn't say, and most people, she knew from experience, don't say a lot of what's important. *Did she?* How honest was she being with herself? Maybe she hadn't worked through her grief about her mom or thought enough about the implications of infertility on her relationship. What would be harder? she thought. Being a single parent or being childless with Cat? Would she be happier now if she'd married someone else? Or no one at all? *Oh, stop it.* These were just cliched questions of middle age, how to reconcile the alternative lives now out of reach.

In the dining room, she opened the small telephone table drawer and found a pencil, a city phone directory, and the old yellow pages that used to arrive on every Toronto doorstep. The black rotary-dial phone sat mutely on a crocheted doily. She lifted the heavy receiver to her ear — no dial tone.

In the kitchen, the flour canister was full of hard candy, mostly Scottish toffees and packages of Wrigley's Spearmint chewing gum. She fished out a toffee, unwrapped it, and placed it on her tongue. A sudden burst of sweetness. The smallest canister, for tea, held a rusty set of Dodge car keys.

Mom would've approved of this house, she thought. Marilyn would've seen it as quaint, a house to love. That was what she'd always said when Laura was growing up, about the house they would one day live in if she ever won the lottery. That it would be a house to love, which meant it wouldn't be large or renovated, or have any curb appeal, but it would at least be theirs.

The thing about this place was that in over seventy years, the homeowner hadn't updated the furnishings or décor, and to Laura that meant grief. She had her own ways of holding on to the past and she recognized when others did it too. She'd never been able to part with her mother's old costumes; they were more than personal mementos, they were sacred artefacts connecting the living to the dead. She needed to surround herself with them for the same reason anyone holds on to old things, she thought, because we don't survive certain losses. Not the way we survive others, by absorbing or integrating them. Some losses are so profound, they pin us to a time and place and leave us haunted by a spirit that can dwell only inside of us. Who had the homeowner lost?

Laura placed her palm over the tarnished brass knob of the basement door and opened it. She hadn't enjoyed playing the "what-if" game with her mom as a child. What if they won the lottery? What if her mother were able to make a living as a performance artist? What if the stars aligned, luck befell them? What if Laura became an archaeologist and one day made a great discovery? Only then, in that hypothetical world, would their lives change for the better. She preferred to invest in a more predictable future, at least one that was within her control.

Once, in the early stage of her disease, Marilyn had told her she didn't understand Laura's interest in real estate. "Whatever happened to your dreams of going on a dig?" she'd asked.

Laura descended the narrow, slanted steps down to the basement using the flashlight on her phone for a guide. The desire to become an archaeologist was so far and so faint now, she could scarcely remember ever having felt it. Any residual dreams she'd had disappeared entirely with the onset of her mother's Alzheimer's. It was impossible to imagine excavating others' lives when the one she inhabited was bleak and time limited and demanding of her full attention. Even if she had kept her internship at the ROM, even if she could've built that career, the soul of every little thing she might've had the fortune to uncover had been stolen along with her mother's fading life. She choked and coughed as her feet swept up dust from the dirt floor. The chilly basement air was thick with it and with the harsh odour of turpentine.

It was dark, despite her small light, a weighty, opaque darkness. Her heart thundered in her chest; she was scared in the way new love is frightening, as if everything is once more possible, and everything could be lost.

Tap tap tap.

She froze, caught her breath.

Light from outside was filtering in through the small rectangular window.

Tap tap tap.

A strange electricity ran through her. Was the house trying to gain her attention? Draw her close? The only other time she'd felt that kind of charge was when she'd first met Cat.

Her dorm mate at the university had been dating an architecture student and invited her along to a faculty party. As the liberal arts major in the room, she'd felt awkward and out of place trying to generate small talk. Then, there, beside the snack table, stood this tall figure listening in on the conversations going on around her with a glass of red wine in one hand, her dark wavy hair and olive complexion hinting at the Italian in an Argentine background. Cat smiled and Laura had instantly felt at home.

Tap tap tap.

Laura closed her eyes and forced herself to take a step closer to the window. She counted to five and peered into the centre of the pane of glass. Her reflection, that was all. Only her there, staring back wide-eyed. She unclenched her jaw, felt her breath even out as rain and wind continued to tap on the other side. The storm was becoming part of the background of her day, like a soundtrack, almost a companion. She was growing accustomed to its restless music and the constancy of cold. The snow and ice seemed a buffer against the rough, abrasive grain of city living. But this storm wanted something, she could feel that, even from down in a dry basement. What was it?

She noted a bit of efflorescence flaking on the brick on the out-side wall. No cracks or leaks in the foundation though. She scanned the ceiling. Lead pipes. Likely asbestos in the walls. To know for certain, she'd have to come back with a home inspector.

Along the back wall, she found a stack of old Somerville and Ravensburger puzzle boxes, a wringer washing machine full of pot-ting soil, a high work table with a hammer and saw, and a row of empty jam jars, each filled with a different type of nail or screw. The original oil tank had been left in place, though at some point the house had been converted to forced air gas, because there were ducts. She knelt. The furnace serial number and installation date showed that it was ten years old. Not energy efficient, though buy-ers would at least get a few more years out of it. A house was only worth what buyers were willing to pay, and with a scarcity of single-family homes in the city, rising demand, and low interest rates, it was a seller's market. People were willing to pay almost anything. The only issue with this house, as far as she could tell, was that its owner was in a coma and a house without an owner was like a marriage without passion. Sooner or later, something had to be done about it.

Laura turned to head back up the basement stairs, and again, her heart leapt. There was an imposing shape in the shadows. "Who's there?!" She extended a trembling arm to aim the dim light of her smart-phone flashlight as far as it would travel, under the staircase. "Oh." She clutched her chest. It was only a pair of overalls hanging on a hook.

There was something peeking out of the breast pocket. A movie program. How thin and aged the yellowed paper felt between her fingers. The program had been for the 1944 film *Laura*. She knew it well, as it had been her mother's favourite movie, and the reason for her given name. It was a moody, atmospheric Otto Preminger mys-tery starring Gene Tierney and Dana Andrews. What a coincidence, she thought, slipping her hand into the hip pocket of the overalls. She fished out a set of door tickets to an event at some place called the Rideau Club on Gerrard Street. They were also dated 1944. Same date as the inscription on her new ring.

Yawning, Laura leaned against the wall and inspected the tickets more closely. The blue block ink had faded, leaving only an echo of the cinema's name, the price of admission — twelve cents — and a six-digit number along each end. They smelled stale, a sweet undertone of cigarette smoke and dust. They smelled like time. What had life been like then? Coming out of the Depression, enduring the Second World War. How did anyone find love surrounded by deprivation? Her mother always said that having relatives who'd perished in Auschwitz was the reason she kept a freezer full of food. Laura suspected that fear of not having what she most needed, love, or of losing that love, was also what drove her mother's independence; the reason Marilyn refused to marry, the real reason she'd never told Laura's father she'd gotten pregnant, was that she didn't trust that anyone else would provide. If Laura were hers alone, nothing and no one could take her away.

Just then, her phone rang. It was the selling agent, Peter Kaminski. "My clients want to accept on the Craven property," he said. "No counter-offer. Can you send the deposit cheque over?"

"I'm on it," she said, dragging herself back upstairs. As she climbed, two sets of eyes, one of them green, were peeping in at her through the basement window.

ANNIE HAD BEEN the only other girl at the brick pit where Eddie worked; the boss's daughter, and she spent her afternoons in Building One answering the telephone and taking care of the books. Eddie saw her now and then, whenever she passed by on her way to the latrine. Once a week they'd exchange a few words when Annie came 'round with the envelopes.

"Pay day!" she would sing as she trotted from one outbuilding to another. She found the men where they were stationed — crushing and grinding shale, moulding or loading or firing brick — and whenever she came upon Eddie she'd sidle up just the same as with the other fellas and call out, "Mr. Ferguson!" Was it playful teasing, Eddie had wondered, or a meanness in her that made a point of drawing attention to her sex in a brickyard where she was the only woman? With the war still on, there wasn't much money for building and Armstrong was the last holdout. There were rumours of dismissals coming or even closure; the boss had been driving over some of the German prisoners of war housed at Todmorden Mills. Free labour wasn't a good sign, especially not for her, Eddie thought. She'd already agreed to stay on at less than half her former wage. How long before that punch-drunk bum, Armstrong, folded?

Then, one Friday Annie came by, same routine. "Here you are, Mr. Ferguson." She held herself high, gave off a haughty confidence. She was an Orangeman's daughter, trim and neat in her smart woollen victory suit and red oxfords — pretty enough to enter the Miss Toronto Beauty Pageant, but she was also bold, armoured, and worldly-wise. A sharp-tongued beauty without a mother, she knew more than she let on and maybe Eddie liked that. Her auburn hair was tucked under a red crocheted snood.

Eddie set the long pole on the side of the kiln and wiped her hand across the sooty leg of her overalls. "Miss Armstrong," she nodded, accepting the envelope. She folded it and stuffed it deep into the bib pocket of her overalls then turned back to the job.

Annie lingered. "I've left you for the last today," she said, leaning up against the chimney.

Eddie's stomach clenched. The year before, she'd taken on a mortgage buying her little house, and the heating bills would be high this winter. Was she being let go? "Is there a problem with my performance?" she asked, bracing against bad news.

"No," said Annie, seeing Eddie's strained expression. "No, no nothing like that. Just a little something I thought you might be able to help with."

"All right."

"I've heard talk that you bowl."

"Every Saturday I don't work," said Eddie.

"And you're the captain of the team?"

Eddie blushed. She glanced around discreetly, worried someone would notice the two of them speaking and get the wrong impression. What if that someone were Annie's father or that skinny boy from Building Three where they did the mixing? He often came sniffing around. Eddie didn't want trouble. "I got four more ovens to clear before end of day, miss."

Annie leaned in closer, lowered her voice. "It's an all-girls team, is it?"

Eddie's throat flashed dry; she felt the tightness of the skin on her face from standing in front of an open kiln all morning. "Why do you ask, miss?"

"Call me Annie, please, Mr. Ferguson." This time Eddie's surname rolled off Annie's tongue sounding vaguely flirtatious, not at
all sarcastic, and there might've been a tremor. "I'm awfully inter-
ested in the game," she said.

THE NOONDAY SUN played across the walls of Laura's home office and lit the top of the filing cabinet where her mother's old top hat and black patent leather tap shoes sat. The shoes were upside down, "soles toward heaven," Marilyn used to joke, "unless you wanted to bring bad luck." A cane lay in the windowsill beside a large aloe plant. A lab coat hung on the back of the door, along with a bullwhip and stethoscope. Laura was comforted by the costumes, having fragments of her mother's creative life decorating her own. She hadn't always felt so appreciative of Marilyn, not when her mother would answer the door to Laura's friends in her bra and underwear rehearsing costume changes, not when she'd turned up to Laura's grade five parent-teacher interview en route to a performance dressed as Dr. Nottalotta Payne, the s/m practitioner known for her commentary on the non-consensual bondage of romantic love. Growing up, Laura had often been mortified by her mother and hated performance art. Now, she appreciated her unorthodox upbringing.

The old movie program and Rideau Club tickets she'd taken from the Condor house lay across her keyboard. It was puzzling, the Pocket would've been a working-class neighbourhood then. A movie and a club would've made for an expensive night out. Must've been a very special occasion.

She heard Cat turn on the radio upstairs and step into the shower. "The storm is paralyzing the city's transit system," said the announcer. "Holiday travellers are stranded." Laura sighed. That Cat needed the news to validate the storm irritated her, an act of redundancy and willful ignorance. Oh, for God's sake, she thought. She could see the vigour of winter with her own eyes, from any room in their house. Why would Cat need confirmation of that? Really, Cat's change of heart about having a family was what was putting her off. What choice did she have except to go behind Cat's back?

She typed, "Rideau Club Toronto?" into a search engine and waited. Nothing came up. She tried "Toronto hot spots 1940s?" Still no useful links. Then, she thought to call and leave a message for her contact at the city archives. "Hey Mohan, it's Laura. This might be a long shot, but if you're in the office, could you please check files on a 1940s hangout called the Rideau Club, and a house at 2 Condor Avenue?"

She'd traced the history of other houses; potential buyers were often curious. Some were superstitious, consulting feng shui or numerology before closing a deal. She'd learned not to argue. For those who believed, luck was an empirical phenomenon, like the homeowner last year whose house had sat on the market for months until he buried a statue of St. Joseph in his garden. The very next day, inexplicably, there were multiple offers. "Thanks, Mohan," she said, and she hung up to review her notes on the Craven house.

Her clients had paid close to $600,000. How much of that was her take? Five percent from the seller, split fifty-fifty between herself and the other agent ... $15,000. Less the $1,600 fee and percentage-based cut to Re/Max, her brokerage. In total, her commission should come out to $12,650 plus tax.

She composed a brief follow-up email to the buyers congratulating them on the purchase of their first home, and reminding them that their new neighbourhood was up-and-coming, a good neighbourhood, with excellent public schools, close to the beach and parks. The value of their house would only climb. Then she cringed reading over what she'd typed. In her business, good and bad were euphemisms for wealthy and poor, those who belonged and those who didn't. Good neighbourhoods were not often where underemployed performance artists, like her mother, lived. Not Parkdale, where she'd grown up. Most days she didn't think about that; today she was feeling introspective.

"Why do we have to live in this crummy apartment?" She was ten and had just returned from playing solitaire for two hours, while her mother cleaned a spacious home in High Park. The owners were on vacation at a resort in Cancun.

Marilyn hadn't responded right away; she was taken aback and needed a beat to compose herself. "We have what we need," she finally said. "And there's no shame in renting."

Laura threw herself onto the daybed where her mother slept. "I know that. Sometimes I just wish things were different." It was becoming more obvious at school who had money and who didn't. Generally, the whiter your skin, the larger your parent's paycheque, and the larger your home, even in a place like Parkdale where lots of people struggled to make ends meet. A few of the kids had piano lessons and March break camps and ate neatly packed hot lunches. Not many of them, but enough of them that Laura was beginning to feel there was a better world out there, one that she wasn't able to access. The house in High Park had confirmed it.

Marilyn plopped down beside her. "I get it. You'd like a big backyard, maybe a basement with a large screen TV. *The Brady Bunch* sort of thing."

"I'd settle for a Walkman. Or a vacation." She looked her mom in the eye. "To literally anywhere. Do you know I'm the only one of my friends who's never left Toronto?"

"Sucks for you," said Marilyn.

"It's not funny, Mom." She folded her arms across her chest tightly.

Marilyn rested her head on Laura's shoulder. "Life's a bit of a lottery, kiddo; what can I say?"

"You could say you'd get a real job."

Marilyn stiffened, sat upright. Laura was sure she could feel her mom's heart pounding through her Cindy Sherman T-shirt. "You might find things aren't so black and white, when you're an adult, Laura. I hate to break it to you, life's not a meritocracy. You can work hard and still not get what you deserve. So, I'm going to keep making art and I suggest you stop comparing yourself to other people."

Laura could tell she'd hurt her mother's feelings and regretted it. Marilyn was the hardest working person Laura knew, carting supplies on public transit to clean houses for families in High Park and Forest Hill and Rosedale and, once or twice, up at the Bridle Path where there weren't sidewalks. She scrubbed and mopped and vacuumed and watered and laundered and dusted and swept and washed on evenings and weekends. She created her performance pieces in her "spare" time. Laura felt a pang of guilt. It didn't really matter that they couldn't afford a big house or even to explore the wider world, did it? Being Marilyn's daughter was always an adventure. They travelled in their own way, up and down the aisles at Designer Fabrics where colour and texture and every kind of person were hers to discover. Their neighbourhood was rich with the aroma of goat curry and roti, and the peal and ring of accents from around the world. Sure, there were shady pawnshops on Queen Street and drug dens that fronted as tattoo parlours, but you could pretend not to see illegal activity and you were safe. Mostly Laura loved their small life together. She wasn't the only latchkey kid in grade five, though she was the only one who knew who Angela Davis and Gloria Steinem were; the only person her age who'd been made to take Wen-Do so she'd know how to defend herself if she were ever attacked. "Sorry," she mumbled. "You're not like other moms, but I like you anyway."

"I like you anyway too," said Marilyn.

They sat in a companionable silence, Marilyn momentarily forgiven for being herself, Laura forgiven for wanting to fit in and have more, until Marilyn pushed up off the daybed. "Let's have the gang over tonight. It'll cheer you up."

"Okay."

Her mother's art school friends regularly camped out smoking pot and playing records on an old turntable; Betty and Boop, transsexual working girls, stopped in for Friday night pancake dinners, and her mother's occasional boyfriend, Thom, shot his documentaries in their building. People and their stories, not any grand fixed address, were her sanctuary.

Now, sitting in her home office in 2013, inside a spacious three-bedroom detached house in one of the city's most sought-after areas, those early years seemed far away, like a parallel universe. A house in a quiet, treed neighbourhood, a good neighbourhood, was a lovely thing, but Laura knew full well it wasn't an option for most people and that fact made her uncomfortable. And then, the thought she couldn't utter out loud, not even to Beth, especially not to Beth, the question that filled her with a purple, bruising shame: as a realtor, was she upholding the very system that ensured a scarcity of safe, affordable housing?

She used to jot down the interesting things she and her mom's friends did, as if cataloguing fragments of pottery. Now, she jotted down room measurements and mortgage calculations. *Oh, why dwell on it?* She didn't take for granted her clean streets, or that she could afford to shop at the farmer's market in the park. She'd even been able to buy her mother a little place when Marilyn was still living independently. It wasn't as if she fooled herself into thinking her financial security was the result of individual effort alone; her childhood had shown her that's not how the system worked. People didn't start from the same place.

She ran her fingertips across the letters of her keyboard, scanned the email to her clients. Cat had been born with a trail of inheritances, investments, and down payments passed from one generation to the next. She'd enjoyed regular vacations since childhood and viewed them as an essential form of self-care. Laura had worked hard, harder without all the safety nets and perks, and she'd bought in, but she didn't feel entitled to an easy life. Someone like her — with a bit of luck, a good enough education, and usually with white skin — occasionally managed to climb up a rung or two, leaving the inequitable social order unchanged. She was an interloper, a guest who could be asked to leave the party at any moment, and she understood that her good fortune had likely come to her at the expense of someone else's.

Laura was about to hit "send" on the email when there came a knock at the front door, and then the sound of someone leaning on the bell. She heard Cat step out of the shower and race down to answer the door thinking it was urgent. They met in the hall.

"It's Matt and Beth," she said. "Their power's out." Cat's white bathrobe was frayed and too short, her wet hair flattened and darker than it actually was, almost black. Water clung dew-like to her long lashes, and the backlight of their entrance cast spider-web shadows across her cheeks. Her beauty was most apparent when she was wet — out of the shower or emerging from a lake — and the hostile indifference Laura had become accustomed to evaporated. Suddenly, she wanted them to be new again and was staring. "Sorry I forgot to tell you. I've invited them to spend the night." She watched Cat dart back up the stairs before opening the door.

Nate, a preschooler, leapt into the hall on both feet, wearing his superhero backpack. He was carrying his treasured stuffed toy, a moose named Hector, and a dreidel. His older sister, Noa, dragged in two small sleeping bags. She was wearing a snorkel and swim goggles. "Sleepover!" she announced. Her father followed, balancing a bag of hamburger buns and a cooler of food. Beth hauled a mixing bowl full of ground beef. "Guess what I was making when the power cut?"

"It's only homes north of the Danforth," Laura said, bustling them out of the cold. The air was glacial, aloof. She felt its chill pass her lips, sit on her tongue, and bite down into her lungs. She stepped out onto the porch long enough to see the sky dressed in a veil of cloud, and cast her gaze eastward. Tomorrow she would begin sorting contents and preparing for an estate sale. It was hard to stop thinking about the place on Condor, and those tickets she'd found. Maybe the special occasion had been an anniversary or the night of a marriage proposal?

The filtered sun danced down over the trees that lined their winding street and the Japanese maple that shaded their porch. Lit, each spindly branch and each pointed leaf was preserved within a thin membrane of ice. She reached out for the closest leaf and ran her fingers across its smooth, cold surface. It snapped in her hand.

The winter she'd begun trying to get pregnant, Beth had told them she was carrying Noa. They were hopeful, certain it would happen quickly for them too. Thirty-five wasn't that old to conceive; many of their friends had had children in their early forties. Her sister-in-law, Abril, Cat's only sibling living outside of Argentina, had been forty-two when she'd conceived twins. When Laura had announced she was ready to try, Cat was thrilled; she'd scooped Laura up and spun her around. "You'll make a wonderful mother," she'd said. "You'll look sexy pregnant." Cat kissed all over her face, tiny, wet stars of gratitude, and then more ardently, upon her lips. They might've sparked a current back then, with all the heat they generated. They might've blown a fuse.

Inside, heading for her office, she called to Beth. "Make yourself at home! I'll be there in a sec." She just needed to send an email.

She and Beth had been roommates during their final years of university; they'd shared other kitchens, even when Beth kept kosher. They shared everything, actually. Well, nearly everything.

They'd never shared a bed, and Laura hadn't told her about the jealousy that obliterated all other feelings, a thick, choking envy that briefly rose inside of her when she watched Beth with the children. In moments, she'd even imagined that Beth's children were her own.

She returned to her laptop and found the unsent message to her clients in her drafts folder. On the other side of the door, Nate and Noa began arguing loudly over some minor infraction. Her stomach clenched. Before infertility, the sound of children had brought her immeasurable joy. She'd revelled in their blunt anger and their unselfconscious laughter. She'd been reassured of goodness by their free-flowing tears and the motherly kisses upon knees and elbows that took pain way. If she hadn't miscarried that last time, she'd have a toddler now.

Out her office window, snow tumbled from stratus clouds, a silent, white downfall. Thick drifts softened the evergreen, and eddies of snow spun between the neighbour's house and the garden shed. She caught the flash of a bright red cardinal perched atop the wrought iron fence that enclosed the yard — a drop of crimson in a papery white world, his feathers puffed for warmth. The fence was coated in ice, the yard covered in snow. She watched as the cardinal struggled to take flight.

Until recently, Cat had wanted them to have a family. At least six kids, Cat used to tease, because she'd grown up with five siblings. It didn't matter to her whether they were sons or daughters or who would change diapers, as long as there were children. This certainty was one of the reasons Laura had been attracted to Cat in the first place. Now, she claimed to be over it, as though Laura's three miscarriages had never happened, and the years they'd spent trying were for nothing. Cat was warm liquid moulding and adapting to reality while Laura was frozen in place. It enraged her. "We need to let it go now," Cat had said, when she told Laura to stop trying. "It just wasn't meant to be."

Well, fuck meant to be! Laura had wanted to be a mother long before she'd met Cat. She'd prayed for it even though she didn't believe. Why not her? For five long years she'd juggled medical appointments around her crazy work schedule, watched younger women with buoyant, hopeful energy push double strollers through the fertility clinic doors and flip the pages of glossy magazines while she waited for blood draws and ultrasounds, for embryos to enter the blastocyst stage, for extractions and transfers, and for a successful pregnancy. Together, she and Cat had celebrated friends and family as they gave birth to their second and third children without going into massive debt while she emptied their bank accounts, miscarried, and continued trying for her first. They were everywhere now, the fresh, naive faces. They didn't look haggard, weary, defeated. How she hated them in their oblivious privilege, for their luck, and especially for their optimism. Not being able to bear a child will break your heart, but hopes raised and dashed, month after month, will bleed all joy from living. As Nate and Noa abandoned their argument and chased off down the hall, she hit send on the email, then closed her laptop.

AFTER FIFTEEN MINUTES tucked across the street in her ankle boots, with a quarry in her stomach, Annie saw a group of girls enter the Danforth Woodbine Bowling Alley together, laughing, cases in hand. Eddie was one of them. They'd knocked, and someone on the other side had opened the door and in they'd shuffled, easy as pie. Annie gathered her nerve and crossed to the north side of the street.

"Password please?" said the voice behind the door when she knocked.

Eddie hadn't mentioned needing one. "I don't know it," she said, plainly. "But I was invited." It was a lie. She'd invited herself, though what did it matter now. Eddie had said she could come, and she was here.

"Name."

"None of your beeswax!" Saturday afternoons were girls only, and rumour had it that the place was full of working girls and toughs, downtowners who dabbled in the drug trade. If it got back to her father that she'd been there, well, she didn't want to think about that.

"I'm only toying with you," laughed the voice. "You're a rook-ie, aren't ya?" The girl opened the door to have a look at Annie. "Who was it invited you?"

"Edna Ferguson." Annie knew from doing the books that Eddie's full Christian name was Edna Marion Ferguson. To Annie's relief, that was all it took, knowing the right people. Or the wrong ones, she thought, stepping inside.

The place smelled of beer and peanuts and sweat. This was a two-floor, sixteen-lane house, the first she'd been in, and Annie wandered through the darkened hallway out into the first level, nervously, scouting for Eddie. Sunlight fell in through single windows at either end. The place was filled with cigarette smoke and the walls were a dirty yellow, splattered and stained, paint peeling. The wood floor was gleaming, and the lanes even more so, straight golden rivers of northern hard rock maple and Mississippi pine, carrying ball after wooden ball to the far end, where pin boys were stationed, ready to re-set for the next roll. Annie strode through the centre of the long room, pretending she belonged; that was her plan for the afternoon, to act just as natural as could be.

When she spotted Eddie, she was milling about with her teammates, at the top of lane ten with a Hires root beer in one hand and a cigarette in the other. Her black hair had been newly cut, high and tight. She was laughing at something one of the other girls had said, and her handsome smile was lit with amusement. Annie's lungs deflated a little at the thought that Eddie might already have a sweetheart.

There were five of them, Annie counted, not including Eddie, each wearing identical uniforms, stiff collared shirts with chest pockets and loose rayon pants, both a dull wartime grey. Annie felt foolish in her knee-length turquoise number, with the back piping and patent belt. It was her best day dress and she'd even taken the trouble to put her hair up in pin curls. Now she could see she was overdone, trying too hard to make an impression. Eddie's crowd appeared effortlessly casual. Rusty hens, her father would've called them derisively, though there were a couple around the scoring table who appeared to be more feminine, like her. One of them had red polish on her nails with fashionable unpainted half-moon tips, and the other, the one holding Eddie's attention, wore her blonde pompadour as though it were the British crown. Annie put on her best smile and, with fawn legs, approached the scoring table. They all turned to stare.

"You lost, honey?" teased Miss Pompadour.

"'Course she ain't lost," said the gruff-sounding girl with slick-backed hair and a pack of Lucky Strike in her breast pocket. She opened her arms wide, to receive a hug. "I'm right where she found me. Hey Sugar, you rationed?"

"She's with me," said Eddie, quietly.

The other two on the team exchanged glances, a chunky girl with a mop of red curls, and another so thin her uniform hung off her bones as it would a clothesline. Eddie's face flushed crimson.

"Ignore Dyllis," she said, of the gruff-sounding girl. And of the two flanking her, she added, "This here is Red and that's Louise." Both gave a nod and went back to their game.

"I'm Evelyn," said the pretty one with the painted nails, making room on the small bench next to her. She wore four fashionable identification bracelets. Annie didn't sit. Her backside was still sore from her father's last outburst, when he'd kicked her. Instead, she scanned the long room. On the wall, a colour poster from the Canadian Women's Army Corp showed a male and female soldier marching shoulder to shoulder. Another declared, "Buy Victory Bonds!" There was an advertisement for Canada Dry Spur, "The Finest Cola Drink," and a new brand of face cleanser with a picture of Asteroid Cold Cream that caught her eye. It purported to keep a girl looking youthful far into the future. "You got a name?" said Evelyn.

"Uh … Astrid," she said, interrupting Eddie before she could finish the introduction.

"Oh, how foreign sounding," purred Miss Pompadour. "I'm plain old Dorothy," she added, without breaking eye contact. "Eddie likes to call me Dot. Don'tcha?"

Annie felt a surge of jealousy, then recovered fast. She knew girls like this, the daughters of her father's Orange Lodge fellows, girls who mistrusted anyone they perceived as competition. With the war on, boys were scarce, and yet there were no boys here, were there? That was the point.

"I've come to play," she said.

"Sure you have," said Miss Pompadour.

THE CALL CAME from the clinic right after Laura had gotten Beth's family settled in the spare bedroom, with clean linen and towels. "Today's the day," the nurse chirped. Laura's last egg had successfully fertilized and was ready for implantation. Could she come now? She hung up and offered the others some excuse about being needed at the office. Out the door she went.

A magnet with a Jesus poem was stuck on the equipment cart in the clinic's operating room. Laura rolled her eyes then read it anyway. Would God finally grant her serenity, as it claimed, or a baby? On the cart sat a beige file folder with her first initial and surname printed in thick black ink and next to her name the words, "high risk."

Let me in.

She flinched when her doctor inserted the cold, steel speculum. Held her breath as he threaded the catheter through her cervix.

You could if you wanted to.

She played with her wedding band for good luck, tried to visualize her open cervix, a wide pink donut glistening with mucus. That ring had belonged to Cat's grandmother, and she'd birthed ten children. Laura closed her eyes, imagined her embryo attaching to her uterus. She was a tree with ripe fruit, peaches, apricots. She was fertile. The rose gold band from the Condor house felt warm to the touch. If this turned into a viable pregnancy, she thought, she'd tell Cat then.

After the procedure, Laura wandered down Bay Street. The sky was overcast, a grey day, with a diffuse sun peeking through. This was it, she thought, her last chance. The days and months and years of fertility appointments might finally be over. *Then what?* She crossed Dundas, heading for the north entrance of the Eaton Centre; after everything her body had been through, she deserved a treat. A Greyhound bus turned at the corner, spewing diesel smoke. Laura tried to hold her breath to avoid inhaling but ended up choking and feeling light-headed.

In Sears, she grabbed a pair of thermal gloves off the discount rack, then rummaged around in some remainder bins. The store's tinny sound system blasted "Jingle Bells." Shoppers filled the wide aisles. Sears had made a surprise announcement last month that it wouldn't be renewing its lease here, the hub store. Everything was on sale.

Laura carried the gloves to the nearest service counter and stood in line waiting her turn. She'd made the right choice years ago, she thought, about residential real estate. Commercial offered the higher yields, potentially, but she'd always known she didn't have the risk tolerance for it. She stepped up to pay.

"Oh, that last customer forgot these," she said. A box of Hanukkah candles had been left behind on the counter.

"She returned them," said the saleswoman. "The colours, I think."

Laura lifted the box to her nose, sniffed, then coughed. *Paraffin.* There weren't many traditions Marilyn had passed along; lighting the candles was one of them. "My mom would've loved these," she said, feeling guilt at having let the holiday come and go without marking it.

"Did you want me to add them?" The saleswoman's hand was hovering over the cash register, waiting to ring the order through.

"Sure, why not," said Laura. "There's always next year." Pink and purple weren't her preferred colours either, though they reminded her of home, her childhood home, and Marilyn's unusual Hanukkah parties.

Laura would be tasked with decorating the apartment, so she'd set out Marilyn's ever-growing snow globe collection and use the bright, bold scarves her mom bought at second-hand stores, draping them over closet doors and the high back of their white rattan peacock chair. Marilyn and Thom were usually stoned by the time the cannabis kugel went into the oven, and Laura would fend for herself for supper. Betty and Boop always turned up last, in frilly aprons and stilettos.

"Knock, knock." Betty, the more reserved of the two, would poke her head around the door, fluttering long, fake eyelashes. She wore a gold Jamaica map pendant in honour of her homeland.

Then Boop would sashay in ahead of her, hips swinging, hair flying, fringes and feathers dangling off her clothes and body. When she opened her mouth to speak, out fell a Newfoundland accent. "What y'at?"

It was years before Laura ever learned that they'd met in a doctor's office, waiting for their respective estrogen injections. It hadn't taken them long to figure that two self-made beauties out in the world together would be safer — and more profitable — than one. In no time flat they'd become roommates, business partners, and best friends.

Laura made her way out of the Eaton Centre, with her shopping bag in hand. What had happened to them since her mother's funeral? At that time, they'd been toying with the idea of making feminist porn.

Across the street, Dundas Square was crawling with skateboarders doing tricks. A religious fanatic stood at the corner wearing a sandwich board that quoted the Book of Revelation, shouting about the end of the world. What about Saffron and Ocean? Laura thought. What were they up to now? She remembered the year they'd announced they were going to become "friends with benefits." It was shortly before her bat mitzvah.

They were all sitting on mirrored cushions on the parquet floor. Somewhere, incense was burning, and the whole apartment smelled of sandalwood. Laura was between her mom and Thom, and had been put in charge of the turntable that was plugged into the wall beside her. "Hounds of Love" was spinning. As the adults passed the kugel around with a spoon, she forked her way through a giant stack of buttermilk pancakes. She accidentally dripped syrup onto the floor and tried to wipe it up by using her socked foot; that only smeared it around. Crossing her legs, the bottom of her sock stuck to the inseam of her stonewashed jeans.

"We just want everything out in the open," said Saffron. "So there's no awkwardness." She was wearing her usual, black T-shirt, black jeans. Her bleached-out bangs were teased and backcombed and standing high on her forehead with the help of a lot of hairspray.

"I think it's great," said Thom, being his usual chipper and optimistic self. Whatever people wanted, so long as they weren't hurting anyone, that was Thom.

"The art will suffer," said Marilyn through a mouthful of kugel. "You'll become distracted and domesticated."

"We're not farm animals," said Ocean, whose real name was Irene Ackermann. She was leaning back onto her arms, with her legs stretched out in front of her. Her bare toes reached Saffron's toes, opposite.

Laura flipped through a pile of records. Thom had brought some of his favourites from home, bands she'd never heard of. She was quietly humming along to Kate Bush.

"We've made ground rules," said Saffron. "Number one, no sleepovers."

Betty cocked a chiselled eyebrow. She'd worked as an accountant before emigrating. Now she charged wealthy businessmen by the hour for the pleasure of her company. She and Boop both knew that where sex was concerned, very little in this life was hassle-free.

"Listen, if you set expectations from the beginning," said Ocean.

Marilyn's lit hanukkiah sat in the centre of their circle on the floor, dripping candle wax onto a dinner plate. The apartment was poorly ventilated, and the incense and paraffin irritated Laura's eyes. Her throat had begun to itch. She got up to open the window. "What about protecting your friendship?" This was Marilyn. She winked at Laura for the fresh air. "Thanks kiddo."

"That's exactly what we're doing," said Ocean.

"Number two," Saffron continued, in a louder voice. "Time spent outside the bedroom should be kept to a group setting." She gestured to everyone around the circle. "Et voilà!"

Ew, thought Laura.

Betty sucked her teeth. "Oh honeys, this is foolishness."

Thom dug himself a large spoonful of kugel. "Such naysayers," he said, reaching over Laura to pass the pan to Ocean. "Let's hear what Laura thinks."

"Me?" Why ask for her opinion? "I dunno." Thom and her mom seemed happy enough together, very happy actually, but that was her only example of a relationship and it was unconventional. They didn't ever intend to live together or marry, and they went long stretches without seeing each other. She slipped a Stevie Wonder album out of its sleeve and set it down on the turntable, one of her own records this time.

Boop tapped one long, red acrylic fingernail on the parquet, *tap tap tap*. "Well, let's hear from ya, then?"

Laura ran her tongue across the front of her teeth and tasted syrup. The pancakes in her belly were beginning to expand. "I don't really care," she said. "But wouldn't it just be easier to actually date?"

"Thank you!" Betty smoothed her apron on her lap.

"We don't feel that way about each other," said Ocean. "We are ..."

"More evolved than that," finished Saffron. She wore a self-satisfied expression that Laura didn't trust. *How was not dating more evolved than dating?*

"G'wan," said Boop.

Ocean tried to sound blasé about the whole deal. "We just don't want to feel limited by any relationship right now," she said.

"I can see that," said Marilyn. She was nodding and squinting at them the way she did whenever she was really high. Laura doubted she could see much.

We, we, we. That was all Laura heard. A lot of *we* from two people who claimed they didn't want to be in a couple.

Boop began to sway her head from side to side like Stevie performing "Part-Time Lover."

"There she goes again," teased Betty. "Running that mouth like a track star."

Everybody laughed, and the candles flickered, softening their faces. They were all so beautiful, Laura thought, Thom included, with his warm brown eyes and newsboy cap. Her stomach was full and the rest of her was brimming with a feeling she could only describe now as love.

She turned onto a side street off Bay, where she'd parked her BMW, wishing she could've frozen the moment, and others like it, to take them out again now, as needed. Whatever alchemy had created the sense of belonging she'd had when her mom was still alive, she'd been lucky. At that thought, her chest tightened, regret settling in like ash and smoke. She hadn't heard from Thom in over a year. Their contact had gradually waned in the five years since Marilyn's death, and now they only spoke on birthdays and holidays. It was her fault, Laura knew, Thom had tried to keep up the connection. "You're family," he'd said after the funeral. But she hadn't known how to grieve then, that grief was a thing best done communally. That, and she'd felt judged for moving Marilyn into long-term care at the end. If Laura hadn't had her own lingering guilt about it, maybe she wouldn't have needed to put distance between them.

She reached her car, unlocked the driver's side door, and tossed her Sears bag across to the passenger seat. When was the last time she'd seen anyone? Was it that summer she'd bumped into Saffron by accident at a laundromat, around the time of Marilyn's yahrzeit? It was her lunch break and she'd darted in to make quick change of a five-dollar bill. There was Saffron, sorting T-shirts and underwear, her face freckled and sunburnt. They chatted about Obama's historic inauguration and the swine flu pandemic. They mentioned the strange circumstances surrounding Michael Jackson's death and the hope provided by Israel and Hamas declaring a ceasefire in Gaza, though the conversation was strained; they'd been open doors to one another and now they were sealed shut. Saffron had received an arts grant to run drawing and painting workshops in low-income neighbourhoods, she'd said, though it barely paid the rent. She was thinking about applying to teacher's college. She'd sounded happy, light. Her hair was longer than Laura remembered, and dyed rainbow colours for Pride.

"It's great to see you," Laura had said, meaning it.

"Thanks, kid. You too."

She'd jotted down Saffron's new number, promised to call so they could get together, but she hadn't called. What was the point, she'd thought, until she stopped grieving? It would only bring up all that pain. Now, she strapped on her seat belt realizing how selfish she'd been; after all, the others had lost Marilyn too. The muscles in her neck and shoulders stiffened. They weren't family by blood, but they were every bit her real family. She fished her phone out of her bag and texted Thom.

ANNIE STOOD AT the top of lane ten in oversized bowling shoes with the ball in her right hand, Eddie's chest pressed against her back, her hand overtop of Annie's to demonstrate the proper swing. "Don't angle to the side," said Eddie, showing what she meant by slowly guiding Annie's arm backwards and then overreaching. "Come straight back and roll fluid. See?"

Annie nodded. Eddie's hand was warm, rough, and calloused — she had worker's hands. Annie's were damp with nerves; the ball might slip right out and hit the floor once Eddie let go. "Check the centre mark on that line in front of you and keep your eyes on the headpin."

At her back, she could feel Eddie's heart pounding through the thin material of her dress. She'd never felt the jitters with any of the fellas she'd been out with, not even that Roy she'd let kiss her for two hours in the movie house. An unfamiliar kind of nervousness rippled under her skin, the need to connect with Eddie, change her life. "Show me once more," she said, craning her neck. "I don't quite have it."

Dot rolled her eyes. Eddie pretended not to see. Annie smelled good, like a garden. What exactly did she mean by coming here? It was obvious she didn't know how to bowl; equally clear she wasn't trying that hard to learn. Was Annie one of those girls who dabbled with danger but always went back to the safety and comfort of some unsuspecting fiancé? Eddie had fallen too many times for that racket, and she wasn't doing it again.

The last girl, a strawberry blonde who bowled for a west-end league, had played her good. Olena was her name. Ukrainian. From the first day their teams met, Olena was hanging off Eddie's sleeve and her every word. Public displays made Eddie uncomfortable, it wasn't safe for one thing, and bowling wasn't a talker's game. Still Olena pressed her for conversation like it was classified information. It turned out she had a boyfriend serving overseas and when he came home all torn up and shell-shocked, that was that. A bit of a relief, truth be told.

Before Olena, there'd been Ailish, the daughter of an Irish pub owner. She'd been discreet. She'd worn her honey-coloured hair down to her shoulders and little white gloves. Ailish put on airs, though, and it was clear by the second outing that she had a taste for finer things than a brick worker could afford.

Marjorie was Eddie's first. They'd met at a victory garden picnic where Eddie had noticed her welcoming smile and modest manner of dress. Turned out Marjorie was a churchgoer. Nothing against God, just that Eddie didn't believe he lived in any one house, and she wasn't prepared to spend her Sundays off sitting on a pew, being proved wrong.

The bowling league had taught her: there were the girls who got their kicks with you and then married men, girls who fell in love with the idea of love, and girls who were so afraid of themselves they couldn't look at you without feeling dirty or crazy or mean. She lifted Annie's arm, guided her through the motions of a proper swing. Which type was this?

"Got it now, *Astrid*?"

The sarcasm fell with hot breath, on the back of Annie's neck, and Annie lowered her voice to a whisper. "What do you want me to tell them? That you're out with the boss's daughter?" With that, she took a step forward and knelt a few inches, bringing her arm back as Eddie had shown, and in one great motion, she swung and let it roll. The ball bounced on the lane making a loud thud, and then veered to the left, ultimately taking out two pins.

"Nice going. Not bad for a first try," said Dyllis.

Annie beamed. When she turned around Eddie's face was red as shale brick.

"Three rolls a frame, unless you strike," Louise said. "Go again. You have to take down the corner-right pin for points to count."

"Tillie Hosken scored a perfect 450 a few years ago," said Evelyn, cheerily. "She's the only girl so far."

Annie faced the v formation at the end of her lane. She'd just be happy not to embarrass herself. She was pleased to see she'd rattled Eddie some and gave a slow wiggle in her dress, before she rolled again, a little something more for Eddie to think about.

By the second frame, when Eddie ran for root beers, Annie was enjoying herself; the solid weight of the ball in her palm, the smooth feel of the wood and its grain. It didn't take long before she'd learned which pin boys did the fastest job of setting, and why Eddie had been made anchor. Whenever her turn came 'round, Eddie easily bowled a strike — three consecutive ones — without being showy, which started Dyllis squawking like a turkey in honour of the play. Eddie was affable, generous with praise for the others, no grandstanding. She enforced proper game etiquette by example and promoted fairness, the sort of person who fostered camaraderie within competition, the sort, Annie thought, she could trust.

An hour later, she was still rolling with too much revolution, making the ball hook left. "You're a bit of a cranker," Dyllis said. A sidespin wasn't a problem if it hit the pins, but more often than not she was leaving deadwood.

"Naah, she's cooking now," said Eddie. She was staring at Annie's bright red lips. "You just need to learn where your pocket is. That's the perfect place for your ball to hit if you want a strike. I think of it as Home Sweet Home."

RETURNING FROM THE embryo transfer, Laura found Beth in the kitchen, teaching Noa, in goggles, how to cut onions without crying. "Why have I never thought of that," she said, giving the child a squeeze as she moved past. She tossed the box of Hanukkah candles in a drawer and poured herself a glass of red wine. "Anybody else?" She waved the bottle and then realized she shouldn't drink, just in case.

From bar stools at the end of the counter, Catalina and Matt each held up bottles of beer. Beth shook "no." The tannins do a number on her head now.

"Everything at work okay?" Cat asked.

"A last-minute fill-in at an open house," she lied. "The agent came down with the flu. How's it going here?"

Cat reached back and opened the fridge to grab more beer. "We're debating whether or not the mayor will declare a state of emergency." She popped the cap off a bottle and handed it to Matt.

"I'm still shaking off a twelve-hour shift," said Matt. "It's a mess out there."

Laura studied him discreetly: his usual blue jeans and Raptors T-shirt. He didn't look especially tired or preoccupied. His mood seemed quiet but jovial. Things had been strained since Beth found those flirtatious texts on his cellphone. Had she confronted him yet?

"Apparently hospitals are relying on backup generators," said Beth.

"You wouldn't believe what's going on," said Matt. "First, we get a dozen carbon monoxide calls. Stupid, fucking people using outdoor generators inside."

"Maybe they couldn't pay their heating bill," said Laura. She opened the refrigerator door looking for the cranberry juice.

"It's a dangerous thing to do."

Laura turned with the bottle in hand. "I know, but if they'd freeze otherwise."

"C'mon, Laura, let the guy finish his story."

She glared at Cat while she poured herself a glass and took a sip, embarrassed to have been reprimanded like a child. There'd been more than one time when Marilyn had had to choose between buying groceries or paying for utilities and rent. "I'm just saying, people only take those kinds of risks when they don't have other options."

"She's right," said Beth.

"Anyway," continued Matt. "We got a record number of bad falls. Then, in comes this call about an eighty-year-old on the nineteenth floor of a high-rise. Ran out of her heart medication two days ago. No power, no elevators. She was trapped."

"Oh my God," said Beth.

Matt nodded and took a swig. "Could've been my Bubbe, you know? We climbed nineteen flights. Carried her down in a chair."

All at once, Laura felt limp, lifeless. Her arms were sore. She'd pictured a chair while Matt was talking, though it had been a wheelchair and she was clumsily helping her mother into it for the first time, hoisting and carrying Marilyn's full weight in her arms, like she was a sleeping child. There was the whiff of urine from Marilyn's diaper that needed changing and a small, dog-eared note that fell from Marilyn's pocket, landing at Laura's feet.

"Gimme that!" Reflexively, Marilyn had tried to grab the paper, but Laura held it out of reach long enough to read it. It was a list. A list, *Things To Remember:*

1) Laura is my daughter.
2) She's an archaeologist.
3) I love her.

Laura stopped breathing for a moment. Her skin tightened. Her windpipe narrowed, then her oesophagus, intestines, the canals in her eardrums, her arteries and blood vessels, all collapsing, shrinking to an economy of pain. If only it were possible to contain hurt to one small place. She pressed the note back into her mother's pocket for safekeeping, her voice trapped at the bottom of her throat. Would they both be defeated by this disease? It was already changing who they were to each other. Who was she if her mother couldn't remember her name? The name she'd chosen out of all others because it had meant something and made Laura special. Names were destiny, she thought. Take them away and who's left?

"Laura? Hellooooo?" Cat waved a hand in front of her eyes. "Where'd you go?"

She shook her head to dislodge the memory. "Nowhere," she said. "Sorry."

WHEN SHE STEPPED out of the bowling alley onto Danforth Avenue with the other girls, Annie felt as though she'd crossed back over an equator, an invisible line on one side of which lay her old self, everything known and familiar, with all attendant expectations and approval, and on the other, some new, untried freedom. Eddie held the door until they were all through. Dot, Red and Dyllis, and Evelyn following behind Louise. The whole gang of them, and other girls too, from other teams. They poured outside, saying their goodbyes, and making off for home.

Annie didn't want to go. In only a few short hours, Eddie's world seemed more familiar than it should've been. That was how it had felt when she'd mastered her maths at ten, when multiplying and dividing numerals finally clicked and she understood the patterns and how to use them; it had been exciting and natural, as though she'd known it all along. Now, she watched the girls laughing together, and her heart sank. They would soon disperse, with Eddie going one way and she going the other, back to her real life. When they'd next see each other, at the pit, she'd have to pretend tonight had never happened. But tonight was what she wanted. Tonight multiplied by infinity. How might she conspire to make it last?

"Thanks for letting me play," she said.

"You were pretty good," chirped Evelyn. "Wasn't she good, Dot?"

"I suppose so." The group walked westward. "Plan on making a habit of it?"

Annie upturned the collar of her coat. "Oh, I don't know." She looked for Eddie's reaction. Did Eddie hope she'd return next Saturday? Her face gave no clues.

Red crossed in the middle of the road, to the south side of Danforth. She lifted her hand. "Catch ya next week." Everyone except Eddie followed, and Annie watched them wind down around East Lynn.

"Do come back!" Evelyn called out to her.

Annie waved. "Bye."

The autumn sky held the oranges, golds, and pinks of turning leaves. Sweater weather, she thought, with a shiver. It was cooler, though not yet cold, more the season for endings than beginnings. She turned to face Eddie. "I guess it's good night, then." Much as she wished to prolong their time together, in plain sight, the two of them could be caught out by someone who would relay the information to her father. She started for the transit waiting station at Danforth and Coxwell. With each step, she felt a gravitational pull away from Eddie.

"Hold on!" said Eddie. "I'll walk with you a ways." The wind rose and a trio of blue-grey pigeons flew overhead. Eddie ducked instinctively at the sound of flapping wings, which made Annie smile.

"They flock up the Don Valley every spring, you know? I've watched them gather by the thousands at the beaches."

"You like birds, then."

Annie nodded. "Every year Father takes me with him to the Royal Winter Fair to watch them award prizes to the best-bred pigeons."

"Pigeons. Huh."

"Don't say it like that. They have noble ancestors. The army enlisted passenger pigeons to deliver messages during the Great War."

"Isn't that something."

"One bird called Beach Comber was even given a medal for bringing back word of the tragedy at Dieppe. Father likes military history, that's all. But I think they're amazing creatures. Some nights, I actually fly in my dreams," she said, then blushed for having shared such a personal detail.

"Do you suppose they're using birds in the war effort now?"

Annie shrugged. She shortened her stride to buy them more time together. "Your friends seem really nice," she said.

"Even Dot?"

"She speaks her mind. I'll say that much."

"Dot's all right. A little wary of newcomers is all."

"Well, she doesn't have to worry a lick about me," said Annie. "I'd be hard pressed to get away again any time soon. I was lucky tonight because Father's lodge was initiating him in as Deputy Master. He left early for a lodge brother's house and won't remember so much as his own name by the end of it."

"My father and brother are both Orangemen," said Eddie. "In Hamilton, where we're from."

Most of the powerful men in the city belonged to a Loyal Orange Lodge, Annie knew; there was little way into local politics or business without the conservative Scots-Irish network, a fraternity known for anti-Catholic hostility. "Would you join if you could?"

Eddie shook her head. Her aspirations were modest, and she held no particular affection for her own kind. "They're not all as broad-minded as your father."

"Broad-minded!" Annie couldn't contain her laughter. "James T. Armstrong? Now I've heard everything."

"More than half the boys at the pit are Catholics."

"Well sure, as long as you're not sitting at his dining table or dating his daughter, he'll tolerate you for a profit."

Eddie looked injured by the remark. "Good thing I'm not doing either, then."

"Oh, I don't share his attitudes. I only meant that ... well ... he's not always what he appears to be."

"How 'bout you, Annie? You what you pretend to be?"

In the distance they heard the rhythmic sound of a streetcar's steel wheels rolling — *inevitableinevitableinevitable* — like fate through the neighbourhood. "My father can't know I was at the bowling alley," she said.

Eddie nodded. "Better for us both that way."

The wind blew and a tornado of dry leaves formed and then disassembled on the path at Annie's feet. "Why did you leave Hamilton?" she asked.

Eddie shuffled alongside wordlessly. She was definitely drawn to the girl. They had an easy connection when it was just the two of them. So easy, in fact, she wanted to take Annie into her confidence. She shouldn't. Best not to forget to whom she was speaking. "Change is good." She shrugged.

"Do you miss your family?"

"At times, sure. But, well ... Let's just say some people get on better with a few miles of road between them." She was trying to sound cavalier though Annie recognized resignation in her voice. Whatever Eddie's family situation, she wasn't welcome home anymore, or felt she didn't belong there. Annie's chest swelled at the thought that, like her, Eddie was an orphan of sorts. "Do they even know where you work?"

"You sure are full of questions."

Annie felt her face redden once more. "That's what my mother always said." She'd crossed a line by coming to the bowling alley, they both knew it, and now she was being intrusive; still she wanted to know Eddie and the world Eddie inhabited. How far was she willing to go to gain Eddie's trust? "I like the name Astrid better than my own," she confessed.

"I think Annie is a fine name."

"You do?" Up until today Eddie hadn't seemed to notice much of the real her, only what she wanted to see: the boss's daughter in a pretty dress, someone forbidden. Didn't most people place upon others the qualities they needed them to possess? What if Eddie knew about the bruises she sometimes wore beneath her expensive clothes? Or that she had a head made for more than numbers? "I don't need an escort," she said, when they reached Coxwell. The streetcar wouldn't take more than ten minutes down Broadview. "I'm accustomed to looking out for myself."

"No doubt about that." Eddie hung back, watching as the streetcar pulled up to the waiting station. Annie boarded. When she sat and opened the window, Eddie approached and stood on tiptoe to be heard. "Listen, if you — or Astrid — happened by the movie house next Saturday, we would run into each other again."

Annie grinned as the car pulled out. "I do like coincidences," she said.

"NOA MAKES REAL good burgers," said Nate, proudly. He was on the floor trying to entice the cat to play with his superheroes.

"Watch out for Sourpuss. She's old and mean," said Laura. "She might take a swipe at you."

"I'll put her in the basement," said Cat.

Nate squealed and dissolved into a fit of tears. "Nooooo! My cat!"

Matt moved to scoop Nate into his arms, swinging him high. "Zoom, zoom, zoom!" he said, mimicking a rocket ship launching to the moon. Cat would be physical like that, Laura thought. She'd be the one their child climbed onto for horsey rides and piggy backs.

Laura watched Cat carry Sourpuss to the top of the basement stairs and set her down gently. If this IVF cycle worked and she carried to term, would their child prefer Cat? How exactly would she announce the pregnancy when she hadn't even told Cat she'd had the embryo implanted? Write it on her belly? Say it with cupcakes? Hide the test results in Cat's wallet, coffee cup, Christmas stocking? What had ever made her think she could get away with it?

After the meal, Matt set the kids up in the spare room with jelly doughnuts and a DVD. Beth kept Laura company while she loaded the dishwasher. The storm blew like thick smoke outside the double glass doors.

"Looks like a scene from a movie out there," she said.

"Thanks again for putting us up tonight."

"Are you kidding?" She loved having Beth around, a friend with the same sense of humour, someone with whom she'd shared so much history, who had known her mother. The two of them had hit it off the moment Beth plopped down in the seat next to her in first-year anthropology class wearing several feminist, anti-racist buttons pinned to her jean jacket. "End Apartheid Now!" "No Means No!" "My Body My Choice." Midway through the lecture, while watching grainy footage of Koko the gorilla revolutionizing human understanding of apes by using sign language, Beth had leaned over and whispered, "I thought this was supposed to be a bird course." They'd both laughed out loud and eventually Laura had had to excuse herself, because she couldn't stop. "Hey, remember my mom's Hanukkah parties?" she said.

"How could I forget?" Beth cleared her throat and imitated Marilyn. "A minor holiday is still a holiday, girls. Pass the cannabis kugel!"

"God, I miss her," said Laura.

"Yeah."

Beth looked tired, Laura thought. Run ragged, juggling shift work at the shelter, making meals for the kids, and driving them to their respective appointments. She was the one who stayed awake in the night if someone was ill, not Matt, and volunteered at Nate's preschool one morning each month. And yet, just as often it was to Matt they ran when they fell or were shoved to the ground by another kid. It was to Matt they headed with open arms.

"A weird thing happened yesterday when I was out," she said. "This street kid approached me. She had a little black dog with her. I offered to take them to Nellie's but she blew me off."

"We don't have beds right now, anyway. I would've had to call around."

Nellie's was a thirty-three-bed shelter full of traumatized women and children and Beth tirelessly absorbed their suffering without judgement. She believed people were more than their circumstances, and more than even they knew they could be. Beth had a knack for that kind of optimism, and the patience for searching out the warm, golden lining sewn into any soul.

"Does that happen often, that you don't have space?"

Beth nodded. "We turn people away almost every night."

"That's brutal," said Laura. "You know what pisses me off? I can think of at least half a dozen houses sitting empty in the east end alone, meanwhile kids like Astrid are out there, cold and hungry, doing God knows what to stay alive."

"Astrid?"

"I didn't want to press her on the name; she barely trusted me as it was."

"So she's a good judge of character." Beth stuck out her tongue, playfully.

"Cute," said Laura. "Thing is, I should've done more. I left her my number and she's probably got no way to call. If she freezes to death, it'll be on me."

"That's how I feel at the end of every shift," said Beth. "Whatever I do, it's not enough. These kids need supports that just aren't there. Secure housing for starters. Free counselling. Someone to love them without conditions. The need is endless and resources are limited. Most people want to pretend it isn't happening."

"I'm afraid I'm becoming one of those people, Beth. I don't know when it happened. It's like I'm harder somehow, detached from other people's pain. Like I have this shell I wasn't born with, or I've used up all my empathy."

"You deal with a different population. It's easy to forget."

"That's generous. I deal with money. Honestly, I don't know how you can still be friends with me."

Beth forced a grin. "I don't know either."

"I'm serious. Remember all those years I volunteered at the food bank? And the fundraisers I used to organize at the brokerage?"

"You wanted to make a difference."

"Where has that person gone?"

"Laura, your mom got sick so young. It was a lot to deal with. That took a toll. Short of a social revolution, and believe me, I pray for that, we all do the best we can."

"That's just it, I didn't do anything for Astrid."

"Well, maybe she'll turn up at the shelter. If you're ever in a similar situation again, try and give out our crisis line. It's open twenty-four hours and it's anonymous."

IN THE SPRING of Marilyn's upper year at art school, the Market Gallery on Front Street held an exhibition of the top students' works. For her piece, Marilyn had built an enormous bird cage by soldering scrap metal she'd sourced at a junkyard. Now, she was sitting on a child's backyard swing set in the centre of the stage, tarred and feathered in a paste of molasses and dollar-store feather boas. In the background, Thom's black-and-white documentary on Margaret Howell Mitchell, a Toronto ornithologist who'd discovered 289 species of birds in Rio de Janeiro, played without sound, while Marilyn whistled like a thrush and sang Prince's "When Doves Cry." Periodically, she would lay a giant blue egg (a.k.a. a croquet ball) into a pile of hay below the swing and scream at gallery visitors, "Bird brain! Bird brain!"

Laura stood with Thom and Ocean and Saffron, in a corner of the main space, watching and cringing. Why had she worn her neon green headband and leg warmers? She'd bought them with some of her bat mitzvah money and now there was no place to hide. She counted patrons as they entered the gallery, sixty-two so far. She inched over to the food table and lingered there, stuffing her face with cheese cubes and grapes, then she found Thom again.

"Isn't she amazing?" he said.

"Amazing," echoed Laura, but she wanted to run or shrink or disappear. Her face burned with embarrassment. She didn't bother to contradict him, Thom always sounded as if he was under some kind of spell where her mother was concerned. It was endearing, even if he was a hopeless case.

"If I had a fraction of her talent," said Saffron. She was all in black, except for her red sneakers and the purple mohawk that was growing out.

"Your drawings are really good," said Laura. "I like them."

"Thanks." Saffron messed Laura's hair, playfully. "Your mom's in a totally different league though."

Marilyn did have a particular way of seeing life. Like how she'd taught Laura "feminist" chess, where the queen determined the win, and the way she insisted that black dogs were as bad luck as black cats, and how she stopped to recite the Mourner's Kaddish whenever they came upon roadkill: *Yitgadal v'yitkadash sh'mei raba b'alma di-v'ra....* She sure was unlike anyone else, and Laura figured that inviting other people to share in her vision was her mother's best definition of love. Naturally, Laura wanted to be included, and to understand what everyone else saw that she didn't.

"So this is good then?"

"It's just so goddamned gutsy," said Ocean.

Ocean was a poet and a conceptual artist, something Laura understood even less about than her mother's performances. She watched Ocean swirl her wine around in its glass and sniff it before tasting. She caught a whiff of Ocean's patchouli oil.

"But why is she dressed like a bird?"

Ocean pointed to where the bold black print of an artist's statement leapt out in contrast to the white wall paint. "Read that," she said.

Bird Brain uses the life of Toronto ornithologist Margaret Howell Mitchell to represent the limitations imposed by our culture on women who attempt to break barriers. Mitchell, whose significant academic credentials and intelligence were overlooked and whose career, though ultimately renowned, was nevertheless confined to the status of volunteer, is shown in documentary form, while the artist performs her entrapment.

"I still don't get it," said Laura. *What barriers?* She couldn't imagine her mother being held back by anyone or anything.

"You will when you're older," said Saffron.

Laura rolled her eyes. Growing up a child among adults, she was used to being condescended to. It was annoying and tedious, but until right now she'd never felt jealous; it was as if others could access part of her mother that she never would. "Whatever," she said.

She leaned against a white wall, grateful there was no one else her age around to witness her humiliation. She studied an abstract painting, stared out the gallery windows.

"Mazel tov again on becoming a bat mitzvah," said Ocean.

"Yeah, thanks." The event had taken place in the party room of Marilyn's professor's condo, with a tacky Hawaiian theme. It was hosted by a visiting friend of her mom's from the Manhattan School of Music, who spoke about the influence of the book of Exodus on Bob Dylan's protest songs. "You almost beat me at the limbo," she said.

When her mother's performance was finally over, patrons ambled through the gallery introducing themselves to Marilyn, people from the city's museums and heritage services, fellow students. Though it hadn't yet been announced, she'd won the school's year-end prize for Best Emerging Artist. She would receive a cheque for one thousand dollars and a gift basket full of wine and chocolate.

Laura got in line to speak with her mom. When it was her turn with Marilyn, she said, "Can we go soon?"

"I'm working, kiddo."

"But I'm so *bored*."

Marilyn leaned in and gave Laura a quick hug, leaving molasses and feathers stuck to her oversized *Flashdance* sweatshirt. "In a few minutes," she said. "And there's no such thing as boredom, only boring people. Now go entertain yourself."

OUTSIDE THE TORONTO East General, two orderlies in green scrubs huddled on a smoke break. A Wheel-Trans driver was rolling patients down the small ramp of his bus. He wore a red-and-white Santa Claus suit. The automatic doors ushered visitors in and out and in.

On the fourth-floor Intensive Care Unit, at the end of an airless corridor that smelled vaguely of urine and rubbing alcohol, a door was partly ajar. Inside, Eddie's gaunt, emaciated body lay high on a mattress, head slightly elevated, tilted to one side. She was hooked up to a ventilator, the long plastic tube covering her mouth. Hers wasn't the face of a young or an old woman, of anyone living or dead. The coma had been a deep somnolence holding her between worlds, outside time where love lies dormant, waiting. Her weak heart beat to the rhythm of the machine, lungs rising and sinking like flat, grey suns.

She listened, and every sound on the ward was magnified, nurses squelching in and out of her room in sticky, rubber-soled shoes, patients shuffling back and forth outside the door in crumpled paper gowns and slippers, pigeons cooing on the window ledge. No one knew for certain that she was in there, trapped within walls of aged flesh, a force that still mattered.

Once in a while a doctor would arrive with a team of new residents and surround her bed in a horseshoe, talking about her as if she wasn't there. They consulted about the catheter emptying her bladder or the stomach tube that brought nutrients. They checked her IV fluid bag and to see whether she'd had her medication that day. Irreversible coma, they'd say. Acute ischemic stroke victim.

Might go on like this for years. And yet, time was of no conse-
quence. For Eddie, there was only this waiting, waiting, and the
uncertainty. What remained of love?

Now, from her hospital bed, she heard the interns making
rounds. Then, someone poked a head in, scribbled a few notes in
pen on a clipboard, and was gone without addressing her by name.

Hearing them from her middle place, between living and not
living, Eddie laughed inside, an unpleasant feeling, like a bubble
that can't burst. She knew what the doctors didn't: the coma was
buying time, not wasting it. There was a reason she was holding
on, why she was still here. When you extended the life of a house,
the men down at the pit called it cut and plug. You hammered and
chiselled in around a crumbling rectangle on a wall, not beating too
hard, mind, not shaking good things loose, just carefully removing
old mortar from the surface of the brick and tapping it into rubble
until there was nothing there except a pocket waiting to be filled.
Slip in the replacement brick, and presto! Restoration. Sure, no one
was immortal, she knew that, but people were like houses, they
could be restored and go on, in a sense. That was what she was
waiting for; that was what would get her home.

THE NEXT MORNING, Laura was in the front hall helping Beth bundle the kids into their snowsuits when Matt's cellphone rang. It was their neighbour. "Hello ... You're kidding?"

Beth stopped what she was doing, wrapping a scarf around Nate's neck. "What is it?"

"Okay, I'm heading up now." Matt slipped his phone into the pocket of his jeans. "That old oak came down on the house last night."

"Kaboom!" said Nate.

"It took out part of the roof."

"Shit."

Cat pulled Laura aside. "I'm working from home today," she said. "Site plan sketches for a new renovation. Can you keep them out for at least two hours? Oh, and if you're by the health food store, pick up those power bars I like?"

"You're not planning to run in this weather?"

Cat had jogged around Queen's Park every morning when they were undergraduates and had run on the treadmills at Hart House. Over the years, she'd become one of those fanatics who ran outdoors year-round and was working up the chain from 5 to 10 to 25K. Her aim was to enter the Waterfront Marathon next fall.

"I've got good cleats," she said.

Nate came bounding up in his red snowsuit and threw his arms around her legs. "Ready!" he squealed.

Laura let herself be tugged toward the front door. "What do you think about our trip?" she said. "Hundreds of flights have already been delayed. I think we should refund."

"Of course you do."

Cat had always resented her reluctance to spend their vacation days in Argentina. It was annoying. Laura got on well enough with Cat's family but there were other places in the world she'd like to visit. "I'll wait another day or two," she said.

She and Beth took turns pulling the children up Logan on a plastic toboggan. The energy of the storm was palpable, contagious, and despite common sense, they'd been seduced outside as if by an irresistible lover who wouldn't take no for an answer. They passed a woman in a purple polka-dot coat. She smiled too broadly, conspiring with them to bring about such an event. A man was out strolling with a black umbrella raised. "Hello," he said, crackling with intensity that would've seemed inappropriate on any other occasion.

Across the street, Withrow Park was unrecognizable. It had transformed overnight from a pearly snow dune to a bleak battlefield of debris and destruction. Huge Norway and silver maples were uprooted, split in half from the weight of ice, their largest boughs — corpses — splayed and scattered across the field. Others clung upside down like broken limbs. They swung, pendulous, in the wind and threatened to drop. "We shouldn't be out here," Beth said.

"Probably not," said Laura, but she didn't care. The ice and snow brought a kind of exhilarating madness; it woke all her senses and invented new ones. It stabbed at car headlights and yet tickled her face while it fell. It glittered white sugar on the ground then swirled in threatening funnel clouds above. Comforting and disorienting, the storm made her believe in something more powerful than her small self. Besides, there were always so many things she shouldn't do, especially when she might be pregnant. She shouldn't eat raw meat or shellfish, or drink so much caffeine. She shouldn't get stressed out or waste energy wondering why good people are stricken with terrible diseases, and she definitely shouldn't ask herself what it will mean for her life if there were no viable pregnancy this time. She was still not ready to be one of those women, marked as barren or broken, or simply unnatural. *Think positive thoughts*, her mother would say if she were here. After so many years of trying, Laura didn't dare allow herself to indulge.

They continued on toward the Danforth while the kids tried to catch snowflakes on their tongues. Passing the dog park, there was a lone standard poodle, black, prancing to the top of a giant hill of snow. Laura watched him stick his snout deep into the side of the mound and toss snow gleefully over his head. She blinked and there was Buddy, or at least a terrier that looked like Buddy — a black speck running circles around the other, larger dog. She searched for Astrid, no sign of her. When she glanced back again Buddy was gone. Had it really been him?

The chain-link swing set at the toddler park was painted in ice, glistening. The tennis courts were blanketed. There was still power on the south side of the street, so she darted into the coffee shop on the corner and grabbed everyone a hot chocolate.

Toby was in line, wearing Jackson in a Baby Bjorn. Laura took her place behind them. "Hey," said Toby as Jackson began to wail.

"Hello again." This was the problem with being a realtor, Laura thought. Can't risk burning bridges. She had to be polite and approachable. Future business depended upon maintaining a wide social network. In fact, networking was one of the reasons she'd joined her book club in the first place. Hockey and golf had proven lucrative for the men in her brokerage. "Your pipes working again?" she asked.

Toby began swaying back and forth, to try and settle Jackson. "The plumber's meeting me there in ten," she said.

"That's good. Listen, if you happen to hear of anybody who's looking for a two bedroom, I'll be listing a great little house on Condor Avenue soon."

They made more small talk about the mayor's crack scandal and Malala not being awarded the Nobel, until Toby advanced to the cash register and scrambled for her debit card. "Gotta get him outta this thing," she said, sounding embarrassed. She grabbed an extra-large coffee from off the counter and hurried outside.

A minute later, Laura and Beth were sipping their drinks, admiring the holiday displays in shop windows, while the steam blew off their cups and warmed their gloves. The kids got busy trying to make snowballs of frozen slush.

"Did you see Toby in there?" Beth asked.

Laura leaned against the coffee shop window. "That baby's got a set of lungs on him."

"I remember those days. Nate was the same."

Laura felt a sudden gulf open up between them, invisible and yet very real. Motherhood was its own country, and she had no passport. "Things with you and Matt any better?" she asked, changing the subject.

Beth looked to make certain the children were occupied before lowering her voice. "If you were me, would you leave him?"

"Leave?"

Beth gave her the look, the one that made it clear they were talking about Matt's borderline infidelities. Beth had shown her the texts a couple of months ago, and she'd assumed Matt would put an immediate end to it, that they'd work it out. "What did he say when you confronted him?"

"Denied it, at first. Then he said it wouldn't happen again. It's still going on."

"What a shit."

"You wouldn't put up with it."

Laura knew better than to insert herself into someone else's relationship, even if that someone was her closest friend. If she told Beth to leave and Beth ended up staying, their friendship could suffer. "It's different for me," she said. "I don't have children to consider." She felt a faint flutter in her uterus then, a tickling sensation. Could this be cells multiplying? Luck turning her way? She was sure it was stronger now, and could almost hear it too, a rapid shuffling, like a deck of cards.

"The crazy thing is, I almost feel like it's my fault."

"It's absolutely not," said Laura. "Matt's responsible for his own behaviour; he's a grown man." Still, she couldn't help thinking that their problems might not all be Matt's fault, either. Relationships were complicated, and rarely as they appeared from the outside. Couples found extraordinary ways to escape the cages they'd built for themselves. Maybe sexting with strangers was Matt's way. Since becoming parents, Laura had noticed that her friends' previous lives were unrecognizable, and their current ones defined by roles they'd fallen into and domestic routines they couldn't seem to change. Matt had been sleeping on the couch for two and a half years, since Nate had come along. Unlike Noa, Nate woke often through the night and that disrupted Matt's sleep. "Mid-life bullshit," Laura added. "But he loves you guys."

"I don't know anymore," said Beth.

"I do. He's just flirting with fantasy. It makes him feel free, like peering into other people's windows at night. You know, trying to imagine different possibilities."

"Not the same," said Beth.

"Okay, maybe not. But you two can come back from this."

Laura sounded certain because she'd bordered on unfaithful too and knew it didn't have to mean the end. Each new house she toured was an alternate existence. *Could I live here?* she'd think. *What if this were my life instead? My home?* She'd also come close to a full-blown affair once, with a client. They'd met at a private viewing and then continued to meet in different homes, where they'd kiss. She'd felt European, mature, and convinced herself she was doing an enlightened thing. After a couple of weeks, though, the other woman had wanted more. Laura stopped it. The idea of an affair was decadent and sophisticated, something that rolled off the tongue full of airy promise. The reality was people were bound to get hurt. She looked across at her friend. "Beth?"

"Honestly, I'm so tired I almost don't give a shit what he's doing. He doesn't know a thing about what I do at home, or what the kids need. Just swoops in after being gone for days on end and plays the superhero. That's what truly kills me."

"He can't help the shift work."

"And neither can I." Beth fished in her coat pocket, found an old, crusty napkin from some fast-food joint. Framed by her wool hat, her eyes appeared larger, brimming with tears. "You're so lucky you don't have to deal with this crap."

"There's other crap," said Laura.

"I know. I'm sorry. I'm just overwhelmed."

"You don't actually know that anything's happened."

Beth blew her nose. "I can feel it. Even when he is around, he's not really with me. I swear, he's either at the gym or out with friends. Or texting." She reached down and pulled Nate's hat over his ears. "I've thought about couples counselling," she said. "It's just, well, I know it's not the thing to say in this day and age, but it's his problem, you know? Not mine. I've got enough to deal with."

Laura nodded. She'd been living with Cat for years without broaching important subjects. She'd given up expecting they could be more honest, and although she was frustrated and stunted by their silent arrangement, she'd accepted it. People can get used to just about anything, with enough time. She felt her shoulders drop. "Cat and I aren't connecting anymore either," she said.

"You've been through a lot."

"I'm not so sure it's the baby stuff."

"No? What then?"

She used to be desperately in love with Cat, a burning, pressurized kind of love she carried in her body every moment of every day. How does that just disappear? Maybe her mother had been right. Monogamy was an expensive lie selling a fantasy of eternal bliss, like real estate. "Never mind about me," she said, watching Nate dig a penny out of sidewalk ice with a stick. "I think counselling is a good idea. Someone objective might be able to help you guys. Before it's too late." Laura had hoped her new counsellor could dislodge the wedge of bitterness and resentment between Cat and her. Remind them not to blame each other for the miscarriages. See their folly. Everything they pretend not to know about their relationship, so they don't have to admit dissatisfaction and make a change. "I've suggested therapy over the years," she said. "Cat always refuses." Beneath her scarf, Laura felt her face redden with embarrassment.

"You've never told me that."

"Yeah, well." She stepped between the children and a passing dog walker with four charges on leashes, one of them the poodle she'd seen playing. "Whatever you decide will be for the best."

"Thanks." Beth's smile was weak, her eyes despondent, unrecognizable, and Laura thought, it's not only houses that are haunted.

ANNIE PAID HER ticket into the Gerrard cinema and selected a seat in the back row, second from the end of the aisle. All the long week, she'd thought about coming here, though she'd made every effort to avoid crossing paths with Eddie at the pit. On Monday and Tuesday Eddie had been stuck filling in for one of the boys digging shale at the bottom, where Annie never ventured. On Wednesday and Thursday Eddie had stood at the ovens all day, and Annie remained in her father's office, in Building One, working more slowly than she needed to. If she dragged out the administrative tasks, she wouldn't be asked to run errands or fetch workers. She'd taken her lunch in the office too, which surprised her father, because normally she ate out of doors. And this morning, Friday, she'd excused herself from going in at all by claiming she had female pains and needed a few hours in bed with a hot water bottle on her abdomen. Her father had asked no questions.

After he'd left, she used the time to plot her evening escape. She would say Widow Davis needed her help again. The Davis house, on Bain Avenue, with three wild boys, always had plenty of housekeeping to be done. It wouldn't sound out of the ordinary. Once the plan was settled, she took a leisurely bath, dribbling a few drops of lavender oil into the water. She selected her clothes — a pair of slacks with kangaroo pockets, in British racing green, and a knit top. The outfit was casual enough to draw no suspicion from her father and flattering enough to show off her figure. Now here she was, scanning in the dark of the movie house, no sign of Eddie. Maybe she'd forgotten?

Half the seats in the theatre were occupied, the entire front row taken over by a rowdy group in bomber jackets and plaid shirts. She thought she recognized one of them from the neighbourhood burger joint where the Withrow Whiteboys hung around acting big, smoking cigarettes, and looking to brawl with Jews and foreigners. She was the only one sitting alone.

The lights dimmed, offering welcome anonymity. The curtains drew open and the projector sent moving images onto the screen. She adored going to the pictures because it felt safe; it was what she and her mother had done together, usually after her parents argued. Her mother would flee the house crying, with a bloody nose or a fat lip, and her in tow. They'd duck into the dark of the theatre where no one would learn their business. On other occasions she'd been to see a movie with schoolmates. Twice she'd lied about being out on dates with a boy.

She and Roy had gone to primary school together and still ran into each other around the neighbourhood from time to time. He played rugby and worked downtown at the Toronto Dominion Bank. On their first date, she'd let him place his hand on her thigh. The next date, he got as far as the outside of her sweater; it was easy in the dark to pretend freedom.

Now, actors' names flashed across the screen and background music set a dark tone. *Laura* was a mystery set in Manhattan. If Eddie didn't turn up, well, she'd at least enjoy the experience. She sunk back in her seat as the opening scene rolled out.

A moment later, a shaft of light from the lobby fell down the aisle as someone cracked the door open and stepped into the theatre. A familiar figure sat down next to her and held out a bag of popcorn. Annie beamed, reached in, and grabbed a handful. Her skin tingled with an excited heat. Eddie leaned over, grazed her ear with warm breath. "Fancy seeing you here."

"Hush," she said, feigning interest in the picture on screen. Really, she wanted Eddie to reach for her with grabby hands, though they couldn't dare behave as she'd done with Roy, and the restraint they were forced to uphold made this experience all the more enticing. Face forward, she kept her eyes on Detective Mark McPherson as he began his investigation into the murder of a wealthy Madison Avenue executive, but their hands in the bag of popcorn periodically touched. After a few minutes, she relaxed her right leg against Eddie's left one, and allowed herself to be swept up in the New York City plot line and captivated by Laura's fashionable apartment. As time ticked on, it didn't even seem unreasonable that the detective would fall in love with a dead girl. A different life carried a different set of rules, after all; that was the magic on screen. A moving picture presented a whole other world into which she could escape, if only for an hour or two.

After the movie they filed outside and meandered up Jones, in the direction of Eddie's house, disagreeing about the ending of the film, with Annie insisting that the premise was entirely implausible. "She was dead for more than half the story, then she wasn't. Whose crummy brainchild was that?"

"But the love angle worked all right."

"And that's another thing." Annie sounded personally offended. "What a lot of baloney having the murderer die with the victim's name on his lips. That's some bad business. In my book, he should've been sent to the Big House."

"It's just a movie," said Eddie.

"Still, it gets under my skin that we're supposed to feel sorry for a creep like him. It's not real love if you're willing to do someone harm!"

They arrived outside 2 Condor still arguing, neither one wanting the evening to end. Eddie shifted weight from one foot to the other, nervously. "I could put on a kettle?"

"That'd be nice."

Inside, Annie inspected Eddie's domestic world carefully — the basic furnishings with a simple décor, the small scale of the place, from room size to ceiling height, compared with her own house.

"It's not what you're used to," said Eddie, leading the way through to the kitchen.

"No," said Annie. "It's much homier." She peered out the back window, into the yard. "Good neighbours?"

Eddie nodded. "The fellow on the one side delivers ice through the winter months." She ran water at the tap and filled the teakettle. "On the other side they keep to themselves. He's overseas. Every now and then I see the eldest girl outside tending the garden." Eddie lit the element on the gas stove with a long wooden matchstick. "I've only been here a year. I used to let a room in a house nearer the pit. Before that, I was still in Hamilton with my parents."

"I've never been anywhere but the east end," said Annie.

Eddie set the kettle down on the lit element. "I figure people are pretty much the same everywhere."

"Oh, I hope that's not true." Annie stepped closer to the window, caught sight of a house sparrow. "You've got room for vegetables too," she said.

"I was thinking about runner beans. Maybe cabbages. Do you garden?"

"Never learned," Annie said, instantly self-conscious. Fresh produce was scarce these days, and prices high. That she didn't need a vegetable garden during wartime was a mark of her class and showed the difference between them. "My mother had flower beds," she added, in haste. "Petunias and pansies, I think it was. Hard to remember."

Eddie took a Brown Betty from the cupboard and set it on the counter. "I'm afraid I'm out of rations," she said, flushing red. She'd done without sugar for a couple of years now and didn't much miss it, but she hadn't been able to afford the milkman this week because she'd wanted to buy popcorn and a ticket into the movie house.

"I take it clear," Annie lied.

When the teakettle squealed, Eddie said, "Let's move into the dining room."

Annie sat at the oval table watching as Eddie set down the teapot and selected cups and saucers from off the tea trolley. Then, Eddie cranked her gramophone and dropped the needle down on a 78 that was already on the turntable. The music began to crackle and play. "I have board games if you'd like," she said. "Snakes and Ladders, or have you heard of Monopoly?"

"What's all this?" Annie gestured to the nearly finished puzzle, a lush pastoral scene, arranged at one end of the table.

"A Ravensburger," said Eddie, taking a seat across from her. "Just a hobby."

"Why don't we finish that? Looks like you're close."

Eddie poured the tea. "I've misplaced a few of the pieces," she said. "This one's destined to remain unfinished."

Annie ran her fingers across the puzzle, through the tall green grass. She lifted one of the loose pieces and began looking to place it. It was amusing how earnest Eddie could sound over something as frivolous as a jigsaw puzzle.

"You'll never die happy now?"

"Exactly right." Eddie laughed, picking up an edge piece and taking her turn.

She was surprised not to mind someone touching her puzzle without permission. Well, she didn't mind when this someone did it. "When I was small my mother would tear pictures out of our old calendars and use a die cutting machine to make her own puzzles. For a while we were the puzzle library in the neighbourhood."

Annie sipped at her tea, relaxing. There was a warm, peaceful feel about Eddie's home. Or maybe it was just that here in private, behind closed doors, they were buffered from the brutality of the world. Here, they could both let their guard down. "What about the rest of your family?"

"Henry's in the navy. That's my brother. He's stationed off the coast of Lunenburg, in Nova Scotia. I write every week but it's rare to receive news. Dad's a steelworker." They'd fallen into a rhythm now, taking turns placing the remaining pieces of the puzzle.

"They don't mind you're not married yet?"

"Mind or not, that's how it is." Eddie gulped her tea. She could've married her brother's best friend and given everyone what they'd expected. Eugene had been sweet on her since childhood, and he was kind. Still she could never quite bring herself to return his affection. "It's like puzzling, isn't it?" she finally said, without lifting her eyes from the tabletop. "Two pieces can technically fit, but not be the right match."

"Or look like they shouldn't fit at all," said Annie, pressing down the knob of a puzzle piece with her thumb and flattening it into place. "And then just like that, they do."

THE SEVERITY OF the weather had set off some previously dormant survival instinct and the grocery store was packed with shoppers stocking up on canned goods, bottled water, and citrus fruit. A rack near the entrance displayed candy canes and Christmas cookies, red and green trees and stars wrapped in clear Cellophane; another inescapable fact of the season, Laura thought, along with mall Santas, and all those merry fucking jingles playing on public radio. She consulted her list. Cat's middle sister, Abril, was coming by for dinner and to pick up a hand-crank radio. As she pushed the cart up the aisle, Laura felt mildly resentful that she was going to be forced to host another person and then realized what she actually felt was dread.

She and Abril were the same age. Like her, Abril was ambitious, with an admirable curiosity about the wider world. Before marrying, Abril had travelled extensively throughout South and Central America, and run her own small import-export business. Now, there was more to be envious about: Abril was a mother to twin boys, a red siren blaring a state of emergency. Being around her made it too easy to imagine a parallel life, the path that still might not work out.

Laura reached for a package of dry lasagne noodles and caught Beth on her cellphone over by the bread and wraps. Both children were tugging on the bottom of their mother's coat to gain her attention. She tried to swat them away. "Matt says the damage to our roof isn't that bad, but we can't get into the house for a few more days."

"We've got loads of room."

Beth cradled the phone in the crook of her neck. "Are you sure? It's a lot to ask. I can book a hotel."

"Don't be silly." Laura glanced at her text messages. Three were work related — a question about a listing, the west-end couple wanting their first purchaser visit, and the office alerting her to a deposit cheque.

"Do you want to check with Cat first?"

"*Mi casa es su casa*," Laura said, imitating Cat's accent. Cat had also texted to ask about having a spontaneous date night tonight, Ethiopian, just the two of them, at their favourite local spot. She responded right away with a thumbs-up emoji.

Beth resumed her conversation with Matt while Laura responded to two more texts — one from Toby with an attached screenshot of a novel she was recommending to their book club, and a second text from Isla, asking if she could drop by. What could that be about? Was she planning to drop off holiday baking? Isla wasn't the sort of neighbour to knock on her door.

Isla had become a regular at book club since moving to Toronto with her boyfriend, Greg. She and Laura didn't enjoy the same kind of literature. Laura read mysteries and favoured magic realism, especially the Latin American writers, while Isla usually recommended biographies of dead rock musicians or Hollywood memoirs that Laura began in good faith, then ended up abandoning and donating to the local thrift store. Wasn't Isla spending the holiday out west with her family?

"Okay," said Beth, after she hung up. "I'm ready for the checkout."

Laura waited by the automatic doors with her one grocery bag and the kids. This was the first year she hadn't thrown herself into the season, making rugelach and shortbread cookies, decorating the house for Chrismukkah. With the trip to Argentina looming, they wouldn't be around much to enjoy any of it, and she hadn't felt like going to all the trouble.

Used to be she looked forward to the holidays, when she and Cat would merge their traditions, ordering in Chinese food and lounging in bed watching a DVD of *It's a Wonderful Life*. They'd find an evening to stroll through the Distillery District, sipping hot chocolate. The cobblestone and crowds, the colourful lights, all made for a romantic, almost old-fashioned tradition. It was there they'd found the star that usually topped their tree, and the last time she'd been pregnant they'd chosen a special ornament, baby's first ornament, they'd called it, from one of the craft stands. Cat had paid the vendor and danced the gingerbread man overtop of Laura's expanding belly. "*Feliz Navidad, mi vida*," she'd said.

"Will you love the baby?" Laura had asked.

"Because it's part of you."

"Will you still love me?"

"Even more."

Laura followed Beth and the kids out of the grocery store, her chest tightening with an uncommon sort of loneliness. She had to remind herself that there was a possibility she was pregnant now. Outside, Beth said she wanted to swing by her place and see the storm damage for herself. She'd meet back later.

"I'll watch Nate and Noa for the afternoon," said Laura. "You could use a break."

"Are you sure?"

She and the kids took Carlaw Avenue, on the other side of the park, for their route home. She pulled the bagged groceries on the toboggan and made both children walk. At the top of the park, they passed the Catholic school where two teenagers were making out in the alcove under the side doors. Only teenagers, she thought, with their revved-up hormones and apparent immunity to winter, would bother to grope each other in glacial weather.

She and Cat had once been as consumed with desire. They'd made love in a narrow stone staircase leading to the university students' coffee house. And the first year they were living together, Cat had slipped her hand down the front of Laura's jeans while she drove along Lake Shore Boulevard. Now, they were numb to each other. Could that be changed? She planted her feet solidly on the ice, determined to alter her life, but each step forward, like each month she'd spent trying to conceive, felt like a step away from Cat.

At the edge of the frozen soccer field, Nate pretended to be skating on his boots and his sister wriggled around on the ground like a minnow. To the west, a clear view of the downtown skyline. Strange not to see the CN Tower lit up. Laura sat on a bleacher with her back to the city, facing the Pocket and feeling a pull to get back there, until a cheerless cold moved up through her. She remembered the chill of the stainless-steel table on her bare thighs during yesterday's embryo transfer. "Come on, kids," she said, standing. "Time to go."

They made their way south along the frozen path with her pulling the toboggan, trying to outpace the memory. The staircase at the far end of the park was littered with fallen branches. Rather than attempt to descend it, they doubled back toward the dog park. A gusty wind picked up, sending flurries swirling across the field. Nate and Noa got away from her, and as she chased them past a large maple, Astrid and Buddy stepped out from behind the tree, blocking her path.

"Oh, you startled me!"

"Are you their mother?"

Laura kept one eye on the children. "That's far enough, Nate!"

"They're yours?"

"Wait at the fence with your sister!" She turned back to Astrid. "No, they're my friends' kids," she said. A sliver of pain entered her heart then. Not a bruising pain, or the tight squeeze of guilt she felt knowing she'd kept her IVF cycle a secret from Cat, but a tiny, niggling sliver: a reminder of loss that burrowed fast and deep and wedged under her skin permanently. "I want to be a mother," she added, without planning to. "More than anything. It might cost me my marriage though." She sounded vaguely noble when, really, she was ashamed. "I don't know if I can give up trying."

"Oh, quit your bellyaching!" said Astrid.

"Excuse me?"

"You've got a roof over your head, someone to love." Astrid sighed heavily. "And you've got time. I'd trade places with you in a second." Then she averted her gaze, as though she'd said too much.

"Time for what?"

"You'll see." Astrid looked up at the sky, at an endless expanse, and may as well have been staring into infinity. "How long do you think it will last?"

"The storm? Forecast says at least a few more days."

"Only days." She sounded disappointed. Or was it anxious? Buddy growled at a dog in the distance, then gave a loud, warning bark.

"I've been worried about you two," Laura said.

Right then, Nate slipped from view and triumphantly rolled down the hill to the baseball diamond. Noa went down after him on the toboggan holding the groceries between her front legs. That was a mistake. Ice concealed beneath a thin layer of snow slid Noa much farther across the field below, almost across the sidewalk and onto Logan Avenue. "Roll off!" Laura yelled. Noa had already been thrown and the groceries fell out around her. A jar of spaghetti sauce smashed, staining the snow with bright red juice. From a distance, it looked like blood.

"Don't move!" Laura hollered. "I'm coming!" She clung on to the wooden fence posts that circled the dog park and crept down the hill as fast as she could, slipping and landing painfully on her bottom. "Shit!" What if she'd dislodged the embryo? Her fertility doctor had told her this was impossible, that she should go about her normal routines and not act like a china teacup. Cat would've said the same, after all, marathoners ran pregnant with no adverse consequences. Women in war-torn countries carried to term, despite malnutrition, drought, and severe stress. But she wasn't other women, her body didn't do what it was supposed to do, and during this phase of things, when she was waiting with fingers crossed and bated breath, she'd always been overly cautious. No hot baths. No strenuous exercise. No air travel.

Nate caught up to Noa before Laura could, and when she finally reached them, he was licking red snow. "Tomato popsicle," he said, smiling up at her.

"Don't do that, there's glass everywhere!" She was breathless, panicked. "Noa, are you okay?" Noa rolled away from the broken shards. "Nothing hurts?" She brushed snow off the front of Noa's snowsuit with her glove and turned the girl around to examine her backside. She removed one glove and felt Noa's head for bumps or cuts. Relieved there were none, she knelt and hugged the girl tightly.

"I want Mommy," Noa said, sounding teary.

It was a natural response for a frightened child, the thing you'd expect her to say, and yet Laura felt a pinch in her chest, her heart forming another small crack. She glanced back up to the empty path where she'd left Astrid and Buddy. They weren't there anymore, and snow was a flurry of tickertape. Then, just as suddenly the wind shifted again and the snow was gone, like a runaway lover.

"Noa, did you see that girl I was talking to on the hill?"

"The one with the puppy?"

"So you did see them." That was a relief; for an instant she'd doubted her own perceptions. She began to pick up the shards and collect the groceries. "Let's go back and watch a movie."

ON MONDAY MORNING, the sky above the brickyard was a powder
blue, the blue a bride carries after something borrowed, the colour
of infinity. Annie watched for Eddie all that long day, eager to lock
eyes, for a sign of recognition of what was developing between
them. Eddie was doing the same and caught the first glimpse late
in the morning when Annie darted between Building One and the
moulding table, to deliver news that a worker's wife had birthed a
healthy baby boy. She caught the next flash of Annie around three
o'clock, when the steam shovel was going strong down in the pit,
and the crushing noise of shale was inescapable. The yardmen were
on break, smoking near the empty dinky cars, and the boss had just
driven off in a hurry, leaving his office door open a crack. So, trans-
porting newly moulded bricks on a hake barrow, Eddie stopped
to wipe her brow outside the office where she had a clear view of
Annie seated behind her father's desk, calculating sums.

Annie chewed on the end of her number 8 pencil, erased a column of numbers in the ledger and then scribbled her final tally.
She was thinking about standard Armstrong-style moulded bricks.
They were the most affordable, and so the most in demand. But
a wealthy customer, an alderman no less, was building a low-rise
apartment for his three daughters. Each girl would have her own
floor. The building was to be approximately 32.88 feet high and
boast a custom order of buff brick.

She lifted her eyes to a slice of sky and there beneath the blue
was Eddie, in overalls, coated in red brick dust. She raised a hand
to wave. "Hi-de-ho," she said. Over the din of the pit Eddie could

only guess at her words. "Quick, in!" she added, waving again, and coming around from behind the desk.

Eddie lowered the wooden arms of the hake barrow, parked it there, away from the office door. She looked for the all-clear before stepping inside.

"He's gone to see the banker," Annie said, as she shut the door. "It'll be an hour." She stepped forward, felt the heat of Eddie's body beating through her overalls. "Were you watching me?"

Pipe tobacco lingered in the air. Eddie shifted her weight from one boot to the other, on the dusty plank floor. "Passing by, that's all."

Annie smiled wryly. "That movie was a gas, wasn't it?"

"Hm hmm."

"And we had fun afterwards."

Eddie blushed and stuffed her nervous hands into the pockets of her overalls. "You enjoy doing the books then?"

Annie cocked her head to one side, threw a hand to her hip. "I suppose you'd choose brickmaking?"

"As a matter of fact," said Eddie. A moment later she added, "Listen, there's a dance at the Rideau on Saturday night. The girls will all be there. Thought maybe you'd come along with me?"

"That what you thought?"

Eddie grinned. "Don't expect much. I'm afraid I'm a bit of a dead hoofer."

"Well in that case I'll have to come," said Annie. "It's my turn to give you pointers."

LAURA AND THE kids approached the house at the same moment that Cat was hobbling up the walk from the opposite direction, in running clothes. Cat moved with a half limp, head tilted painfully to one side. "Did you slip?" Laura's instinct was to add, *I told you so*. Instead, she shuffled the children inside and helped Cat onto the porch.

"It started out as the best run of my life. No cars. Each foot down was a victory over winter. Now I know what mountain climbers feel like."

"I hope you haven't broken anything."

"The wind picked up and the limb of a giant oak snapped and landed on my shoulders. It knocked me right to my knees. I got nailed by a tree, Laura," Cat said, trying to make light, and then anticipating Laura's derision she added, "It could've happened to anyone."

But it hadn't happened to anyone, and Cat should know better. Now there could be broken bones or a concussion. It was hard mustering compassion when they might have to cancel their dinner out. "Let's just get in the house," she said. She held the door open and, for an instant, felt like an imposter. She should've wanted to be home, she did want that, but where was home anymore? She saw the future laid out before her and that future was too quiet, free of obligation. What if there was no new love? She reached down and patted her abdomen. *Anybody in there?* She could smell the ice, its ruinous, metallic tang. She tasted its threat. Unless something thawed soon, there would be nothing left of them.

"My sister cancelled," said Cat.

Laura pulled the door shut. "Good."

After Cat was settled on the couch with an ice pack for her head, Laura made the kids a large bowl of popcorn and set them up with a movie. She called her brokerage to check in and her call went directly to voice mail. "I'll try and swing by to collect that deposit cheque tomorrow," she said. "There's still a lot to do at the Condor house, but it should sell fast once I list. I'm available if you need me." Then, she saw that Mohan at the city archives had texted. His message said he was still searching files for information on the house, though he had found an address for the Rideau Club: 1300 Gerrard Street East.

THE SMOKY BACKROOM of the Rideau Club was popping with New Orleans jazz. Annie followed Eddie in front of the half-moon stage where the trumpet player belted out "High Society." Eddie's friends were offside, near the scruffy-looking saxophone player. Annie took the chair next to Evelyn. "Thought you might not show," she said.

"I had trouble getting away," said Annie, pulling the cuff of her sleeve down to cover her swollen, bruised wrist. She noticed that Louise had her arm around the back of Evelyn's chair. Louise was wearing a yellow plaid shirt, with the sleeves rolled up, and khaki trousers. Dot sat across from them on Red's lap. They were sharing a cigarette.

"You call this music?" Red muttered, a little too loudly. Annie noted three empty beer bottles on the table, and Red pulling a silver flask from the pocket of her bomber jacket.

"Place is packed tonight," said Eddie.

Annie slipped out of her spring jacket and draped it over the back of her chair. A braid of electricity tightened under her skin and seemed to pass right through her to the chair, the floor, the table, every solid surface her body contacted. She could hardly keep herself in her seat. She'd once heard an Orangeman from her father's lodge railing against this club. He'd been on about a backroom full of perverts and queers, and how the place should be shut down. Now here she was and in the dim light it was rather common, she thought, nothing remarkable, well, nothing to fear.

She straightened the skirt of her shirtwaist dress and scanned the room: ten square tables, two of them occupied by volunteers wearing Canadian Women's Army Corp suits, a few more tables were taken up by factory workers in overalls. On the outside wall there ran a row of steamed-up windows. There was a long counter and bar at the back of the room. The waitress moved busily between the bar and the tables with a tray in hand. She wore wire-rimmed glasses and spoke with a French-Canadian accent. A shallow chandelier hung over centre stage, shining a halo of yellow light down onto the trumpet player. He stuffed the rubber end of a toilet plunger into the mouth of his instrument, turning it into a screaming cornet. A red, white, and blue banner hung on the wall behind the musicians promoting their band: The Everlasting Hot Jazz Band. They were the only men in the room. Annie leaned into Eddie. "They don't mind us here?"

Dot snuffed her cigarette in the ashtray on the table, hopped off Red's lap. "They don't mind us, and we don't mind them!" She mussed Red's hair on her way to the dance floor.

"What does she mean?" asked Annie.

"They're Jews," said Evelyn.

Annie couldn't get a good look at the piano player; he was tucked farthest back on a baby grand, behind the trombonist. The banjo player sat on a high stool. Annie didn't think she'd seen a Jewish person in the flesh before. She certainly hadn't been in one room with so many kinds of people. Her father didn't believe the races should mix. He also said that the Prime Minister was right not to take in that steamship from Germany at the start of the war. It wasn't Canada's problem, he said. The Jews were getting what they had coming to them, and he said it the same spiteful way he said it about her before he'd slug her. "Is it always so cosmopolitan here?" she asked.

"They push in," Red slurred.

Everyone pretended not to hear the comment, but Louise and Dyllis exchanged a look.

"Don't start," said Eddie.

Red set her flask down forcefully on the table. "You're always bustin' my chops these days." She stood, unsteady on her feet.

"Oh, look," said Evelyn, gesturing to the dance floor. "I think Dot's waiting for you." She winked at Annie as Red shuffled off, and she leaned in to say, "Red's on the sauce is all."

Annie knew better than to believe it was just the alcohol talking. Her father and his friends felt the same superiority, so did most of the men at the pit. What did Eddie think? And what would James T. Armstrong say if he knew she was here, in this place, with these people? She suppressed a smile. She should be afraid at that thought and yet tonight she'd vowed to be afraid of nothing.

Sweat was flying off the drummer as he deftly handled his sticks. The saxophone player's long thin fingers teased the shiny keys of his instrument confidently, although it was the bandleader, on trumpet, who made a real impression. He wore brown-and-white leather spectators, a snappy violet-coloured dress shirt, and a black pork pie hat with an electric blue feather on the crown. He looked to be the youngest, maybe twenty. His dark wavy hair peeked out under the hat, and his rich voice was arresting, endearing. He played in conversation with the other instruments, and they responded. The music, not the players, was in charge; the players were merely conduits for a more powerful force. When he sang, his voice filled the room with energy and momentum. Annie thought he must be the kind of person, like her, to make the best out of a situation.

"Hey, is it true Dot lets a room at the YWCA?" she asked.

"Sure does," said Evelyn. She held out a small package of black liquorice for Annie to share. "Don't tell her I said so; her parents won't allow her back home. C'mon," she said, standing and pulling Louise onto her feet. "'The Saints' is my favourite number."

"You want to dance?" asked Eddie.

"Maybe later." Annie popped a morsel of liquorice into her mouth. "Right now I'd rather sit here with you."

Eddie felt a rim of heat burning around her collar. "I told them who you are," she said. "Who your father is."

"Let's not talk about him tonight." Annie tapped her foot on the sticky floor to the lively beat of the song. "I've been studying that bowling handbook you lent me."

"Yeah?"

"Page 5. Under 'eligibility' it says membership is open to any individual who voluntarily wishes to join."

"You thinking about joining, then?"

Annie surveyed the club. Girls were dancing with each other like married couples. A pair at the adjacent table was holding hands. No one was looking over their shoulders for parents or the police. The real world, the world outside, seemed far, far away. "Tell me something about you I don't know?" she asked.

Eddie leaned back in her chair. "Not much interesting, I'm afraid." She was still undecided about Annie, her motivations for wanting to be here. Were they on their way to being steadies now?

"I've seen you hauling bricks and taking orders," said Annie. "Nobody works that hard for so little unless they're reaching for better."

Eddie waved at the waitress, signalling with two fingers for two beers. "Suppose that's true," she said. There was more to her than that brickyard, at least there would be, she thought. She had the house now. One day soon, if she got lucky, she'd have someone to share it with. "I'll tell you about me," she said. "But only if you agree to answer a question first."

"Depends on the question," Annie teased. The corners of her eyes smiled when she did. Her auburn hair was loose tonight, framing her face. Eddie couldn't decide if she preferred it like this or pinned up. Annie sure was pretty, though, and that blood red lipstick.

"You ever been in a place like this before?"

"Once. About a year ago," said Annie. "I found this broadsheet tucked into the back of my library book. It advertised a girls-only dance in the west end."

"What was the book?"

"What? Oh, I don't know," said Annie, laughing. "I don't remember that."

The waitress set their drinks down on the table and the band slowed tempo for a bluesy rendition of "A Good Man Is Hard to Find." In the centre of the dance floor, Evelyn had her arms around Louise and her head on Louise's shoulder. Red and Dot were pressing up against one another, swaying in unison, but Red was getting handsy and loudly insisting on a kiss. When Dot gave in, they staggered around, turning, and Annie saw the embroidered patch sewn on the back of Red's bomber jacket: Withrow Whiteboys.

"That was two," said Annie shrewdly. "Two questions, not one."

"All right, something about myself you don't know?"

"Better make it good."

Eddie turned her chair to face Annie's and took Annie's hands in hers. They were trembling so she squeezed them. "Bet you don't know what I'm thinking right now," she said. Eddie's touch sent a shock through Annie's blood. She shook her head. "Your mouth," said Eddie. "I'm thinking about your delicious mouth. It's all I think about at the pit and all I see at night when my head lands on the pillow."

"That so?"

"Yes."

Annie's heart sped. Eddie sure wasn't wasting any time tonight, she thought. And she was good at keeping the attention off herself. Emboldened, Annie flipped Eddie's left hand over and traced the lifeline on her warm, rough palm. "Let's see what this tells me." She ran the tip of her index finger from Eddie's wrist to the base of her pointer and then slowly back down again, reading the unbroken line. "Looks like you'll live a long time," she said.

"Glad to hear it. Anything else? About romance, maybe?"

Annie grinned, giving away the flirtation. She let go of Eddie's hand. "Well, I don't know much about that, but they do say you catch more bees with honey."

Eddie leaned back, folded her arms across her chest. "Is it working?"

Annie felt her cheeks flush and pretended to fuss with the hem of her skirt, revealing more leg. "Aren't you just the cock of the walk."

"You're the first girl I've asked here," said Eddie.

Annie's breath loosened at that. She uncrossed and crossed her legs, self-consciously. "Exactly how many others have there been, Mr. Ferguson?"

Eddie lifted her beer, took a swig.

"You mean to say you've never had a sweetheart?"

Eddie burst out laughing. "I didn't say that."

Annie scanned the dance floor. "What about Dot? Or Evelyn?"

Eddie shook her head. "Just friends."

"I had a boyfriend named Roy for a time," said Annie.

"How was that?"

"Fine, I suppose. Boys always seem to like me more than I like them."

Eddie sat up straighter. "And you think it would be any different with girls?"

Annie shot a piercing look, desire flickering across her face. "I know it would," she said.

All of a sudden, the band came to a jarring halt. The trumpet player stopped singing and the drummer leapt out from behind his kit with both drumsticks in hand. "What did you call us?"

"Greedy kikes!" Red repeated. She was posturing in front of the stage, ready for a fight.

The drummer threw his sticks at her feet and leapt down from the stage. "I don't care if you are a girl," he said.

Eddie screeched her chair back and stood to see what was happening. The trumpet player had joined the drummer on the dance floor and Dyllis was trying to broker peace.

"Cool down, Red. Give 'em back the hat."

"I'll give him a knuckle sandwich!" Red jangled the few donated coins around in the hat, tossing them like kernels of corn in a pan. "Who let the Jew boys in, anyway?" she said. "Their kind don't take up a church collection."

"Aw, lay off, will ya." The trumpet player was holding the drummer back with one arm. "Nobody wants any trouble here."

"Then you tell that long-nose to keep his eyes off my girl!"

"That's it!" spat the drummer, fighting the trumpet player's hold.

The table of factory workers peered over Red's shoulder. The girls from the Army Corp were watching to see who would make the next move. Eddie felt the walls closing in. Unless someone acted fast, a scene was going to erupt and that would bring police. She reached the dance floor as Dorothy began taunting.

"No Jews and no Krauts. That's fair, see?"

"Shut it, Dot!" Eddie grabbed Red by the forearm, spilling coins from the hat. "This ain't how we're gonna play it," she said.

"Get your grubby meathooks off me!"

"I'm calling it, Red."

"They got no business being here and you know it."

Eddie squeezed harder. "The way I see it, they're good music men, that's all."

Finally Red let go of the hat and yanked her arm away from Eddie. She pushed through the crowd and the doorway into the front of the club.

Dot ran after her. Slowly, the others dispersed, heading back to their tables, chattering.

Eddie straightened the flat top of the hat where it had bent. She read the Bollman Co. label on the inside. "Here," she said, holding the hat out to the trumpet player.

"What's your name?" the player asked.

"Eddie."

"You keep that, Eddie."

"I couldn't," she said. "It's yours."

A warmth spread under Annie's skin. Eddie was the opposite of her father — kind and generous. Respectful. Eddie was a safe, soft place to land.

The trumpet player hopped back up onto the stage, leaving the hat to Eddie. "In times of war," he said, "us misfits have to stick together."

Eddie gave a nod, popped the hat on her head. "I'm sorry about all that gobbledegook," she said. Then she took Annie's hand and led her away, across the dance floor, and back to their table.

LAURA TOOK THE only available booth at the restaurant, closest to the kitchen, and ordered their favourite: the vegetarian platter for two. The rich, heady scent of buna filled the space. "This is nice," she said, peeling out of her winter layers. "I'm glad you felt up to it, after all."

Cat hung their parkas and scarves on a rack beside the booth and sat to compose a text message. "My subcontractor is proving hopeless," she said, as her thumbs flew across the tiny screen. "I'll be quick."

Laura turned her own phone off and slipped it into her purse. "Let's not talk about work tonight, okay?"

"You're right," said Cat. "Sorry." She set her phone face down in the centre of the table and moved to squeeze in next to Laura on her side of the booth. Cat was still moving with a limp, less gingerly so. She gave Laura a kiss. "That a new shade of lipstick? You don't usually wear such a bright colour."

"Nope, same red as always."

"It suits you."

Cat used to notice the smallest details about her appearance, from a change in hairstyle to the slightest shift in her expressions; these comments had made Laura feel appreciated. Cat would spontaneously invite her out for dinner or a show, and frequently surprised her with small gifts of exotic fruit or a box of truffles, for no reason. There'd been an assumed green light on their every interaction, as if part of each belonged to the other. Now they were awkward at intimacy and basic conversation felt unnatural. This is what happens when you stop having sex, Laura thought, recalling having read it in a book. An uneasiness develops and wedges in. Sex is the connective tissue holding couples together. She snuggled closer to Cat, resting her head on Cat's shoulder. They needed to connect tonight.

The waitress set a large round platter in between them, and Cat tore a piece of injera and used it to scoop a mouthful of yemiser wat. "My parents are asking if we'd like to say something at Dad's retirement party."

"When's that again?"

"Day after we arrive."

Laura helped herself to some collard greens. She scanned the restaurant, a small hole-in-the-wall they'd been coming to for years. Everyone around them was engaged in animated conversation, mostly in Amharic. She let the sound of the language wash over her without understanding a word.

"Let's order coffee tonight," said Cat. "It smells so good in here."

Laura nodded. Jasmine and bergamot, she thought. And some kind of citrus.

"I know you want to cancel our flights because of the weather," said Cat, "but I think we'll get out okay. I don't want to miss this. It's important to my dad. Maybe we can take in some tango on this trip?"

Laura scooped cabbage and potatoes. "I'm pretty tied up with work," she said. "Getting away will be a challenge. I mean, the Condor house is turning into a bigger job than I expected."

Cat wagged a finger playfully, "*Sin hablar de trabajo.*"

"Right." It was so easy reverting to neutral subjects like work. What she'd meant to say hadn't come out properly. "Cat, what if I don't come this time?"

Cat's hand holding the injera fell open and a plop of spiced lentil hit the tabletop. "Really?"

"Maybe just explain how busy I am?"

"I thought you loved Argentina?"

"I do, it's not that, and I enjoy your family. I just think some time apart would be good for us right now."

Cat's face reddened. "Why is that?"

Laura reached up to tuck a rogue curl behind Cat's ear. "I think you know."

Cat licked her fingers of berbere and clarified butter. "Not sure that I do."

"We're at an impasse with the kid thing," said Laura. She hadn't expected resistance and was beginning to feel awkward. Cat wouldn't look at her now, as if by not associating her words with her face, this conversation wasn't happening again. "Are you angry?" Laura asked.

Cat pushed her water glass across the table. She began to fidget with a small square alcohol wipe.

"Catalina?" Laura was prepared to argue, arguing was engagement, and yet what she saw on Cat's face was a kind of surrender. Maybe Cat no longer cared enough about the relationship to fight? Or maybe she was finally relenting? "Unless we're not at an impasse anymore?" she said.

"There's someone else, isn't there?"

"What? No!" People in the adjacent booths were looking over now. Their waitress glanced up from behind the counter.

Cat slid away from her. "Bullshit! You've been so preoccupied lately. Falling asleep in the middle of the day. Daydreaming. You jump at the first chance to get out of the house and half the time I don't know where you are."

"I told you, I'm busy with that place on Condor."

"Yes, so you've said. And I've heard that kind of thing before."

Laura leaned back on the pleather seat. "Okay, wow." Cat was alluding to the "affair" she'd almost had a few years earlier — a minor event in their long relationship that Laura had thought was well behind them. Confessing to some heavy petting after the fact didn't seem like such a smart choice right now, and yet for the first time in a long while, she felt that Cat still wanted her, wanted them, even if Cat didn't want a baby anymore. "You sound paranoid."

"It's that new member of your book club, isn't it? The one you're always talking about, with the vanity plates on her bicycle? ART GAL. Who even does that?"

"Isla?! She wanted to be an art therapist," Laura said, evenly. "Before she decided to become an animal rights activist. And you've got to be kidding."

"Apparently I don't know much about you these days." Cat slipped out of the booth and back to her side.

Laura sat straighter, aware the people next to them were eavesdropping. "You're being ridiculous," she hissed. "There is no other woman, Cat. I can't believe I have to say it." Then she lowered her voice to a whisper. "But it wouldn't be so bad to feel desired once in a while!" She landed the next dig under her breath: "I bet Isla wants children."

Cat pushed the platter of lentils and greens aside. Her face was flushed. The vein in her forehead, which throbbed whenever they fought, had popped out. "I may not know exactly what's going on, but I know when you're hiding something." She waved to gain the waitress's attention. "I've lost my appetite. Let's just get a doggy bag and go."

"Seriously?" Laura couldn't believe how quickly their night out had soured. She hadn't realized Cat would protest her staying behind. She'd thought she could just drop the idea into the conversation and not have to explain. She sounded impressively indignant though, for someone who was sidestepping the truth about hiding an IVF cycle and a possible pregnancy.

"It's fine, don't come to Argentina," Cat said, waving both hands in the air dramatically. "I'll make up some excuse."

"You know I hate that word." Fine meant nothing. Fine meant, I can't be bothered to say how I really feel so I'll just throw this waste-basket term at you instead.

"*Por el amor de Dios*, Laura!"

"So you don't think we have issues?"

"Of course we do," said Cat. "You're never satisfied."

"Oh, I see. It's all my fault." Was she the only one feeling lonely in her marriage? How could they not at least share that? She would prefer that Cat not have to be strong-armed into motherhood. "You knew when you signed on to this relationship that a child was part of the deal."

"Yeah, and people change. Circumstances change."

Laura shoved the platter across the table and stood. "Not me. Not about something so important."

Outside, on the Danforth, Laura stood holding their uneaten meal in a Styrofoam container, while Cat scraped the car windows and kicked densely packed snow from around the wheels and tail pipe. They'd taken Cat's Range Rover to the restaurant, not Laura's Beemer — a boxy green 1990s stick shift inherited from Cat's sister, Abril, when her twins were born. King of the road, Cat liked to call it.

"I can do that," said Laura, meaning she should be the one on her feet, exerting herself; she hadn't fallen earlier.

Cat unlocked the doors. "I'm good."

Laura tugged her door open and climbed onto the cold leather seat. She set the doggy bag on her lap and belted herself.

Cat turned the key in the ignition, unsuccessfully. "Fuck, c'mon!" She tried again and smacked her palm against the steering wheel. The engine wouldn't start.

"Looks like we're calling a cab or walking," said Laura.

Cat tried once more and the engine engaged. "*Aqui vamos*," she said.

They drove in silence, the car heater slow to blast. Laura pulled her scarf up around her face. She stared out the window at falling snow, wanting to reach for Cat's hand on the gear shift, soften this moment between them. Cat was freezing her out and she couldn't bridge the distance. Cat was good at turning her emotions on and off. It was a form of self-protection, Laura knew, but that didn't make it any less hurtful.

The last time she'd been pregnant, when they'd been told to expect another miscarriage, Cat had wanted her to book a D&C and be done with it. She couldn't face anymore loss, she'd said, couldn't stand not knowing whether the baby had stopped growing, whether the heartbeat was waning. The thought of Laura carrying death around inside gave Cat a sinister feeling. She'd avoided Laura the rest of that day, avoided touching her that night as they squeezed past one another in the bathroom brushing their teeth. That was when they'd stopped making love. Were they ever going to be close again?

"I hate this," said Laura. "We don't communicate anymore. Cat?"

"What is there to say!"

"That you're frustrated? Or angry and disappointed. You tried to make us a nice evening out," she said.

"So much for that."

They careened through the first intersection, past the dollar store at Pape, and Laura thought, best to just give her some space. When they pulled up at the light at Logan, she bit her lip, didn't want to make things worse by pushing a conversation. What she should do was confess about the embryo transfer, get it out in the open. What was stopping her? Cat might dismiss her as chasing ghosts again and point out the obvious: that if she were pregnant, it could go as badly as it had the other three times. They turned onto Albermarle and Laura couldn't stand the silence anymore. "Just because I don't want to come to Argentina this once, you don't have to pout!"

Cat stared ahead at the road, white-knuckling it.

"At least say *something*. Anything!"

Cat parked at an angle, wedged between two snowbanks, and cranked the emergency brake. "Matt and Beth will still be up. Let's keep this between us."

"And let's try again soon, okay? My turn to make the reservation."

Cat pushed open the driver's side door, her back to Laura. "I won't get my hopes up," she said. "You might bail on that too." Then she stormed into the house.

ANNIE CLIMBED INTO bed in her cotton pyjamas and tucked herself in neatly between the sheets. The milk glass shade of her bedside lamp lit the emerald-coloured wall on her side of the room. She was restless, and the Agatha Christie she'd signed out of the local library was not going to be enough of a distraction. Her bedroom door was shut tightly. She'd heard the men come in downstairs and begin pouring Scotch and dealing for contract bridge: twenty points in clubs and diamonds, thirty points in hearts and spades.... They'd be at it all night. She'd pushed her waterfall dresser against the door, just in case anyone stumbled in. The real trick, she thought, was how to get some sleep with so much on her mind.

Flipping onto her side, she hugged a pillow. Tonight at the club had sealed it; she belonged with Eddie, in Eddie's world. If she'd had any doubts whatsoever, about Eddie or the life her friends led, she had none now. It was clear as consommé; despite their differences, she was like those girls in how she loved, who she could love. They shared a common nature. Did they see it in her too?

She ran her fingers across the dust jacket of the mystery novel on her bedside stand and glanced at the bedroom door where the dresser stood like a heavy-set man, blocking the entrance and exit. The windows were open an inch, and her coral pink curtains billowed in the breeze. There's always a way out, she thought. There has to be. This was how her mother must've felt, desperate to escape a life she knew would otherwise destroy her. Until now, Annie had supposed that running away was a cowardly act. The better path would've been for her mother to have shown more moxie standing up for herself, and stayed with Annie no matter what, but she was beginning to see that running was survival. The worst thing about living in fear wasn't the moment of violence itself, those moments were over fast enough, and she healed. The worst things were the hours and days and months of dread in between those moments, waiting on tenterhooks for his temper to erupt, blaming herself for not being able to prevent it, the shame of hiding the bruises and knowing that even if people knew what was happening at home, no one would save her. She understood her mother better now; a person can be broken and die in a thousand ways, not only physically. And maybe Frances hadn't wanted to leave her behind at all? What choice did any woman have when her life was on the line? Annie choked back tears, tightened into herself like a woolly caterpillar. She was already halfway to a dying spirit unless she did something to stop it.

Downstairs, the men were laughing, shouting their game points at each other, her father's deep voice in the mix. It would be so much simpler to hate him, she thought, to want him dead. But she only wanted to be free of him. Outside, the pitter-patter of rainfall on the shingles, the smell of fresh wet earth and hyacinth wafting in, a gentle, fragrant baptism. *Where are you now, Mother?* she thought. *What's become of you?* If she knew, if she had an example of how to escape this cage, perhaps it would serve her going forward. Problem was, she didn't have a clue. Had her mother found a new man, had she made her own way somehow, or had she met with ruin? The possibility that Frances was in another violent relationship or destitute and no better off now than she had been married to Annie's father was the most likely scenario, and that stopped Annie from searching her out. Sometimes it was better, she thought, living with uncertainty than it was having your worst fears confirmed.

She sat up in bed, pulled the chenille bedspread up around her. Out the window, a dark sky; the moon obscured by cloud cover. It was the law that a man could beat his wife with a stick no thicker than his thumb, and it was law, Annie knew, that girls like her and Eddie were sick in the mind and belonged behind bars. Her mother had kept the violence hidden too, just as Annie was now hiding it from others. After all, a daughter, like a wife, was only a man's property.

She reached over to her bedside table, lifted the mystery, and flipped open to the first page. She read a few lines and slammed the covers shut. It was no use trying to read when her mind was elsewhere. She'd grown so accustomed to concealing her scars and bruises that she'd become adept at concealing everything, including her feelings, even from herself. Eddie had changed that. Once a thing was known and felt it couldn't ever be unknown or unfelt. She shoved the book off her lap and onto the floor, then pulled the cord to turn off her lamp. She didn't know how she'd afford to live, if not here, or what it would feel like being shunned. There'd be no inheritance to count on, that was for certain, but staying in this house much longer, she would be crushed by more than her father's rage.

LAURA WOKE IN their king-sized bed with that familiar tightness making it hard to breathe. She lay there beneath the goose-down duvet, listening to Cat's ragged breath, while the storm continued to blanket the city.

Her phone was face up on the night table. Thom had returned her text. Sweet, sweet Thom. He wished her happy holidays and was looking forward to seeing her. He offered to corral the others, if she wanted to see them too? Laura felt a soaring sense of relief as guilt lifted. That would be wonderful, she thought, just what she needed, and the next best thing to connecting with her mother.

From her side of the bed, closest to the ensuite, her bedroom looked like any number of boutique hotel rooms she'd stayed in: off-white wall-to-wall carpeting, blue damask drapes, a tallboy dresser, the narrow door to a walk-in closet. She felt Cat's back, warm and solid against her own, and wished last night's argument had been resolved. Now tension would follow them into another day. She faced the small seating area with two leather club chairs and a navy pouffe. Stagers had left it behind in a house she'd once sold in the Bluffs. There's too much of nothing in here, she thought, too much white space and a generic kind of grandeur, no sense of intimacy. *Why?*

Cat preferred neutral décor — no bold colour — and no trinkets. Laura was the opposite. She was most comfortable in a space full of warm earth tones, wood and texture, and personal touches, yet she'd let a decorator pick the wall colour and the fabric for the drapes and pillow shams that tied it all together. Maybe because of that, it had always felt a bit like a show home. Staging a house to sell it, she knew, was about removing all evidence of the current owners, and any trace of personality, so that prospective buyers might more easily project their own life onto the "blank" space. Had she done that with her own home?

Sourpuss leapt up onto the bed, settling between her and Cat, and purring loudly. Cat stirred but didn't wake. Would she also sleep through an infant crying? Cat had been known to sleep through ambulance sirens and thunderstorms, so it was possible. Laura lay there a minute longer, stroking Sourpuss, before finally giving into the idea of waking. She grabbed her phone and tiptoed into the washroom. Siting on the toilet, she returned Thom's text. Yes, she did want to see the old gang. She could get together early in the new year. She flushed and ran a hot shower.

Laura caught her own reflection staring back at her in the vanity mirror. Messy hair, roots beginning to show, bags under her eyes, her mother's heel of a chin. She left her pyjamas on top of the laundry hamper and stepped into the shower. The waterfall showerhead massaged her neck and shoulders while her mind flashed among random images: Noa hurtling down the hill in the park, Toby's stroller, Cat's angry tone when they'd argued last night. Cat at her old drafting table. Cat when they'd been in university.

The first year of their relationship they'd met every Saturday morning in Kensington Market and then, after breakfast, walked back to Cat's dorm room on campus to spend the rest of the day making love. Cat had broken up with a cute women's studies student who worked in Diablo's, the coffee house on campus, because the girl hadn't wanted to be exclusive. For months Laura had been jealous. She was always trying to impress Cat, reading up on subjects she knew would be of interest, seducing Cat with garter belts and thigh-highs and a willingness to try anything. Had she felt intimidated by Cat's intelligence? Her family's wealth? The fact that Cat could've had just about any woman she wanted? Then one

Saturday everything between them changed. Cat hesitated before opening the door.

"I have a surprise," she said, pulling a red bandana from the back pocket of her jeans. She made to tie the blindfold around Laura's forehead and Laura blushed under the stiff cotton. "It's not what you're thinking," Cat said.

"How do you know what I'm thinking?"

Cat cupped her breast and kissed the back of her neck.

"Okay, you do know," she laughed.

She heard Cat slip a key into the lock and turn it, felt the press of Cat's warm lips to her ear. Cat whispered, "Happy anniversary, *mi amor*," and guided her inside where she tugged off the blindfold.

On a wooden table in front of the window sat a cardboard model of a house. "Is this what you've been working on?"

The model showed four bedrooms and three balconies, each wrapping around a wall of cathedral windows. It was three storeys high, with a sloping roof and two chimneys. "I imagine it sitting on five acres of land," Cat said. "Jutting out the side of a mountain."

"Impressive."

"*Abre la puerta.*"

Laura bent down and tugged open the tiny cardboard door. A thin residue of glue came off on her fingers. "What's this?"

A miniature envelope, one of those found on the counter at any florist's shop, lay across the threshold of the house. She lifted it, slid out the card.

"Welcome home," it said. "IOU."

That was the moment her insecurities fell away, and she knew Cat was the one. She threw her arms around Cat's neck and they kissed until kissing wasn't enough and then they stumbled across the room and fell onto the futon.

"Let's vow to not grow bored with one another," she said.

"Or become boring," Cat agreed. Bed death wouldn't get them, as it had other couples they knew, they'd be exceptions; build careers and a family and hold on to each other; nothing would be sacrificed. Somehow, they'd both assumed they could do what most people aren't able to do: avoid the depreciation of their relationship over time and win the happiness sweepstakes.

Well, guess what? Laura thought, stepping out of the steamy shower onto the bathmat. Love doesn't always retain its value and loss has a way of blasting apart all good intentions, reducing even the most magnificent plans to rubble. She should've known better than to think a romantic gesture was a guarantee; when they'd bought this place, on Albermarle, that model home was lost in the move, or thrown out.

EDDIE AND ANNIE descended the streetcar at Queen's Park, walking north along the path, toward the Legislative Building. Behind it, they crossed into the park. Sunshine cut through the tree canopy. Two black squirrels chased around the base of a statue of King Edward VII atop his horse. Ahead, in the distance, gleamed the pale yellow brick and limestone of the Royal Ontario Museum, their destination. Beyond it stood the impressive Park Plaza Hotel.

"I've never been to the museum," said Annie. "Have you?"

Eddie wouldn't admit that the ticket price was steep, or that a day trip to look at dead birds was not how she would normally spend her time or money. "This'll be my first visit too," she said.

"Oh, I can hardly wait." Annie was practically skipping ahead in her knee-length smocked dress in British navy with the matching bolero jacket. The dress had full, turned-up cuffs, piped trim, and a Peter Pan collar. The jacket had rhinestone buttons. She felt lucky for the cuffs and the accents; fabric shortages these days meant clothing with feminine touches — pockets or cuffs or hoods — were hard to come by and very expensive. She was tired of wearing boring old wartime rayon gabardine. "I understand they house the largest collection in the country, one of the most impressive in the world."

Eddie did know this. Since the Rideau Club she'd been thinking long and hard about how to impress a girl like Annie who had every material thing she could need and more, certainly more than Eddie could provide. Then, she'd seen an article in the newspaper about a museum researcher, Margaret Howell Mitchell, a woman ornithologist, if you could believe that, who had, and this is where luck came into it, written not one but two groundbreaking books on the passenger pigeon. Well. There it was decided. Her next Saturday off work, she'd take Annie to see the collection. "Shouldn't be crowded this early in the day," she said.

Annie lifted the small black binoculars hanging from around her neck. "Father thinks I've gone out birdwatching. Not a lie, technically. Actually, I'm an ace at identifying them by now."

"How about that one?" Eddie had stopped on the path and pointed at the low-hanging branch of an eastern white pine.

Annie lifted her finger to her lips to signal silence. The bird resumed tapping, first along the thick branch and then from the side of the trunk. "Hairy woodpecker," she said, proudly. "Looks like a little soldier, doesn't it, with such erect posture."

"Holy mackerel," said Eddie. "You're in the know."

"Oh, I just read too much. Father says my head's full of useless information."

"Not at all," said Eddie, trying not to be intimidated. She had no formal education beyond grade eight and was too busy working to read or take up any of the activities Annie must do. However, she did enjoy her paper on Saturday mornings, and she had a respectable amount of common knowledge, maybe even more than the average soul.

"Have you spoken with Red since the other night?" asked Annie.

"I hate it when she drinks too much. I'm sorry you had to see that."

Annie approached the grand limestone steps of the museum's front entrance. The bronze handrails shimmered in the mid-morning light. "The drink's just an excuse," she said, climbing. "It can't bring out what isn't already there. I dare say many people these days feel as Red does about the Jews."

Eddie took two steps at a time, beat her to the top. "That don't make it right or true," she said, and she held open one of the heavy oak doors.

Annie passed through into the rotunda where a half-dozen other patrons were standing, removing their coats and jackets and reaching for their wallets. "Well, I'm glad you feel that way," she said. "Speaking up can get you into hot water, though." She'd often paid that price at home.

Eddie gazed up at the glittering, ornate ceiling. It was covered in gold glass tiles, a geometric pattern. The floor was a sunburst mosaic of different coloured marble. "What's my brother risking his life for, if not freedom?" she said. "Silence carries a price too."

Annie nodded, felt her heart swell. They were allies, of a sort, because Eddie understood the double bind of living under an oppressive hand, the need to hold on to some part of yourself, even if it was just your voice. Even if there were consequences. The alternative was a life without integrity and not worth living. She leaned in close and whispered, "Maybe one day someone will fight for the likes of us." Eddie blushed and hurried off to line up at the counter where she paid their entrance.

A moment later they carried on through to the central staircase that wound around four enormous totem poles. "Have you ever," Annie marvelled. "That one must be eighty feet high." On the second floor, a bird of flight display dominated the Gallery of Birds. Annie craned her neck. "What do you suppose it feels like?"

"Flying?" Eddie hadn't considered the question before, but she didn't want to sound like a drip. "My guess is it's a little like swimming underwater," she offered. "Or floating?"

"I think so too." Annie stepped around the other side of a glass display where stuffed birds, some of them extinct, were enclosed. She beamed at Eddie through the diorama, leaving Eddie weak in the knees.

For the next hour and a half, they wandered the gallery, taking turns with other visitors reading about the many species and their habitats, opening and closing drawer after pullout drawer of eggs and feathers and footprints and nests. Eddie found it hard to retain information; there was so much to take in and she had trouble concentrating on anything other than Annie in her fitted navy dress, and the people around them. Were they drawing attention? She took extra care not to stand too close to Annie or accidentally brush up against her because it was all she wanted to do.

"There they are," said Annie, finally approaching the passenger pigeon exhibit. "They're even more beautiful than I'd imagined."

"Yes," said Eddie, staring at her, not the birds. "They sure are."

They fell out of the museum laughing, both hungry and not saying so, neither one wishing to interrupt the feeling of having been united by a shared experience. They'd made special memories, passed for friends in public. What else might they get away with? The stone pillars of the Queen Alexandra Gates, with their wrought iron lamps, stood impressively at the top of Bloor Street and Queen's Park Boulevard. After admiring them, they headed west and took Philosopher's Walk south through the university campus. Piano music drifted down through an open window in the conservatory. There was a welcome breeze.

"There's a crowd up ahead," said Annie. Farther along the path a group had gathered and there was shouting. "Why all the hoo-ha?"

"Must be a scrap drive," said Eddie. As they approached, she didn't see any aluminum pots and pans, though, or piles of metal for the war effort. Maybe it was another bond rally?

They stood at the outer edge of the group on tiptoe. Annie glimpsed a woman in a blue box coat and round wire spectacles, up on a wooden crate. She addressed the crowd with a megaphone.

"Many husbands are on relief or killed overseas!" the woman shouted. "A great number of children can't be fed or cared for. Why should you go on having more?"

Eddie scanned the crowd. No police officers, but the rally was drawing attention from other passersby.

"Neglecting women's health care only contributes to our subordination," said the woman on the crate. "What do we need?!"

"Birth control reform!" shouted someone in the crowd.

"And when do we need it?"

"Now!" they all chimed in.

They were so gung-ho, Eddie thought. A breed of woman she'd heard about and never known, those with time, *leisure* time, to organize and be out hollering in plain sight. She tugged at the sleeve of Annie's jacket, to pull her away. "Let's not mix in."

"But what do you suppose they mean?" said Annie.

A chirpy voice came from behind. "Don't you know her?"

They turned and found a plump brunette holding a placard that read: University College Women's Association. "That's Dr. Bingham, come to speak to us about birth control reform."

Bingham? Eddie remembered that name from her Hamilton days. "The one they say does the devil's work?"

The girl laughed. "Men on pulpits don't bear children, or raise them, do they? Dr. Bingham has opened many eyes to the need for family planning. There's no shame in it." The girl lowered her placard. "Here," she said, shoving a flyer into Annie's hand. "Our meetings are held on campus the last Monday of the month. We could use your help."

Annie scanned the first lines of the sheet and then handed it to Eddie.

FAMILY PLANNING REDUCES THE NUMBER OF IMBECILES AND UNBURDENS THE POOR. PLANNING IS GOOD FOR THE HARMONY OF A MARRIAGE AND THE FULFILLMENT OF THE COUPLE.

"Are you a student here?" Annie asked.

"Second-year nursing. You?"

Eddie heard the click of a camera beside them. There was a

newspaperman wandering the crowd, snapping photographs. "Thank you," she interrupted. "This isn't for us." She handed the sheet back to the girl. She didn't know much, but she knew enough; the concerns of this group were for married women and women of certain means. She and Annie didn't need to get involved.

"I want to hear," said Annie, and she pushed deeper into the crowd. Eddie had no choice except to follow. Her heart began to pound, her mouth was a desert. Instructing people on how to use contraceptives was illegal. They could all be arrested and thrown in jail.

"Reform!" shouted some onlookers.

Dr. Bingham cupped her ear. "I can't hear you?"

"Birth control reform!"

Annie tightened in next to Eddie. "Aren't they marvellous?"

Eddie nodded, feeling unsure and out of place. It was well and good to teach girls how to prevent pregnancy by promoting devices, but it wasn't the worker whose lot would be improved. The girls she knew in the bowling league weren't the ones who stood to gain, either. They'd be the ones these activists wanted sterilized or blamed for being poor.

Dr. Bingham raised her fist in the air to rile the crowd. "The maternal death rate remains high!" she shouted. "Women suffer physical problems from bearing many children. Some die trying to rid themselves of a pregnancy. There is another way. Our mothers worked for suffrage. We must all work to end our quarrel with fate!"

The crowd cheered. Dr. Bingham stepped off the crate, passing the megaphone to a tall woman with sparkling blue eyes, who reminded Eddie of her childhood Sunday school teacher, stern and unflinching, with a passionate message.

"On behalf of the University College Women's Association we'd like to extend our deepest gratitude to the good doctor for her tireless work, and for coming to speak with us here today. Now, we invite you all back to Whitney Hall for tea and to continue planning."

"Shall we go with them?" asked Annie, as the crowd began to disperse, and then she and Eddie burst into laughter. "Could you just imagine?" Much as she'd like to go, they'd be found out as interlopers the moment they struck up a conversation.

"I could stand to eat, though," said Eddie.

Annie took her by the coat sleeve, pulled her into a narrow laneway offside, behind the law library, and leaned in to kiss her.

"What are you doing?"

"Thank you," she said. "For the best day of my life."

Eddie glanced around furtively. Everyone was gone, all turned down Hoskin Avenue, heading for the dormitory. "You can't mean that," she said.

Once again, Annie moved closer. "I feel inspired," she said. Her mouth was only inches from Eddie's. "Don't you?"

Now Eddie couldn't hold back; she fell hard and fast, recklessly pressing Annie backwards against the brick wall, not caring if they were caught. She sank into Annie's body, into that navy dress that was a little too tight, the haughty attitude Annie wore with it, and then, into her warm and willing mouth.

Annie tasted of black liquorice. She smelled of rosewater and lavender. Eddie's knees buckled, and the world fell away. It was the same disorienting sensation she had whenever night fell and before dropping down into sleep, only this time she wasn't going under alone.

Annie loosened the buttons on the front of her bolero jacket and guided Eddie under the skirt of her dress. "Your hands," she whispered, as Eddie slanted her other hand inside Annie's jacket, overtop of the dress and brassiere. Annie spread her legs, opened her mouth wider, and when Eddie entered her, she gasped. A kiss like that warps time, bends it to a circle. Nothing before or after could ever feel as good.

LAURA SLIPPED DOWN Logan, a propulsive sort of energy tugging her forward, as though she were a magnet being drawn to its opposite pole. Such was the kinetic nature of the storm. The farther she got from home, the faster she wanted to move, and the more necessary it became to get where she was going. Biting winter air grated against the exposed skin on her face and neck and cut across her teeth. The air smelled fresh and exhilarating, hints of earth buried deep beneath the freezing rain. Winter was the cleanest, meanest season, she thought, and she wanted to be purified by its icy embrace, made new again, and if not new exactly, then clear and wide-eyed and available to newness.

She arrived at the address, at the corner of Gerrard and Redwood. The Zero Gravity Circus was housed there now, and above it what appeared to be a few rental apartments. She walked around the side of the old brick building, then back in front. What had felt so urgent about coming here? Did she think she was going to find a nightclub from a bygone era? Some clue as to the mystery surrounding the house she was preparing to sell?

Gerrard Street was deserted. The streetcar rails were covered in snow and there were no tire tracks on the road. Where had everyone gone? A fleet of yellow cabs was parked across the street, outside the taxi depot. A little farther east, in the parking lot of the Lahore Tikka House, she glimpsed two rickshaws decorated in a blaze of red and orange and fluorescent green. The floral patterns and pop art dazzled against the icy backdrop of the city, and for an instant Laura felt a surreal and reassuring intimacy with this neighbourhood; the world had shrunk and all that existed was this place, and this moment, with her in it. Then a fierce wind blew, and she ducked under the circus marquee for shelter, almost tripping over something on the ground.

"Get back!" Astrid bolted upright, was instantly on her feet. Buddy was barking and baring his teeth.

"It's me, Laura," she said, freezing in place.

"Jesus H. Christ!" Astrid rubbed sleep from her eyes, gave them a second to adjust. She soothed Buddy with her hand on his back. "You could scare the stripes off a zebra sneaking up on a person like that."

"Is this where you've been sleeping?"

Astrid fastened the top button of her coat, to close it around her thin, pale neck. She tucked her chin into the ivory velvet collar and hopped from one foot to the other, somehow looking more natural out of doors now, Laura thought. Not as pasty when set against the white backdrop of the storm. "It must be so scary," she said. "Being out here alone."

Astrid scooped the dog into her arms. "I'm not," she said, kissing Buddy.

Laura moved to the front windows where hoarfrost had formed on the pane, small white ferns covering the glass. She scratched a clear spot with her gloved finger to peek inside. The walls were dark red. "Well I'd be terrified."

Astrid joined her. "I've been here before. This very spot, on this exact street."

"The circus you mean?"

"The Rideau Club," she whispered in a daze.

Laura shivered. An enervating chill blew through her; the cold outside was inside her now, draining her of warmth. "What did you just say?"

Astrid broke from her reverie, looked pointedly at Laura's reflection in the windowpane. "Why should I tell you anything?"

A rush of blood through Laura's veins, a drum in her chest. She was astonished by Astrid's comment. It had to be a fluke, her mentioning the Rideau Club, and yet the way she was staring at Laura now, wordlessly, almost knowingly, Laura suddenly felt that curiosity wasn't all that had brought her to this address. There was something else, about Astrid, about this place, that felt coincidental, more than comfortable, nearly inevitable. Standing there, she was part of some strange pilgrimage. To where? And why? The vintage army surplus bag and Buddy were strapped across the front of Astrid's body. "You want something," she finally said, not meaning to sound accusatory.

"Do you believe in second chances?"

Laura braced against the December wind blowing north from across the surface of the lake. She pulled the hood of her parka overtop of her hat and tucked her hands into downy pockets, holding them over her abdomen protectively. "Yes, I do," she said. A moment later she added, "What do you know about the Rideau Club?"

Astrid set the puppy down and he soon had his head buried in a milk crate full of discarded clown noses and a broken aerial hoop. "No, my turn to grill you," she said. "Tell me the worst thing you've ever done."

"I don't understand."

"C'mon, sing."

Laura couldn't think of anything worse than hiding a possible pregnancy from Cat, but she wouldn't confess that to the girl. "Stole stuff, I guess. An angora sweater in high school. Cheated on an exam."

Astrid scoffed, unimpressed. She adjusted the army surplus bag. "Do you have a sweetheart?"

"A what?"

"You know, someone special."

Laura's pulse quickened. How honest should she be? If she came out to Astrid now, it might scare her off just when she was finally winning her trust. "I used to," she lied. She felt a sharp pain in her chest, erasing Cat from her life.

"I have a used-to-be too," said Astrid. There was a slight change in atmospheric pressure then, an alteration only she detected, and it altered her mood, bringing a renewed sense of purpose. She scanned the lobby and beyond, invigorated, reassured, as if life again held meaning, and she wasn't a mere flicker but part of some vast infinity, moving within the circle of time. "Eddie worked for my father," she added. "We had to see each other on the sly."

"Sounds dramatic," said Laura. "Hanging out with me must be boring by comparison."

"Oh, you're nothing like Eddie," Astrid laughed, loosening, relaxing, thawing into the conversation. "For one, Eddie's a gas."

Laura laughed now too. "Gee, thanks." It was the kind of comment her mom might've made to get her to take herself less seriously and she liked Astrid for it. The girl wasn't going to be easily impressed or intimidated, which meant Laura could be herself.

Buddy waggled over with a sword swallower's blade between his teeth and Laura lowered herself to his level. "Drop it, boy." He clamped down and shook the blade vigorously, eyes on her. "I said, drop it!" She tried to wrestle the curved sword from him. He wouldn't let go and she accidentally nicked her glove on the point. "Ouch! It's sharp," she said.

Astrid crouched down and wrapped her bare hand around the blade. She yanked it easily from the puppy's mouth, without drawing any blood.

Laura stared, bewildered. "How'd you do that? And aren't your hands freezing without gloves?"

Astrid scooped up the puppy, stuffing him into the front of her oversized coat. She stared back, teeth chattering. "I honestly can't feel a thing," she said.

Laura felt a sense of urgency then, a restlessness pressing on her from behind her ribs, that she needed to do something, or had forgotten to do something, and now a bad thing was going to happen because of her negligence. What would Beth do in this situation? Through the window of the circus, she caught a glimpse of an old movie house projector and hoped Astrid's tough exterior belied a soft centre. The red walls of the lobby flashed like freshly spilled blood. "C'mon," she said. "I'll buy us lunch."

AFTER TAKING ANNIE to the museum, after their first kiss, love had been like a spinning top set into motion; Eddie could feel it turning and turning and turning inside of her until she felt it might spin her right out of control. All that week at the pit she could think of little else but being alone with Annie again, the smell of her, the impossible softness of her skin. It was unbearable knowing Annie was near and yet a world away with her father in Building One.

Until Annie had pushed into her life, companionship had been infrequent for Eddie, and kept to a discrete compartment. This intoxication was spilling out into all areas; whether she was with Annie or not, Eddie thought about her, whether she was sleeping or working, Annie was the dream that sat behind her eyes.

On Friday, facing the prospect of another cold supper alone, leafing through bowling league newsletters, Eddie was dizzy with impatience. When Annie finally came 'round near closing time, with the pay, Eddie contrived a way for them to be together.

"We could be alone whenever his lodge brothers set a meeting?" she said.

"I could try," said Annie.

A few days later, there came a knock at Eddie's back door — twice rapidly and twice more — as if it was their secret code. She pulled Annie safe from view inside the kitchen, and into her arms. They didn't stop to boil water for tea, or pause in the dining room to puzzle, they'd moved beyond formality and pretenses; what they wanted was each other, no mistaking it.

"How long have you got?" Eddie said, between kisses.

Annie caught her breath. "I just want to be close to you."

Her face was flushed, and there was a sheen to her skin, from running in a light rain. What a topsy-turvy world, Eddie thought, when something so wonderful can be forbidden. Her other earthly friendships hadn't felt like this, as if there was no end in sight, as if they would swallow her whole. The other girls, those situations, had each come with ready-made limitations — one-sided feeling or a boyfriend in the background or a kind of self-loathing that dampened every moment. Before Annie, she'd been in competition with church and family for scraps of love — and made to feel unnatural because of it. Eddie knew that most girls, if they could act the part, would ultimately fall in line as wives and mothers. Who could blame them? But with Annie everything had felt possible, even if it wasn't.

As Eddie led Annie into the dining room by the hand, she felt for the first time that the girl she wanted, wanted her back; a wild, untamed nature rose inside of her. It frightened her. Open devotion could land a body in jail, in the madhouse, or in an early grave. The force of their mutual feeling made it all too real and she let go and stepped back, knocking into her tea cart.

"Aren't you glad to see me?" said Annie.

"Of course, I am."

"Then what is it?"

"The laws of the land are against us," she said.

Annie took her hand once again, squeezed it. "Devotion doesn't need to be worn publicly," she said.

Eddie squeezed back. "Is this really for you?"

"I won't be some man's property," said Annie. "I won't be forced to spend my life serving fruitcake to a bunch of Orangemen's wives, dull as dishwater."

Eddie grinned. "No, I don't suppose you would."

Annie shrugged out of her trench coat, letting it fall to the floor. She pressed her soft, powdered cheek to Eddie's rougher one and wrapped her arms around the back of Eddie's neck. "One day at a time," she said, and that was that.

SUN WAS SLANTING through an overcast sky; beautiful, soft, even, light. It was the hopeful side of the storm. The brilliance and possibility that destruction brings. Laura and Astrid crossed the icy intersection at Gerrard and Greenwood, Buddy trotting alongside. They headed a block north, to Maha's, a small Egyptian brunch place. There, they stopped to read the sign in the front window. It read: CLOSED.

"Tell you what?" said Laura. "We'll go to my house." She wasn't going to let them disappear again without making sure they'd eaten and had a safe place to go.

Astrid stood transfixed in front of the sign. "No, not there," she said.

Laura stepped closer to read over her shoulder.

Dear Valued Customers,
See you on January 2, 2014.
Happy Holidays!

"Guess we'll just have to try another time," she said.

Astrid jabbed at the air, impatiently. "The ddddate!" she stammered. "The year." She couldn't seem to catch enough breath to form a sentence and hugged Buddy closer, too close, until he whimpered.

"What's happening?" said Laura.

"I think I'm gonna spew!" Astrid began to dry heave and Buddy squirmed to be free of her coat, so she set him down on the ground between her feet. As she bent over, her pants lifted, revealing bare ankles. She wasn't wearing socks inside her boots. "It's not possible," she said, gulping air.

"What's not?"

Astrid clutched her stomach, doubled over. Time had been interrupted for much longer than she'd realized, and it was all coming back to her now — the fights and the fear, and that final brutal night. She heaved and heaved, to rid herself of the memory, and a chilling emptiness from within.

Laura scanned the streets for anybody who might help. No one was around. "Astrid, can you hear me?" she said, sounding panicked.

Astrid nodded. She could hear everything and see it, and worse, feel it all again. The cold, in her feet and in her hands, in every muscle and bone, her body, ice. "It hurts so much," she said. She called Buddy over to her and tried to bury him under her coat once more. So many years had passed! Where had she been between then and now? She squeezed her eyes shut. What had happened to Eddie? Was Eddie even alive?

Laura reached out and placed a hand on Astrid's shoulder. "Hey, it's okay," she said. A current of electricity fused them and for a heartbeat Astrid radiated heat through her coat, until her eyes flashed open. She gulped air. Laura yanked away. "What the hell?!" Her hands and arms were tingling and then they felt numb. There was buzzing in her ears.

"I never said you could touch me!" Astrid's face was implacable, wary.

"I shouldn't have done that," said Laura. "I'm sorry. Are you all right?"

"Well, I'm not crackers, if that's what you mean."

"No, that's not what I —" The powerful current between them was dying and Laura was growing sleepy, and then she felt ... nothing.

"I used to be just like you, you know?" said Astrid. "I must be unlovable, I thought, or jinxed. There had to be a reason why bad things kept happening." She sounded angry. "If only I tried harder or planned more carefully or waited it out, then I would finally happy, but that's not always true, is it? I know better now. Too much is beyond our control, and we can never be free, if we're stuck in the wrong life."

Laura averted her gaze. It was painful having her inner world so crudely summed up, and by a girl who barely knew her. "I'm not sure I follow," she said.

"Sure you do," said Astrid. "You just don't want to admit what's right in front of you."

Sunshine surged through a break in the clouds, illuminating her face. Still impossibly white, her skin held a hint of pink. Alabaster. Her skin was almost translucent, Laura thought, and filled with colour when light shone through it. Somehow, though, she appeared healthier than she had an hour before. Her lips even showed a hint of colour, red.

Laura, on the other hand, felt her strength depleting, she was tired and she couldn't generate enough body heat, despite the layers she was wearing. Now that she thought about it, all day she'd been growing colder and more tired, and her muscles feeble, as if her very essence was somehow being leeched from her. Being cold made sense given the temperature, but maybe she'd caught the flu?

"I guess I'm just confused," she said.

Astrid pressed the heels of her palms into her forehead, grimaced. Snow swirled around her feet. "There are guns in my head, Laura, and I need to make them stop."

"Guns?!"

"There it is again. Bang!" Astrid covered her ears. "And blood everywhere."

Laura reached into the pocket of her parka for her cellphone. The girl was hallucinating or in danger, or both. "I'm calling my friend," she said. She was way out of her depth dealing with this situation.

"No! Don't do that!" Astrid's eyes were frantic and imploring. "Please," she said. "You'll only make things worse. We're running out of time."

"But I don't know how else to help you. You're not making any sense. I think you need to see a doctor."

Astrid blinked, then blinked again. Frost coated her eyelashes.

"We could go to emerg?"

Just then, an Out of the Cold van rolled past, searching for people in need of sleeping bags and dry socks. *Should she flag them down? Enlist their help?* Laura hesitated and before she knew it the van was gone. Then came stillness, no cars, no more wind, just the long, cold silence of the storm, a muted separation that blanketed all sound. The roads were empty, she and Astrid the only two people out there, except for slow-moving shapes in the distance, lumpy grey figures shouldering through the blizzard with anonymity. They hid in plain sight or was it disappeared to nowhere? Like phantoms, the shapes were there one second and swallowed by snow the next. Love was like that too, Laura thought. Stealthy, ambiguous. It could charm and then completely disappear.

"Astrid? Did you see that van? There are street outreach workers nearby."

"You're not my mother!" she spat. "Stop acting like you are."

Laura's throat tightened. She pressed back tears. "I'm just trying to help."

"No, you're not. You're trying to keep things under control, which isn't the same. If you really wanted to help me, you'd do what I've asked."

"Not the house again."

"I deserted Eddie. I can see that now. It ruined everything."

The cold was pressing against them, closing in. "It's not your fault," Laura said. "Whatever happened."

"I was robbed, Eddie and I both. We got a bum rap." A dark, rancorous expression fell across her face. "But since when is life fair?" There was a bizarre, almost inhuman, aspect to her voice now. It had dropped an octave and was scratchy and distorted like a record slowing on a turntable. Her posture was ethereal and had lost its three-dimensional quality.

Laura gripped the cellphone in her hand, worried the ridges of the plastic case with her thumb. *Try not to panic,* she thought. *Remain calm, de-escalate the situation.* If there were mental health issues here and possibly a serious crime to report, she'd deal with all that later. Right now, there was Astrid. "It's not fair," she said. "It's not." She meant it. In a more just world, or even a slightly better one, kids like Astrid wouldn't have to choose between living in violent homes and living on the street. If life were fair, Marilyn would still be alive. She looked across at the girl, really contemplated her for the first time. Her skin, like the snow, reflected the light at twice its natural intensity. Her green eyes burned. For what? Love? Saving?

"What do you want to do?" she asked.

"There's only one way to make things right," said Astrid. "I have to get back to Eddie."

"Is that safe?"

"There's no such thing," she said. There never was. "But I want to see something first, before we go."

Laura nodded. "I'll come along."

"I've just been feeling so ... so alive." Astrid sounded breathy, eager, as if she could hardly get enough of the feeling. "I hate to give that up."

"It's weird," said Laura, teeth chattering.

"What is?" Astrid's voice was steadier now, as if she knew what Laura was about to say and yet wanted to hear it confirmed.

"Lately I feel like …"

"Yes?" Astrid's bright eyes sparkled like the crystals falling all around them.

"Like the life is being drained right out of me."

EDDIE'S FAVOURITE DUTY nurse moved efficiently around the side of her bed. The nurse hummed while she worked, rolling Eddie's body onto one side, and reaching over to tug off the sheet. Eddie didn't recognize the song today — something jaunty, which was appreciated; a little music broke up the monotony. "How you doing today, Miss Ferguson?" the nurse asked, rhetorically. Eddie wanted to reply. She'd been feeling impatient and unusually restless. Today love was a current running right through her; she could practically feel Annie's touch. "Don't you mind me," continued the nurse. "I'll just be one minute more."

Eddie didn't mind. The only physical contact she had was when a nurse moved her limbs to keep her from losing muscle, or an attendant ran soapy water across her skin to give a sponge bath, or this: changing her sheets and repositioning her body to help prevent nasty bed sores. The nurse bent down; her face so close to Eddie's ventilator mask that Eddie caught a note of cocoa butter face cream. The nurse gently slid her hand under Eddie's head, holding its weight, while she slipped the pillow out from underneath. "Fresh linen does a body good," she said, and then she hummed some more.

The scent of a woman, any woman, was a reminder of her own humanity. Eddie wanted more than anything to reach out and touch the nurse's face, to resurface, drag herself up toward the light, but of course she couldn't move. She couldn't speak or see, almost every part of her was trapped yet itching to escape. The ventilator did the work of inhaling and exhaling for her, keeping an even pace. Still, she longed to breathe on her own and feel the satisfaction of filling her lungs to bursting. *At least open your eyes*, she thought. *Open your goddamned eyes!* Just then, the nurse gasped, as if she'd somehow heard Eddie's thoughts. She set Eddie's head flat down on the mattress and leaned over her chest to press the intercom. "I need a doctor in here, stat!" What was it? Eddie wondered. What was happening out there? Footsteps raced into the room. There was a second voice now, the young nurse who never trimmed her nails and often scratched Eddie by accident.

"Something the matter?"

"Look at her eyelids. Did you see that?"

"Oh my God, they're fluttering!"

Eddie felt the hard hospital mattress pressing beneath her back, and the soft dip of her own coil spring at home. The past looped around, unfolding time like stiff sheets.

It was late fall when they'd tumbled onto Eddie's bed fully clothed, with the yellow moon shining in through the small window.

"Have you ever seen a woman?" Eddie whispered.

They were face-to-face, Annie's warm breath landing on her.

"No."

She traced Annie's lips with her pointer finger, spotted a thin white line, a tiny scar that was barely visible. "I've never noticed that before," she said.

Annie tried to turn her head, but Eddie parted her lips and kissed the corner of her mouth where she touched. "Are you frightened being here with me?"

"No."

"I can stop," said Eddie.

Annie shook her head and they both scrambled under the quilt. Eddie unbuckled the belt of Annie's dress and pulled her sweetheart neck aside, exposing one bare shoulder, kissing it softly. She inhaled Annie's scent, rosewater. Annie's lips were warm and insistent, and

Eddie helped her to lift the dress over her head. Annie lay back down in her silk slip and garters.

"Do you like what you see, Mr. Ferguson?"

Eddie kissed the other shoulder, and then Annie's mouth once more. She didn't need eyes for this. She wasn't worldly, though she had some experience and there were instincts to follow. After a few minutes kissing, she got up the nerve to reach around behind Annie's back and try to unfasten her brassiere. The clasp was fussy, and she lost confidence.

"Never mind," said Annie, fiddling with the clasp herself. She guided Eddie's hand around to her breast and arched her back. Her mouth was more urgent now, her tongue searching. This made Eddie feel urgent too, as if she might tear Annie's slip off altogether. Instead, she fumbled under the skirt of her dress.

Annie reached over to undo Eddie's pants, but Eddie stopped that. She pressed her weight into Annie's body, rolling her onto her back. Annie's skin was impossibly soft — her breasts, her navel, and between her legs, a fresh rain.

"First, let me hear you moan," she said.

LAURA ENTERED HER mother's long-term care home pulling off her gloves. She signed in at the front desk and then waited for the elevator. When the doors parted, out clomped Nomi, her mother's favourite personal support worker. Good. Whenever Nomi was on shift Laura knew Marilyn was being well cared for. Nomi helped Marilyn with the old VCR in her room and she was never condescending with residents. She kept kosher, but snuck Marilyn her favourite — bacon pizza — whenever Marilyn wanted to order in.

"Morning," said Laura, stepping in as Nomi stepped out.

Laura's snowy boots left wet prints along the second-floor hallway where Mr. Cooperman was pacing up and down in his best suit and tie, making clicking and sucking noises. Howard was in a wheelchair at the long table in the lounge doing one of his million-piece puzzles. Jean and Mildred sat outside their rooms, propped in wheelchairs, staring at the floor. It had been less than a year since Marilyn had moved in and already Laura knew most of her neighbours. Cartoons blared from the common area where someone was watching an old *Looney Tunes* episode.

Laura kicked off her boots outside her mom's room, left a puddle of melt. *Will she know me today?* Without realizing, she'd crossed her fingers for good luck. She could never be certain anymore which version of Marilyn would be waiting, the one who knew her or the one who tried to trick her into seeming that she did. She knocked. No answer. The picture of her mom that was taped to the door in case of fire had been updated with a more recent likeness. A little thinner, Laura thought, eyes a little more vacant. She turned the knob and pushed inside.

Marilyn was lying on a twin bed, with her back to the door. She spoke without turning over. "Twenty-four hours, twenty-seven minutes, and," she made a show of reading the extra-large face of her wristwatch, though she could no longer navigate the concept of time, "fourteen seconds," she finished, sounding indignant. Somehow she'd sensed that Laura was supposed to have been here already.

Laura sagged, late, again. The cheap care-home calendar hanging on a wall beside Marilyn's dresser showed Laura's name under yesterday's date, where she'd written it the week before. "I know," she said. "Work has been intense lately, and yesterday completely got away from me. Sorry." Marilyn didn't move. Not an inch. "C'mon," said Laura. "I'm here now. And I brought you something."

Marilyn rolled over. "A moving truck?"

Laura felt a tiny ice pick chipping away at her heart. "Funny," she said, relieved it was a bit of the old Mom today, with her sense of humour intact. Still, a foreboding feeling of wrongdoing rose in her chest. If Marilyn was "all there," aware of how much she didn't want to be living in an institution, she also knew who had put her here. Laura didn't know what was worse anymore: when her mom forgot she'd ever been an artist who valued independence above all else, or when she remembered. Laura held out the paper bag. "There's a new French bakery near my house. Best croissants in town."

"Thanks."

Laura scanned the room. Everything was in order and as she'd left it, nothing missing, nothing lost or stolen. Her mom's small brass menorah on the bedside table, the rattan Peacock Chair in the corner by the window, their old television and VCR on a stand, with a framed photograph of Marilyn performing at the Lula Lounge for the Mayworks Festival of Working People and the Arts. Beside that sat another photo — the two of them riding horses on a white sand beach in Costa Rica. *Was that only five years ago?* It was the last trip they'd taken together, and the last Marilyn would ever take now. On the dresser, her mother's prized snow globe collection — all thirty-four of them, one for each year of Laura's life.

"You finally unpacked those."

"Nomi did it."

Laura sat on the end of the bed. "I saw her in the elevator just now."

"She wants a dog," said Marilyn. "But they won't let her bring one to work."

"Small, medium, or large?"

"We have therapy animals. I don't see why not."

"Maybe until it's trained?"

Marilyn grimaced through a mouthful of croissant, a big, exaggerated, pouty grimace, and Laura thought, *that's new*, never seen that expression before.

"Is she still your favourite?"

"Who?"

"Nomi. Is she still your favourite staff?"

"Not anymore." Marilyn raised her croissant as if it were a glass of fine wine. "You're my favourite now."

Laura pressed back tears. She'd been forgotten again, erased from Marilyn's mind like chalk on a blackboard. They sat in silence for another few minutes, chewing. Then, Marilyn asked, "How come you look so tired?"

It wasn't seasonal affective disorder and a lack of sunlight. The thin film separating Laura from the rest of the world, from other people whose lives carried on unaffected by diseases like Alzheimer's, had again slid into place. Peering out the window, she said, "I've been having trouble sleeping."

Marilyn wagged her finger and in a familiar maternal tone said,

"Working too hard again! You should try ... Oh, what's it called? That botanical the Romans and Greeks used? You know, that flowering thing that helps with insomnia?" She pinched up her face as she sifted through her words. "Starts with a *V* ..."

"Valerian?"

"That's it! You should try and score some valerian root."

At the sound of her mother's concern, Laura was once more hit with a wave of grief. "You're probably right," she said, determined not to cry on every visit.

"Talk to my daughter," said Marilyn. "She works long hours too."

Laura pushed up off the bed. "Want to watch cartoons?"

"No."

"Howard's doing a puzzle?"

"All day, every day."

Marilyn sat up cross-legged. "They keep telling me I have this Alzheimer's thing. Why would they say that? Where's my daughter anyway?"

"You've got lots of colouring books," said Laura, deflecting. "We could make art?"

Marilyn pinched up her face, as though a foul odour had filled the room. "She promised she'd be here on fish and chips day. Fish and chips are always on Saturday. Can you check the calendar?"

Laura pretended to look at it again and hid the tears she could no longer control. The disease had finally won, she thought. It had robbed Marilyn of her very soul.

"I want to see my daughter!"

The best strategy when Marilyn became agitated was to deflect and distract her. Laura had learned that from consults she'd had with people at the Alzheimer's Society, and from some recommended readings. Don't argue the facts, they'd advised, don't correct her memories. Don't try to fill in the blanks. It would only make her more upset. People with Alzheimer's get angry and worried, and on occasion they see things that aren't there.

"Let's go outside," said Laura. "Fresh air will be good for us."

Marilyn started rocking back and forth on the bed, forward and back, again and again until she noticed Laura's tears and stopped. "You're sad?"

Laura wiped her face with her hands. "I've lost something I really love," she said.

Marilyn held out her left hand, palm down, wrist limp, as if showing off a new engagement ring. "This is how I keep track of things," she said. "See?" On her hand she had written the word *Me* in blue ink.

Laura stood. "I have to go but I'll come back soon," she said, choking on her words. She'd almost added "Mom" to the end of that sentence, though reminding people of what they'd forgotten was cruel. She was beside the dresser now, pointing at the wall calendar. "How about I come on lasagne day," she said. "Tuesday?"

Marilyn shrugged. "Not in the afternoon. That's when I do my exercises."

"Okay, here, Monday afternoon. It's tuna casserole." Laura sounded impatient. "Day after tomorrow. We'll go for a walk then, okay?"

Marilyn turned away and grabbed one of her snow globes. She shook it, starting a blizzard inside the small glass dome. She watched the snow settle over the ceramic figure. Then she watched the snow start to blow outside her window as if everything important rested beyond this room. "Don't come back," she said.

"What?"

"Don't come back unless you're taking me home."

AFTER THE NIGHT that Annie disappeared, Eddie found it hard to face an empty house, so the next day, a Saturday evening, she dragged herself into the new Barking Dog Pub that had opened on Jones Avenue. Women were welcome in a separate section so long as they didn't come at midday, when men took their working lunches. She entered through the women's door into the basement, closing out winter. Her friends would already be there, they'd taken to sharing a pint when they didn't have bowling. She pulled up a chair and ordered a draft, the only alcohol served. The place was toasty warm, and she immediately removed her hat and coat.

"I've been to the recruitment office," said Louise. "I'm thinking of joining up."

"Navy, army, or air force?" asked Dyllis.

The player piano rolled out a medley, though Eddie barely registered it — the notes banged and tinkled and bled into an indistinct sound. She was sleep-deprived, weary from the week working at the pit, and sunk in her grief. Her toes still ached from frostbite, but it seemed she'd caught it early enough and wouldn't lose any fingers or toes.

"Don't matter to me which," said Louise. "It's all room and board."

"You'll look smashing in uniform," chirped Evelyn.

Eddie was silent; thoughts of the future, any future, were impossible. She was trapped in the deep, dark underworld of loss and secrecy, the way a bug is trapped in amber. She couldn't speak of what had happened, not even to her closest friends, so she'd best not speak of anything and risk the wrong words escaping. Instead, she guzzled her beer and waved the waitress to bring another.

"They need clerks and radio operators," said Louise.

"Maybe I should join up too," said Dyllis. She enjoyed working at the Colgate factory, and it wasn't far to get to, but she only earned thirty-three cents packaging for every dollar the men earned making soap and toothpaste and cleaning products. "What does it pay?"

"Come with me tomorrow and ask," said Louise. "The real advantage, as I see it, is gaining skills and training for the future. What do you suppose is gonna happen to us when the men return?"

"We'll all be out on our arses, that's what," said Red. She made aircraft windshields and had gotten used to a good wage and spending much of it getting sauced.

"Things are changed now," said Evelyn. She was feeling modern in her new Elizabeth Arden "victory red" lipstick.

"Not for us," said Dot. "And not forever."

"She's right," said Louise. "When the war ends, most girls will be back in kitchens feeding husbands and babies."

Dot smirked. "Is there a difference?" When she wasn't stuck in a clothing factory sewing buttons on for fourteen hours a day, she turned tricks to make ends meet, so she knew men.

"I don't mind the babies," said Evelyn. She and her mother had taken in a dozen local children while their mothers went out to work. "It's the husband I don't want."

"You'll have to have one," said Louise. "If you haven't got an alternative."

"I thought you wanted to be a streetcar driver like that girl on the 506 route."

"Pie in the sky," said Louise. "They won't let too many of us in, but there's always a job in the service." She turned to Eddie. "You're awfully quiet tonight?"

Eddie hadn't heard her; the drink was dulling what senses she had left.

"Hey, you listening?" said Red.

"The war could end soon," she said, mechanically.

"Everything all right, Ed? You don't seem like yourself." This was Louise again.

Eddie gulped the dregs of her second beer. "Just tired," she said.

"It's that highfalutin girl, isn't it?" said Dot. "I knew it; she's finished slumming it with you."

"I like her," said Evelyn. "She's different but I like her and I hope she sticks around."

"Don't talk about her that way!" Eddie slammed her palm down on the tabletop. "Don't talk about her at all!"

"All right, all right," said Dot. "You've got a bee in your bonnet tonight."

Evelyn reached over and placed her hand overtop of Eddie's. "Ed, it's not like you to raise your voice? And I don't think I've seen you drink so much."

This was her chance, the moment to blurt it all out and find absolution, but Dot had given her another option: let them all believe their own worst assumptions about Annie, that she'd never been one of them, not truly, that she'd toyed with Eddie's affections and then deserted her when the life became too real.

"I should go," said Eddie, trying to stand and faltering.

Dyllis caught her. "We'd better get you home," she said. "C'mon Louise. Let's take her now."

"You'll feel good as new in the morning, after some shut-eye," said Evelyn.

"We'll stay with her," said Louise.

"See you," slurred Red.

Eddie let Dyllis and Louise prop her up. It was as if she had no bones or muscles anymore, no will of her own. She had friends, though, and when hope is gone, when life as you knew it has ended, that can sometimes be enough to carry you forward.

THE SUN WAS barely pushing through the glassy trees as Laura and Astrid approached the Greenwood rail yard under a sky the sepia tone of brick dust. Every solid surface was gleaming and slick — the roads, the hydro poles, a bus shelter. Patterns stood out on shrubs, the trace of green veins in frozen leaves, the red pop of serviceberries encased in the transparency of ice. Laura removed one glove and ran her hand atop the roof of a parked car, scratched along the frozen surface with her fingernails. The city had grown an exoskeleton.

"Why are we here?" asked Laura.

"Used to be the smell of this dump wouldn't wash out of our clothes," said Astrid. "The smell and before that, the red dust. There it is again."

Laura sniffed the air but took in only the near-antiseptic odour of freshly fallen snow. She peered down into the vast expanse of the rail yard, twelve hectares. The subway cars were lined up in rows, like silver caterpillars.

"That's where my father's brickyard sat," said Astrid, flinching, as if startled by a loud explosion. "Oh, I hate that sound!"

Buddy yelped.

"I don't hear anything," said Laura. She snuck a peek at her cellphone. The brokerage had texted twice to say they were still waiting on those photos from her last job. She texted back to say she'd already asked the photographer to forward them and would follow up.

"Building One," murmured Astrid, under her breath. "The kilns. Harper's Dump ..." There was that gauzy curtain again, separating

172

her from everyone else. One day she'd been over there, on that side of it, with Eddie. Now she was over here on this side. She shuddered. Until today, it hadn't felt permanent. "Do you suppose there are others like me out here?" she asked.

"I know there are," said Laura, tucking her phone away. Homelessness was all over the news again this winter, people were dying of exposure. Beth had told her that a disproportionate number of kids in shelters identified as queer. *Did Astrid?*

Astrid bristled, her eyes widening, and she glanced fearfully over one shoulder. "He could still be after me, then?"

Laura slipped her hand back into her glove. "You're safe now," she said. She was struggling to find the right words, still reeling from the thought that Astrid was involved in some sort of violent crime, and yet she was determined to help her. They had to get off the street and out of the cold soon.

"I know what it's like to want someone to love you," Astrid said, softly. "I mean, when they don't."

"Eddie?"

"No, my father."

This confession hung in the air between them, thick and dense as a winter's fog. Laura opened her mouth to speak and said nothing. Astrid's tone had been casual, forcibly nonchalant, but she was fidgeting with her chalky hands.

"That's really sad," said Laura.

Astrid shrugged. She snapped her fingers to pull Buddy's attention back from the road. "After a while you figure there's no point waiting around for things to be different. A souse won't change if he doesn't have to. And you can't warm a cold heart."

A souse? Laura had only heard drunks referred to that way in old movies.

"Our Durant got stuck in the mud over there once," Astrid said, pointing. "Some Red Hander fans pushed us out. Toronto Ulster

United FC had just won the National Soccer League Championship. That was Father's team. I hate sports," she added. "All except for bowling."

There was another long pause, and then Laura said, "I don't mean to sound insensitive, but you talk about him like he's ... like he's dead?"

A sour, pained expression drew across Astrid's face, like a curtain. "Don't use that word."

"What, dead?"

"Sssh! Stop it!" Astrid winced. A sudden, dreadful sensation fired through her body as if she were falling into a deep sleep, being pulled down, away from breath and air, from touch and time, into a sinister hibernation. She struggled to remain alert, counting backwards: *10, 9, 8, 7, 6, 5, 4, 3, 2, 1, 0 ...* Numerals flashed behind her eyes. Sums, simple equations, whole numbers, and prime; before they'd always given her a solid, sure sense of herself, grounding her in quantifiable fact. Now they deserted her. She grew faint and reached out for Laura's arm. A second jolt passed between them, momentarily stealing Laura's energy. "That's better," Astrid said, recharging.

Laura tried to pull away, couldn't. The girl's face flashed dewy and red. Beads of sweat pearled on her upper lip. She grinned at Laura, a slightly calculated expression.

"What are you doing?" said Laura. "Stop it!"

"Thank you," said Astrid, and then she let go.

Laura had lost feeling in her fingers and toes and yet her hands were trembling. *Was her life in some kind of danger?* She chewed her bottom lip. *What was that shock she'd felt pass between them? An electrical impulse?* That didn't make any sense, and Astrid didn't strike her as violent, only fearful and anxious, the kind of PTSD response Beth would say comes from having suffered a traumatic experience. Pins and needles started in her hands as the feeling returned. She could be imagining things? Or, another unsettling thought: what if she were wrong about the girl?

"C'mon," said Astrid, starting the long walk back down Greenwood. "Time's a tickin'." Her voice sounded stronger now, there was more energy to it. She spoke as though they were a team, and wherever they belonged, it was together. It was sort of sweet, Laura thought. If it wasn't getting so out of hand. She reached for her phone again, started dialling, and got Beth's voicemail. She struggled to hear through the crackle in her ear.

"Hey," she said. "Remember that situation I mentioned the other day? I really need your help. Sorry to sound cryptic." She whispered into the receiver, "Call me ASAP." She pressed "end."

"You call that thingamabob a telephone?" Astrid had turned from the rail yard and was facing her with Buddy at her feet, tail wagging eagerly.

"I wish you'd tell me what's going on."

Astrid walked backwards, speaking. "If wishes were fishes, we'd all have a fry."

Laura folded her arms across the front of her parka and waited in place. The road, behind Astrid and Buddy, rolled out like a white ribbon, with the lake in the distance, darker than the sky, slate grey, flat and smooth, the water a grave. *Goodbye*, she thought for no reason.

"I just wanted to see the pit one last time," said Astrid. "Before you let us into the house."

Laura sighed, exasperated. "Listen, I like you, you seem like a great kid, but none of this adds up and the bottom line is I'm being paid to sell that place. It's private property." Buddy chewed noisily on an icicle by the side of the road. "You can't stay outside forever," she added, "your dog is practically starving."

Astrid grimaced. "Forever is a really long time." She turned and marched off ahead, the army surplus bag slamming against her chest like an angry fist. "I just want to be loved," she called over one shoulder. "Is that so wrong?"

Laura was speechless. The snow shifted and compressed under her weight; the frozen ground less stable than it had been before. The city was full of people like her, she thought, abandoned, homeless, refugees from love and others, who didn't know where to place their hearts. Was she one of them now?

Astrid took a right at Wagstaff Drive just as Laura caught up to her, and they made a shortcut through the alley, past the new craft brewing company. "Mr. Wagstaff was my father's biggest competitor," she said.

"Slow down," Laura said. "Who?" Her boots crunched on the ice. She was trying not to slip and fall while she listened to her voice mail. Cat had left a message to say she was sorry. She felt badly about their fight.

"Those two fat heads were the last holdouts with family plants," said Astrid. "Up until the coal shortage, they used coal in the kilns, while others stuck with wood."

Laura hung up. Her feet were suddenly heavy, dragging through the thick snow. With each step she felt she was leaving some part of herself behind. Her muscles ached and her breathing became laboured. The cold air bit into her, sapping her of energy. "You're starting to scare me," she said.

Astrid raised an eyebrow. "What a whacky thing to say."

At the corner, Buddy lifted his leg but didn't pee on a red Canada Post box. Astrid stopped to take a close look, she pulled the lid open and peeked inside. "Is this a letter box?"

"You're pulling my leg, right?"

"And what's that, up ahead?" Astrid was pointing at a construction site.

"Another condo going up."

"Condo," Astrid repeated, as if pronouncing a foreign word.

"You act like you've never seen one before." Out of the corner of her eye, Laura thought she saw Buddy trot off to dig a hole in the side of a snowbank. "I'm certain my friend is going to help with your housing," she added.

"I didn't ask for that!"

"No, I just thought —"

"That you know what's best for me?"

The orange glow of a flickering street light illuminated Astrid's face. She was like the storm, Laura thought, a beautiful and dangerous proposition. But chance encounters led to risky obligations. How much more was Laura prepared to give?

She'd been asking herself that question a lot lately, how much work was she willing to put into her marriage to make it better? How far was she willing to go to have a baby? "I guess I deserve that," she said, shivering.

"Sure," said Astrid. "That's how I used to feel when my dad would blow a gasket."

"I hope you don't mind me saying, your dad sounds like he was a dick. Is there someone else? Your ex? Your mother, maybe? I could help you contact her."

Astrid gave a brief, amused laugh. "Frances Armstrong is long gone," she said. "And you're very persistent. But that's not why I followed you."

Laura stopped in her tracks. "What the hell does that mean?"

Astrid's expression softened, the muscles in her face relaxed, even her star tattoos seemed to slacken with grace. "At first I thought it was because you're the one with the key," she said. "Now I see, we want the same thing."

"What's that?" asked Laura.

"To have our old lives back."

A chill rippled down Laura's spine. Her temples began to throb. For so long she'd wished she could have her mother back, and before that, she'd wished for Marilyn's memory to be restored — or at least to slow the progression of her Alzheimer's. "You know we can't really do that, right?"

Astrid adjusted the strap of her bag, impatiently. "But if you could," she said. "Just for one day. If you could return to where you left off and start again, wouldn't you?"

Start again?

Astrid was watching her, waiting on a response. Whatever she said next could strengthen their connection or jeopardize her being able to help get the girl off the street. She glanced up and caught the waning winter sun breaking through the clouds. Some of the most beautiful skies happen just before sundown, she thought. Or right after sunrise. Dawn and dusk were the beguiling "in-between" times when the soul of a city was most visible, its inhabitants raw, revealed. All around them, hundred-year-old trees were shimmering against the light of the dying sun, oak and Norway maple giants, spread out into a frozen canopy. Beneath it, she felt small, mesmerized. "I don't know," she said. "Maybe. It wouldn't be the same."

"No, not the same at all." A bitter irony lined Astrid's voice. "It doesn't have to be," she said. "As long as —" she interrupted herself.

"As long as what? What, Astrid!?"

"As long as the love goes on!"

Laura studied the girl and a fuzzy awareness came over her. They'd both lost their mothers. They'd both known that grief. It doesn't matter how old we are, she thought, or what our lives have been like, tucked away in every soul there is a yearning for home. She hardly knew Astrid, that likely wasn't even her real name, and yet she felt she did know her; not the details of her life maybe, but the tenor of it, the colour of it. In a matter of days Astrid had managed to occupy Laura's mind as stars occupy the night sky, piercing vacant space with light.

"Time to find you a shelter," she said. "And I'm not taking no for an answer."

"It cannot be stopped, Laura." Then, in a whisper, "It's already in motion."

The blowing snow surrounded them, dense and impenetrable, making it impossible to see. "Astrid?" The wind rose, flurries erasing the three of them; Laura appeared to be gone, even to herself. "I can't see anything," she said, panicking. "Where did you go? Astrid? Buddy!" Seconds later, the tempest subsided, and she found she was alone.

Laura approached the Condor house expecting the girl and her dog to be there. They weren't. Everything had turned white, the sparkling sugar crisp found in a storybook. She crossed the front lawn and walked around the side where she lay down in the middle of the backyard gazing up at falling snow. It came down slowly, at first, like her heart rate, and randomly, yet each flake was a frozen fractal bearing a knowable pattern. The air was nippy and the flakes that fell landed as delicately as glazed gossamer on her eyelids, her lips. Kissed by the sky, she let her body sink into the snow and press against a bed of ice.

DOWN AT CHERRY Beach, the snow-covered lake was silent and still. The frozen expanse was an unmade bed, miles of rumpled white sheets, as far as the eye could see. Ice was densest around the legs of the wooden dock by the lifeguard station. It spread from the shore in sheets of white and grey, indigo and baby blue. Ice covered every track or trace of foul play. But if someone had been there, if someone had been listening, they might've heard the faint hymn, the sunken note of red regret.

LAURA POKED HER head into the second upstairs bedroom, the smaller one. It fit a single cast iron bed and a jade art deco night-stand with two drawers. On the stand sat an oil lamp, a wind-up alarm clock, and a set of nail scissors and file. She was scouting for items to set aside for the estate sale. It was her job, and it was also a good distraction. How could a girl and a dog simply disappear? Soft light filtered through the only window, a narrow unadorned rectangle overlooking the backyard. She entered and sat on the edge of the bed. The springs creaked. Who'd slept here? Had they been well loved? She ran her hand along the smooth press of the top sheet, the hand wearing the rose gold band.

The bed had been made with cream linens and covered in a patchwork quilt. The wallpaper was a washed-out ivory with delicate green vines and billowy white flowers. The green carpet with its large white peonies matched. The room's décor was romantic, Laura thought, it lent an austere and timeless quality to the space, hearkening to a bygone era. But these days, clients wanted modern, sleek, and expensive looking.

Over the bed hung a large rectangular frame in gold leaf, with a floral oil painting. At her feet was a small oval rag rug, and across from her, a weathered straight-backed chair. It would maybe bring fifteen bucks at the St. Lawrence flea market.

Looking out the window she saw into the neighbours' yards, all of them fenced. The trees were leafless and wrapped in ice. The snow-capped houses lined up in neat rows, typical of the city's old grid-style urban planning. *I don't want to empty this house*, she thought. Nothing here felt out of place.

She and Cat had every modern convenience — dishwasher, heated bathroom tiles, custom built-ins. On the advice of one of her colleagues, she'd hired a decorator ten years ago, when they'd bought the house. The decorator was the one who'd taught her about sightlines and flow, how to create a distinctive moment, turn each room into a unique experience. She stood to try the small room from another angle. *This is more like me*, she thought. The person she used to be, the one she'd forgotten about, who enjoyed foraging at rummage sales with her mother to find that one-of-a-kind item that told a story. How many stories did this house tell? She flashed on the Rideau Club tickets. How many stories was it hiding?

At the foot of the bed sat two brown leather suitcases, one stacked on top of the other. The bottom case boasted engraved initials, AKA, and a stitched leather handle. She wrapped her fingers around the handle, felt the cow's hide warming her palm. The top suitcase was smaller. Pressing open its metal rivets, she lifted the lid. A musty scent and, under it, stale rosewater. The fitted interior was patterned shot silk. In the case, neatly folded, lay a burgundy knee-length dress with pleats. She lifted it out and the skirt flared. The dress had hip pockets and a narrow belt and the tag inside the collar read: T. Eaton & Co. Limited. There were a few wrinkles in the fabric. She held it against her body and a shudder of excitement rippled through her, as if she were a child playing dress up, or a teenager sneaking out on a date. It smelled of cedar mothballs.

Also in the suitcase, a hat with a blue feather, a cream-coloured silk slip and brassiere, and matching garter belt and stockings. Her heart sped. She'd secretly tried on clothes and shoes and even jewellery in other houses before. Waiting for an open house to begin, or for a home inspector to turn up, she'd spooned ice cream from freezers and spritzed herself with expensive perfume, and once, when she knew she was the only one with keys, she took a bubble bath in a heart-shaped Jacuzzi.

Quickly, she tossed the dress across the bed and unbuttoned her blouse. She struggled out of her pants and tugged off her shoes and socks. The garter belt was confining around her hips, its metal clasps cold against her inner thighs. She sat on the chair and gently, ever so carefully, so as not to put a tear in them, slid the sheer silk stockings over her toes and up her calves. She was slipping into another skin. Fastening the clips to the top of each stocking, she puzzled her way into the stiff brassiere. Today she wasn't just trying to amuse herself; she felt compelled to be here, needed to feel something she hadn't felt in a long, long while. What was that? Alive? Free? The dress went over her head easily and slid snugly down against her silhouette. The fit was perfect. She cinched the belt and lifted the wine-coloured oxfords from the shoe pockets in the suitcase. She stretched the elasticized heels over her own and plopped the hat onto her head. Then she found her reflection in the windowpane.

AT HALF PAST eight, Annie sailed down the back staircase of her house in a killer-diller burgundy A-line with knife pleats swishing around her legs, the slip teasing her thighs. She'd splurged on silk stockings, an extravagance most girls had to do without. She hoped Eddie would appreciate the effect.

In the vestibule, she set her black handbag on the mantle of the marble fireplace and checked her image in the square mirror above it. Spiffy, she thought, pinching her cheeks. She dabbed on a bit of lipstick.

"Where the hell do you think you're going?"

She stiffened, didn't turn around, instead she forced herself to find his image in the mirror. He was standing in the doorway, lighting a tobacco pipe. His brow was sweaty, his chrome dome shiny under the overhead lighting. *Why was he here?* She'd heard him leave over an hour ago. "Just out to the park," she said, in a phony casual manner.

"Painted up like that you're not."

She smeared the colour from her lips with the back of her hand and turned around to face him. He was holding his cherrywood pipe in one hand, puffing on it. He didn't appear to be drunk. There was no smell of alcohol. "There's a baseball game tonight," she said. "I'm going to take the Davis children to watch. I would've asked you along, but I thought you had a lodge meeting."

He stepped forward and blew smoke in her face. "Who is he?"

"Don't be silly, Father." She coughed, despite trying to suppress it. Any reaction only showed weakness on her part and weakness drew his ire.

"You've been different lately," he said. "Don't think I don't see it. An extra spring in your step. Distracted at the pit."

Her heart was pounding so hard she was sure he could hear it; her palms were sweating, and now the narrow belt of her dress felt a little too snug. "It's not a boy," she said, to disarm him. "Still, aren't you clever to notice. I suppose I have been distracted lately." She was scrambling to think up her next move, what lie she might tell to get out of this trap. "With thoughts of business college," she added.

"Business college?" The woodsy blend of his MacBarren filled the vestibule.

"I wanted to bring it up once I'd looked into it, see if you agree, but here you are as usual, one step ahead."

"Hmm." *Puff, puff.* He leaned against the carved walnut banister, inspecting her from her oxfords to her hair, with the pipe hanging out one side of his mouth, as though he were a gumshoe and she were a criminal. "That's right," he said. "Nothing gets by me." Her flattery had massaged his sense of importance.

She slipped the tube of lipstick into the hip pocket of her dress and discreetly lifted her handbag from off the mantle. If he took notice and demanded to look inside there'd be hell to pay. She'd forgotten to discard her museum ticket.

"As I say, I haven't thought it through. Widow Davis mentioned a girl she knew who'd attended classes and she helped save the family bakery from going belly up." This part wasn't a lie, so it came off sounding sincere.

"You manage the books all right, as is."

"That's true enough."

"Sounds like a cock-eyed plan," he said. *Puff, puff.*

She shrugged. "If that's what you think." Anything to avoid his temper and get going.

"If you want my two cents worth, take up volunteer work. Make yourself useful. This war isn't over."

"Good idea," she said. "I'll do that." She took a step toward the hallway entrance that led, they both knew, to the back door of the house where freedom might still be found. He blocked her with one arm, the hand holding the lit pipe.

"You'd better not be lying to me," he said.

The air in the space between them seemed to thin. The walls pinched in. His tobacco smoke turned her stomach. She wasn't going to get out of here unharmed after all. "I wouldn't dare," she said, matching his stony eyes with granite of her own, a change of tactics for his changed tone.

He was holding the bowl of his pipe tight up under her chin now, its heat threatening her face. She could hear the faint burn of tobacco leaf and smell the blend of wood fire and berries on his breath. She stood perfectly still, holding her breath, not even the slimmest gesture or evidence of life detectible. She was brick and she was mortar, as hard as she needed to be to flatten this moment, and just as lifeless. It was what he wanted.

Finding no great opposition, he retreated, dropping his arm, allowing her the victory this time. Then, before she could move to leave, he turned the pipe over and dumped its contents out, onto her shoes and the hardwood floor. "Clean that up," he said. He tucked the pipe into her empty skirt pocket. "I'm going upstairs." He took his time ascending.

Annie watched him go, until he passed the Clan Armstrong crest that was nailed to the wall at the top of the stairs. The crest featured a muscled arm from the shoulder in the centre of a strap and buckle, framed by the Latin motto, *Invictus Maneo*. I remain unvanquished.

THE LARGER SUITCASE was locked. Laura tugged on the rivets; she reached for the nail scissors on the bedside stand and poked around inside the small keyhole. Why lock it unless something intriguing lay inside? She lifted the case, and it was heavy, too heavy to carry home. Just then, her phone rang. She dropped the case on the floor with a thud and fumbled around in her bag for the phone. It was the husband from the Craven house. The bank had declined their mortgage application.

"Don't panic," she said, in as soothing a voice as she could muster. "Give me the numbers." She wasn't really listening; the suitcase had popped open to reveal a stack of faded newspapers. Crouching down, she peered inside. The *Toronto Star* headline at the top of the stack declared: "Father and Daughter Missing After Blizzard!" With the phone wedged between her ear and her shoulder, she riffled through the papers, trying to sound attentive and reassuring to her client. Another article from *The Sentinel* announced: "Foul Play Suspected in Disappearance of Local Orangeman." The *Globe and Mail* wrote: "Stolen Money Possible Motive in Armstrong Mystery." Armstrong? That name was familiar, but she couldn't think why. And why had the homeowner saved these clippings? Was she somehow related to the man and his daughter?

"Apply with a different lender," she told her client. "Half my buyers are rejected on the first try." His wife was despairing, and felt the property was "meant to be" theirs. The notion offended Laura, even as she indulged it. Predetermination was for those who couldn't live with ambiguity or unknowns, and those who'd never had to try. "Let's just wait and see what else you can find," she said.

"Call me back tomorrow." People wanted to believe in a hidden power, she thought. Control over the future. It absolved them of responsibility. *What did she believe in?*

She hung up and stared at the suitcase full of sensational headlines. *Shit.* If it turned out some heinous crime was linked to the homeowner or this property, she'd have a hell of a time selling the place. A flush of guilt spread under her skin. In her jurisdiction, an agent wasn't legally obliged to reveal that a death had occurred in a house or even to share rumours of a haunting. Not unless a prospective buyer asked outright, and few would think to do that. She closed the suitcase without locking it and dragged it off the bed, across the room, and noisily bumped it downstairs. One. Step. At. A. Time.

An hour later, she was sitting in her home office with a hat on her head, conducting an Internet search while Beth, Matt, and the kids were in the backyard having a snowball fight. Cat called from the kitchen. "Laura, can you come?"

"I'm in the middle of something!"

She tried "Armstrong Murder Toronto" and got three links, all to articles written by a local historian about the brick quarries that once dominated the east end. Choosing randomly, she clicked on a link about a brick pit owner, James T. Armstrong, who was suspected of having been murdered, though his body had never been found. The article also said that his daughter's frozen body had turned up in a local dump weeks after a big blizzard with an army surplus bag containing cash. A puppy had been found with her, also dead. No one knew how they'd gotten there or why.

A puppy? Laura scrolled through the pages, her palms sweaty. What breed of dog? Did they say? Without realizing it, she was holding her breath. Then, the words leapt off her computer screen. A Scottie, one paper had noted. A black Scottish terrier!

"Laura, hurry!"

Her heart fired inside her chest like a pistol. Frantically, she searched "Annie Armstrong Missing" and half a dozen links popped up; finally one offered a grainy photograph. It appeared to have been taken at some sort of demonstration. A woman was holding a protest sign. The angle of the shot made it impossible to decipher the words. Laura instantly recognized the face in the image, though. Astrid! But that was impossible. She leaned in closer to the screen.

The face was unmistakable, even in black and white, with a poor-quality image. Those eyes ... Laura fiddled with the rose gold ring on her finger. Astrid must be a relative, she thought. Of course, a descendant of the victim. That would explain her interest in this house. A bubbly, expansive feeling pressed under her skin. The bonus of being a realtor, aside from the money, was that every so often she became privy to someone else's secrets, this time maybe even unearthing a crime!

"I need your help, Laura!"

She removed the hat, set it down on her keyboard, and rolled the chair away from her desk.

Cat was standing by the gas stove, in a reddish-brown puddle, face flushed and shiny from tossing a stir-fry. The fragments of a broken bottle of soy sauce were scattered across the floor. "My vision is blurry, and my hands don't work," she said. "One second, I was holding it, and then I wasn't. Made a mess of my sketches too."

Laura bent over to pick up a large section of glass before they stepped on it and carried it to the recycling bin. "We should've gone to the hospital," she said. "What if you have post-concussion syndrome?"

"Matt examined me."

Laura mopped up the soy sauce with a tea towel and they sat at the table. Years ago, she'd sold a house to a client who'd been in a motorcycle accident in California before there were helmet laws. He'd spent years with amnesia before regaining partial memories.

Suppose Cat had lost a permanent part of herself in the storm. "At least get x-rays," she said.

"*Bueno, mañana.*" Cat's eyes held a distant gaze and for an instant Laura wanted to cup Cat's face with her hand, bring her back, kiss her fast, forget the last hard years that had fallen on them, and confess the recent embryo transfer. Instead, wordlessly, she let Cat take her hand.

"This is new?" Cat said, meaning the rose gold band.

"What? Oh." It was stacked on top of the ring Cat had given her, the one she'd worn for ten years, representing their vows, family, the closed circle of a life. She fiddled with the ring, sliding it on and off her finger, guiltily, then moved her hand to her lap, beneath the tabletop.

"There's something I need to tell you," she said, heart pounding. "I'm not sure how you'll react." She took a deep breath. It was hard to push the words out, hard, after their recent fight, to make herself vulnerable. How angry would Cat be? Would confessing what she'd done jinx her chances? Sweat trickled down her sides and she shifted in her seat uncomfortably. She'd start in gently, easing toward the truth. "I'm not ready to stop trying," she said.

The sour, fermented odour of spilled soy sauce grew more pungent. The clock hanging on the kitchen wall ticked loudly.

"We've been through this already."

"I know. But what if we just do one more cycle?"

"That's what you said last time."

"Just because we haven't been successful yet doesn't mean we won't be."

"Successful?" Cat looked at her with a mixture of pity and regret. "When was the last time we laughed? We used to laugh, remember? Before all this started, we were enough for each other. I'm sorry, I just can't go back there, and I don't know how to make you understand that." Then she powered up her smart phone and was surfing the Internet.

You could if you wanted to.

Blood flooded Laura's temples. She wrung her hands. It was one of those banal moments that might pass for insignificant to someone watching from the outside, but which actually revealed the insurmountable hill of ice that had formed between them. The delighted outdoor squeals of their friends' children grew louder, which only amplified Cat's silence, a silence that enraged Laura. It was an aggressive move, the ultimate expression of control. "So, what, you make a unilateral decision and I'm just supposed to live with it?!"

"You're obsessed, Laura!"

"Well maybe I am!"

IVF had taken a physical and emotional toll; failing month after month haunted her and made her question the meaning and purpose of her own life. She'd thrown herself upon the world of reproductive science to see what it would make of her, and yet she'd never been able to fully trust it. Maybe that was part of the problem? That cells could be frozen and thawed, that the building blocks of life could be manipulated within a lab, and her body reduced to a container. Believing in miracles became a daily challenge. It was possible, she let herself think, that a miracle was already in progress.

"It was so easy for you," she said. "All you had to do was hold my hand and show up at the clinic once a month."

"I was there every morning! We spent my savings too. And, just for the record, five years of hanging out at a fertility clinic is not my idea of a good time."

"Face it, you're punishing me because you can't buy your way out of this."

Cat recoiled. "Wow! That's fucking insulting! And unfair."

"I'm sorry. I didn't really mean that. It's just —"

Cat raised her hand, fingers spread to say, *stop*. "You know what? I can't talk about this anymore. I wanted kids, okay? I still do, if that's what you need to hear. I always thought I'd be a parent, but I've accepted that it isn't going to happen for us."

"Cat —"

"*No mas*." She looked back down at her phone and started scrolling through Facebook.

Laura could've pressed the issue, but what would be the point? Cat related to the world by analyzing it, understanding, explaining, and then redesigning it, and there was no explanation for her infertility. Cat had never wanted to carry a child or wished for more family the way Laura had. She still didn't get it. The three pregnancies were just abstractions to her. Underdeveloped concepts, no more real than her initial renderings in the early stages of a renovation. "Coffee?" Laura asked, standing to brew a fresh pot.

Cat didn't look up. "Thanks."

Laura paced in front of the sliding glass doors that looked out onto their backyard. She flicked on the porch light to see better. On the surface, the world outside was clean and clear, and suffocating, she knew, under all that ice. Their smoke bush would not likely survive the winter. Two limbs from their oak had snapped off; one, crashing down on the fence they shared with their neighbour, had crushed a section of it. The other had knocked out the tool shed. She glanced back over her shoulder at Cat, engrossed in the small screen at her fingertips. Then, she turned to the outside once more.

AFTER MONTHS OF dating Annie on the sly, Eddie was summoned to Mr. Armstrong's office by the skinny boy from mixing. "Hey, you! Boss wants to see you." Her stomach turned. Bile filled her mouth. *He knows,* she thought. *Somehow, he knows about Annie and me. I'm done for!*

On her way to Building One, Eddie lit a cigarette, puffed on it furiously. She passed a line of German POWs being led across the grounds, then Joey and Antonio from blasting, two roughs who usually stared her down like dogs do to those lower in the pack. Today they averted their gazes. From the top of their heads to their boot heels, they were covered in clay. Their dry grey faces resembled painfully cracked sculptures.

She would lie about Annie being any more than an acquaintance, deny having taken her to the ROM or out to the club or having ever had Annie inside her home. She would pretend to know nothing about Annie joining the bowling league, and display no feelings for the girl, even though their connection was more than that now. But what if Annie had already confessed? Eddie stood outside the door, checking to see if Annie were anywhere near, trying to conceal the tremor that had taken hold of her body. She was surely going to lose her job. What about her life? Armstrong had a quick, ferocious temper, everyone knew. Some said he kept a gun in his desk drawer. Eddie dropped her cigarette, snuffed it with the toe of her boot. She balled her right hand into a fist and, with her left, turned the door handle. "You wanted to see me, sir?"

The coal-fired air inside was no better than it had been out in the open brickyard. A fine red dust coated the floor, Armstrong's desk, even the back of his balding head. "About time," he said, turning with a tumbler of whiskey in hand. The engraved star insignia on his Orange Order ring caught the light. He licked the rim of the tumbler and his moustache twitched. "Pannito from blasting was injured," he said, taking a gulp. "Joey will fill in for him. I need you to take over as the signal man."

Dominic Pannito was the pit's detonator, the head honcho — he knew where to light the sticks, and how to aim the blast so no one was buried when the overhang crumbled and fell. If he could be in some kind of accident out there, she would be in danger.

"I'm not trained for that," she said.

Armstrong downed the rest of the whiskey. "The boys are shaken. Just do what you're told and keep your eye on that working face."

Eddie had heard tell of his drinking binges and he often stank of the stuff; they all knew what it meant when he didn't turn up to work. For him to be drinking here, in front of her? Well. Whatever had happened must be mighty bad. She wanted no part of it.

"What about my ovens?"

Armstrong gripped the tumbler in his thick palm as though he had his hand around the back of her neck. "They're my ovens!" he shouted. "And I need you to stand signal today. If you can't manage that, maybe you can't handle your job anymore, either?"

"Father?" Annie swung the door wide. "Everything all right in here?" She nodded furtively at Eddie, scarcely an acknowledgement, as she ambled over to her father's desk. "It's only just the noon hour," she said, lifting the tumbler from his hand. "This can wait." She behaved as a beleaguered wife might — mechanically, neutrally, settling him into a comfortable dependence that served her own best interest, though Eddie knew she was afraid of him precisely by the way she hid that fear, navigating his unpredictable temper without inflaming it. Like a soldier stepping through a minefield, she was clearly practiced at sidestepping his moods.

"Show Ferguson to the blasting crew," he said, taking a seat. "We've got a new signal man today."

"Her?" Annie looked shocked and for a moment Eddie thought she was going to protest and give them away. "All right, then." She set the tumbler down on the desk. "This way." Once again, she sounded stiff, formal, pretending she and Eddie were little more than strangers.

Eddie tipped her hat and followed Annie outside. She felt the muscles in her stomach unclench; they hadn't been caught out after all.

They rushed between the buildings of the brickyard and into the secluded wooded area to the south where a city of wayfarers pitched tents at night. As soon as they were out of earshot, Annie let down her guard. Her voice wavered. "The boys say they were working about forty feet high and fifty across this morning. They fired a round of six shots into the face first thing and left the overhang for a couple hours to fall on its own. It didn't. Dominic was all clear when he detonated, but he was standing too far under the crest of the ridge. A large chunk came down on top of him. Oh, it's awful," she said. "It's something terrible awful! Both legs were crushed. His lungs were punctured. They don't know if he'll live and Father acts like it's nothing at all!"

Eddie's gut was in knots again. Clay was a tough, rubbery substance that broke in heavy slices or large blocks. She pictured Dominic's face, his large forehead with the serious brow, dark eyes that were almost black, and the stubble that darkened his chin and upper lip. Dominic was one of the hardest workers at the pit, and the strongest. "Is your father always like that?" she asked.

"On the hooch, you mean?" Annie scoffed. "You've heard the rumours."

"Cold I mean. Detached. What'll he do if he finds out about us?"

Annie moved closer, placed one hand on Eddie's chest, overtop of her heart. "You are the one good thing I've been waiting for." She took Eddie by the hand, moved them farther into the woods. "Let's steal away from here," she said. "Someplace without the dust and noise, where we won't hear the blasting in our sleep."

"It's food on the table."

"Inglis has thousands of girls working at his munitions plant. You could try there."

It would cost gasoline to travel to the west end and back every day, and Eddie had no interest in machine guns, but she saw the pained way Annie's eyes tightened in around the edges, as if they were being sewn up with a needle and thread. She heard the inflection in Annie's voice flatten. Annie was right; everything was different now that they had each other. Everything was worth more. "I'll work something out," she said. Then, she spied around to make certain no one was near. Satisfied that they were alone, she pulled aside Annie's scarf and quickly kissed the exposed skin of her neck. "Can you get away tonight?"

Annie shivered with pleasure. "I don't know." Her green eyes flashed like emeralds. "Eddie, he's got plans to sell. The Taylor brothers have been after him for years to consolidate. I heard him on the horn last week saying there's been less and less demand since the Depression. The brick business is done. He's getting into trucks."

Eddie kissed her once more, on her neck, then all the way down to her clavicle. Annie flinched, painfully. "What is it? Are you hurt?" A red heat spread up Annie's neck and coloured her face. She avoided Eddie's eyes. "You are. Let me see."

Annie tried to pull away, but Eddie held her by the arm. She tugged aside the collar of Annie's shirt to reveal a dark, purple bruise that spread into a sickly mustard halfway down her shoulder. "Did he do this to you?"

Annie yanked away now. "Nobody did anything!" A beating was one thing to endure; she would not also suffer humiliation.

"Annie?"

"Worry about yourself!" She straightened her shirt, adjusted the collar, and fixed her hair around her neck as she'd had it.

The steam shovel in the pit slammed against a wall of shale and they both felt its vibration underfoot. "Let me help you," Eddie said. She locked eyes on Annie's and was about to say more when they heard rustling in the woods.

"What was that?"

"Might be a fox," Eddie whispered, scanning through the trees. "Or a coyote."

Again a rustling, farther away this time.

"Eddie, I think someone saw us."

LAURA ANSWERED THE doorbell to Isla and her boyfriend, Greg, who were wearing colourful Ecuadorian wool hats and stoned expressions on their faces. They matched, a set of grinning sock monkeys leaning into one another. She'd forgotten how beautiful Isla was, or maybe it hadn't occurred to her before. Seeing her in the doorway now, face framed by her hat, the blue of her eyes cutting into the night, Laura was struck by how a person who can be ordinary in one moment can be extraordinary in another. She automatically went into work mode. "Welcome," she said, ignoring the skunky smell of weed fuming off their clothes. "Come in."

"Thanks for texting back," said Isla.

"Sure, what's up?" Laura pulled the door closed behind them as Nate and Noa chased down the staircase in pyjamas and tore around her through the house, screaming.

"Indoor voices!" she heard Beth shout.

"Oh, Beth's over?"

Greg opened his large backpack, the kind she and Cat used to take on summer camping trips to Algonquin. He retrieved a rolled-up document and passed it to her. "We found this in our apartment."

"I didn't want to recycle it without showing it to you first," said Isla. "Because I ran into Toby at the Carrot Common, and she mentioned you're selling a house at this very address. Coincidence, right? I figured you'd know if it has any value?"

Laura unrolled the yellowed paper and scanned the page. "A Deed of Trust." Someone had sought to share their property, in trust, with a second party. It was dated 1944. She jumped down to the description section and caught her breath. The lot was located

at 2 Condor Avenue! Her eyes darted to the trustee's section naming
Edna M. Ferguson as homeowner, and below that, the beneficiary,
Miss Annie Armstrong. And right there, was Annie's signature.

"You found this at the co-op?"

"In a crawl space in our bedroom," said Isla. "Should I just toss
it?"

"Let me check it out," she said, heart pounding. "For fun." Her
fingers tingled, and a tickling sensation crawled up her arm. Armstrong again. The name from the newspaper clippings! It belonged
to the missing brick pit owner and his daughter. The one who
looked like Astrid. Laura's hand began to tremble. The document
had been witnessed by a lawyer, notarized, and officially stamped.
None of this made any sense. The Office of the Public Guardian and
Trustee had done due diligence, digging back fifty years to check
for outstanding liens, title issues, or deeds. Apparently, they hadn't
searched back far enough and now the past had reached out and
grabbed on to her.

"Are you okay?" Isla asked. "You look pale."

Laura rolled up the deed. "I'll let you know what I find out."

Cat appeared in the hallway. "Thought I heard the doorbell."

"You remember Isla, from my book club?"

Cat extended her hand. "The night Laura hosted that Giller
Prize winner, right?"

"Good memory." Isla pulled off her hat and her blonde dreads
crackled with static electricity. "I still don't see what all the fuss
was about."

"And this is Greg. Greg, my partner, Catalina Bottino."

"Coming in for a drink?" asked Cat.

Greg and Isla exchanged a look. Greg shrugged. "If you don't
mind us crashing."

Cat had spiked the eggnog with a bottle of rum and now Laura regretted not downing a glass. It would've helped her to sound more

gracious than she felt. "Follow me," she said, leading the way down the hall, gripping the deed in her hand. *What are the odds?* First thing Monday morning she'd consult with a real estate lawyer. But something told her that wouldn't be the end of it.

In the living room, Matt looked up from the couch and flashed Isla a charming grin. He stood to shake Greg's hand. "Hey man."

"I don't think you've met my husband, Matt," said Beth. Then turning to Isla, "Aren't you two supposed to be in Vancouver?"

"Yeah, the flights are all grounded. My folks are pretty bummed."

"Where'd the kids go?" asked Laura.

"I bribed them down to the basement with video games."

"Then it's official," said Cat, clapping her hands. "We're having a fiesta!"

Matt moved to stand a little too close to Isla. "The more the merrier, right? People shouldn't be strangers during the holidays."

Beth was fast to move in between them, a proprietary gesture. "People shouldn't do a lot of things," she said. It was an odd comment, and the room fell silent, until Laura broke the tension.

"We've got an Italian red and a dry French white. Name your poison."

Matt disappeared into the backyard for a smoke and Laura headed into the kitchen with the Deed of Trust. Beth was right behind her. "Shit, I'm sorry. I didn't mean to make things awkward."

"Don't worry about it."

"He likes her, I can tell."

"Already?" Laura poked her head around the corner, peering into the living room. Greg was settling into their gold wingback, flipping through an old *National Geographic*. He appeared relaxed in a faded orange MEC fuzzy and a pair of blue jeans. His thick blonde hair was tousled on top and short at the sides, and he sported the trim fashion beard of so many young urbanites. Isla, on the other hand, lingered around their upright piano with her macramé shawl over a grey turtleneck. She touched middle *c* without pressing hard enough to make sound. "Shame about the hair," Laura said, to make Beth feel better. "White people shouldn't wear dreads."

Laura struggled to pop the cork on the red, took a sniff. A burnt, fruity aroma. Her mouth watered as her unsteady hand poured for the others. Ever since she'd taken on the Condor house, peculiar things had been happening. First, Astrid and Buddy, then those newspaper articles about an unsolved murder, and now this, a Deed of Trust found at the co-op. There had to be a logical explanation, didn't there? What if there wasn't? Her mother might've said something absurd like she'd conjured the girl and her dog to quell her own loneliness. Was that possible? She'd heard of women with phantom pregnancies, why not just phantoms? Don't be ridiculous, Laura thought. Since when did she believe in ghosts!

"Hey, did you try and call my cell yesterday?" asked Beth. "There's a garbled message from your number."

"Yeah, I ran into that homeless girl again. Astrid."

"She's still out there?"

"Hmm hmm. But don't ask me where." Laura scrunched up her face. "Listen, I've done something," she said. "It's big."

"I hope you didn't involve the cops? That rarely helps."

"It's not about that. I did another IVF cycle," she said. "I used the last embryo. Without telling Cat."

"Holy shit."

"I just couldn't leave it, wondering for the rest of my life. What if that was the one?"

"So was it?"

"Too early to tell," Laura said. "What should I do?"

Ding! The oven timer went off.

"Well, the hors d'oeuvres need to come out."

"Smart ass. Pass me those oven mitts."

A few minutes later, they headed back to the living room, with a tray of wine glasses and a large round platter of assorted canapés. Isla was in the corner, running her hand along the surface of Cat's old drafting table, now a repository for junk mail and loose change. "I'm totally into antiques. They're so ... um, old."

Laura set the tray down on the coffee table and an ache of yearning rang through her. She and her mother had found that table at an outdoor antique show in Aberfoyle during Cat's final year of architecture school. It had been a birthday surprise. Cat had insisted on holding on to it for sentimental reasons. She'd been full of promise then; they all thought so. She was going to be the Argentine Zaha Hadid, another brilliant architect. Their life together had been pointed in the direction of family and success. Laura felt a lump in her throat. Marilyn had been proud of Cat's career ambitions. She would've made an even prouder grandmother.

Laura watched Cat join Isla in the corner of the room. "So, you're in the book club. And you have good taste in furniture. What else should I know?"

"I'm an expert tarot reader," Isla chirped. "And a Gemini. I can be impulsive."

Laura observed them with bemused detachment and a stab of jealousy she hadn't felt since before she and Cat had moved in together. Was Cat attracted to Isla? Isla's face was serene, smooth. Not a hint of a wrinkle. Her voice was absent of irony. "What sign are you?" she asked. Then she moved over to the piano bench for the second time since she'd arrived.

Laura asked, "Do you play?"

"Not really. I had lessons when I was a kid. I'm more into electronica now. You know, EDM, synth-pop, ambient?"

Laura didn't know but nodded anyway. "Well, feel free." Discreetly she scrolled through her recent texts. Thom had given a thumbs-up to her last message. He was in South Africa putting together a CBC documentary on the legacy of Nelson Mandela and would be back in Toronto in a few weeks. They could get together then. Ocean had disappeared into an ashram or some commune south of the border, he'd said, but the others were still in the city and looking forward to seeing her. He'd attached a heart emoji. A colleague from the office had also messaged to suggest she find a better real estate photographer, because the photos from her last job had finally come through and they were out of focus. She sighed. One more thing to add to her to-do list.

Isla sat at the piano and placed her hands overtop of the keys. How much younger she appeared from behind, Laura thought. Almost childlike. Her movements were tentative, and yet she was soon striking the keys decisively. Laura watched her play, imagining what she made of the music. Why that particular song? Maybe Isla could see it as well as hear it, the way Laura could visualize accent walls and paint colours for a home that hadn't yet been fluffed. Was the song Isla played deep purple? Vermillion? Smoky grey? Her hands knew the chords without her having to think where to place them. Isla closed her eyes and Laura closed hers too. Funny, someone she barely knew was playing the old upright as though it had been put there especially for her, and Cat, in ten years, hadn't touched it. Then, another irony hit her: she found people houses for a living and yet no one had been willing to take up residence inside of her.

A minute later, she caught Cat alone by the front staircase. Sourpuss was hiding inside the wicker basket that held their hats and scarves and miscellaneous items. "Should we be concerned?" she asked.

"About what?"

"Our guests." She lowered her voice. "The co-op is full of bedbugs."

Cat sighed and shot her a look of tedium. They had this same sort of dynamic in many of their exchanges: Laura found Cat's blasé nature dispassionate and personally insulting, Cat found her demand for emotional engagement exhausting and believed she had a need to create drama where there was none.

"It's fine, Laura."

"Of course, it is. She's pretty."

"What is that supposed to mean?"

Through the stained glass in the front door, she saw a hint of the waxing moon. "Everything is always fine with you. Never too hot or too cold." Just once, Laura wanted to provoke a strong reaction. "You were flirting," she said.

Cat lifted a mitten from the basket and flung it down the hall to entice Sourpuss, who didn't budge. "Don't overreact, okay?" There was an extension cord in the bottom of the basket, and a flashlight. "I was wondering where that was." She lifted the flashlight and pressed it on. In shadow, her features appeared distorted, grotesque. She grinned, teasing. "This is romantic."

Laura couldn't help smiling, although she was still feeling singed from their exchange. "You really do have a concussion," she said.

Cat shone the light at Laura's feet, then higher, and higher, to reveal the outline of her thighs through the material of her A-line.

"What are you doing?"

"Feel that?" The yellow glow of the torch scanned her body and Cat's eyes pored over her. Maybe because the moment had taken her by surprise, or because it'd been so long since they'd shared any intimacy, she felt the heat of illumination on her skin, ever so lightly. She felt warmer.

"Yes."

She heard Cat's shallow breathing. If having company over made manifest the cracks and fissures in the life they'd constructed, a bit of levity obscured resentment. Reading an opening in her voice, Cat pulled her close for a kiss.

Laura's body tensed. They were no longer easy or familiar with each other, but maybe if she tried harder they would survive, after all. City workers were repairing power lines and infrastructure, why couldn't they repair their relationship? So she went along with the kiss, letting Cat tighten her grip and press their breasts together. She felt the insistent warmth of Cat's tongue in her mouth, trying to coax desire. Then Cat moaned — low, guttural — and Laura felt the vibrations of it on her lips. She pushed Cat away. "I can't do this."

Cat faced her, time suspended. Laura's rejection had turned them into strangers again. "What's wrong now? Are you still thinking about Isla? She's not even my type."

"I didn't know you had a type anymore."

Cat looked injured by the dig, aware that it had been months since they'd made love. "*Te extraño*, Laura," she whispered. "I miss us."

"You do?"

Cat stepped closer once more. "*Claro.*"

"Then let me use that last embryo."

"Oh, for Christ's sake." Cat slid the flashlight onto the console, scooped Sourpuss out of the basket, and tossed her up the staircase. "I have a pounding headache." She tramped off down the hall, leaving Laura standing alone in the dark.

Laura reached down with one hand and ran her fingers across the wainscot to hold her bearings. The storm had a soul and that soul had entered their home, forcing them to be colder here too. She was grateful for a moment alone, invisibility that edged off her need to keep up pretences. Down the hall, Matt and Beth had begun to argue in hushed whispers outside the first-floor bathroom. Laura strained to hear what was going on.

"What's the matter with you?" Beth's voice was sharp, cutting. "Your children are right in the next room!"

"Don't be paranoid, we exchanged numbers, that's all."

DAYS BEFORE CHRISTMAS, Eddie carried Annie's suitcase upstairs. "Second bedroom's all yours," she said, dropping the case on the landing outside the closed door. "I've set out fresh linens and a new face towel."

Annie placed her hands on her hips. "I'm a boarder, then?"

Eddie fidgeted, straightened the framed photograph of her bowling team hanging on the wall between them. "I didn't mean that." She intended to do things right and proper, that was all, and was making no assumptions about how Annie would want to present their arrangement.

Annie lifted her suitcase by the handle and carried it to the master bedroom. "I think I prefer it in here," she said.

From the hall, Eddie watched as Annie opened the suitcase at the foot of the bed and began unpacking. It didn't matter that they couldn't have a church wedding or an official marriage licence. She'd used her meagre savings and had rings engraved. They could exchange them privately, make their own vows.

Annie set a hand mirror, brush, and comb on the bed. "Are you just going to stand there staring?" She pulled an army surplus bag out of the suitcase as Eddie stepped into the room. "I want to show you something."

Eddie leaned over Annie's shoulder to admire a black-and-white photograph in Annie's hand. "You look just like her."

"I found it in the milk chute after she left us. That was always our hiding spot. She'd hide me a sweet or a stick of chalk. Once, a doll with a cloth face. For years, she'd been keeping money there, in my piggy bank. It was the one place he'd never think to look. After she left, I checked each day for a year, still playing. I never really stopped waiting for her; if she'd already come back once, then she might come back again. At times, I would look over my shoulder with a feeling that she was watching me. Then on my tenth birthday, there she was. Well, this picture." Annie's eyes were a little less guarded, a little less sad. "I sometimes wonder where she is now. If she's still watching over me or if she's even alive." She turned back to the suitcase and set the photograph inside the satin pocket, for safekeeping.

"We could try and look for her?"

Annie smiled. "He would hate that." Out the window, a wintry sun was already setting, that final gasp of December daylight.

Eddie lifted Annie's long hair and kissed the back of her neck. "What did you tell him?"

Annie turned. "I left a note to say I've gone to the YWCA."

"He'll learn the truth eventually."

"Yes, and by then there'll be nothing he can do about it."

Eddie gave her a squeeze. "I will be your shelter."

Annie pressed her lips to Eddie's. Warm. Eager. They were meant to be together. They fell onto the bed kissing and pushed the suitcase to one side. Lying side by side, Eddie traced Annie's fingers with her own, planning to surprise her with the proposal on Christmas Eve.

"What's your mother's name?" she asked.

"Frances Kathleen Hall," said Annie. "Before she married my father, that is. We share a middle name. It was after her own mother." Annie snuggled in closer, nuzzling Eddie's neck. "She smelled of lily of the valley," said Annie. "And had the voice of an angel. She learned to sing as a child, in English church choirs. If I close my eyes, and my mind quiets, I can still hear her moving through our house with a song in her heart."

"What is she singing?"

"'Amazing Grace' or 'I Love My Baby.' She liked that one be-cause Elsie Carlisle was from Manchester too."

Eddie tucked a strand of Annie's auburn hair behind one ear. "She had no other family here?"

Annie shook her head. "All left behind. I once heard her tell my father it was leave or starve; so, she left." Annie stared at a diamond shape in the quilt. "She's good at leaving."

"Don't say that."

Annie buried her face in Eddie's chest. "Do you suppose she ever thinks of me now?"

"She does. I'm certain of it." Eddie pulled the lip of the quilt up higher around the back of Annie's neck and Annie lifted her face.

"It's very kind of you to say, even if it might not be true."

Eddie was impressed by the sadness those green eyes betrayed. "I know this much; you would be impossible to forget." They kissed once more, and then Eddie pushed up and swung her legs around the side of the bed. "I have something to show you too." She turned and from out of the top drawer of her armoire she lifted some sort of document and a pen. She held one page out for Annie.

"What is this?"

"Read to the bottom."

Annie skimmed. "I see my name typed," she said. "Beside yours."

Eddie pointed to a line on the page. "And there's a place for your signature. I'd like to make you beneficiary of this house. If that's agreeable to you."

"But what does that mean, exactly?"

"If anything were to happen to me, the house would remain yours."

"Nothing is going to happen to you, silly."

"The point is, we would be joined formally, on paper, Annie. In the eyes of the law."

Annie reached for the pen. "Natch, I'll sign," she said. It was too good of an offer to pass up. Then, in cursive and with flourish, she wrote her full name on the line. "There, it's official, together forever."

Eddie bent down and gave her a kiss. "There's one more thing," she said. "Wait here."

Under the window in the second bedroom, she reached into a Hires root beer crate to retrieve a sleeping puppy from his bed of rags. She carried the tiny black bundle into her bedroom and set the dog on Annie's lap. "Three makes a family," she said.

"Oh! A puppy, I don't believe it!" Annie scratched under his ears, as he licked her excitedly. "Hello little buddy." She laughed. "Aren't you just the most precious thing."

"So you like him? I considered a pair of canaries; I know how fond you are of songbirds."

"I love him," she said, hugging the puppy to her chest and beaming up at Eddie. "He's perfect in every way." The puppy chewed her wrist, and then leapt off her lap into the open suitcase.

Eddie reached across the bed and plucked the photograph of Annie's mother out of the suitcase pocket before the dog could damage it. "I'll give notice at the pit tomorrow," she said, propping the black-and-white image against the mantel clock on top of her armoire. "The girls will help me find something else."

"It'll be a good life together," Annie said, rubbing the puppy's belly as he rolled around in her suitcase. "Now, what are we going to call this little fella?"

"CHECK HER OUT." Greg held the *National Geographic* magazine open to an article about an anthropological discovery in Peru. "The Ice Maiden," he said, flashing the picture of a mummified girl who'd frozen to death five hundred years ago. "Just looks like she's sleeping, eh?" He used his hands while he spoke, animated, expressive.

"There was this Argentine mountain climber," Cat said. "Discovered him after twenty-three days frozen solid. People said he eventually revived."

"That's impossible."

"It's a bit creepy," said Isla. "Kind of comforting too. A rebirth, you know?" She helped herself to the mini empanadas and impressively balanced three on her cocktail napkin at once. "These look delicious, Laura. What's in them?"

"Pork, I think. Maybe beef."

"Oh." Isla set her napkin on the coffee table discreetly. "We're vegan."

"I'm sorry; I forgot." Laura leaned in closer and saw that Isla's hands were chafed and worn, a touch of eczema, perhaps. She was definitely a nail biter. One nail was chewed right down to its bed. "Can I at least offer you something to drink?"

Isla looked up at her with those big round puppy-dog eyes, and a guarded innocence she found touching. "Do you have any soy milk?"

"Milk?" No one asked her for milk except Beth's children and the request made her feel, strangely, maternal.

"I'm not drinking alcohol these days," Isla explained.

Laura snuck a peek at the girl's abdomen. It was flat, practically concave. Surely she wasn't pregnant? "Be right back," Laura said, trying to slow her breathing.

She headed through the kitchen and carried on into her office where she pulled the unmarked folder out of the bottom drawer of her filing cabinet. Had she been carrying a boy or a girl the last time? She suddenly had to know and couldn't remember if there'd been any indication of sex on the obstetrical ultrasound report.

Gestational age:	8 weeks
Gestation:	single, intrauterine
Yolk sac:	0.78 cm
Gestational sac:	1.06 cm
Crown rump length:	0.2 cm
Foetal heartbeat:	yes, 109 bpm

The pregnancy had been viable, the technician had registered a heartbeat, but the embryo had appeared to be only six weeks when it should've been developed to eight. So, too early to know the sex. She'd had a fifty-fifty chance of miscarrying.

She slid the folder back into the cabinet, lingering, rearranging her mother's old top hat and tap shoes, slipping her hands into the shoes and making them dance. *I miss you*, she thought, *wherever you are*.

Marilyn believed in ghosts, well, spirits. She claimed that people were souls housed within bodies, energy contained within matter, stardust originally. She said that when she died her energy would carry on, somehow. It was a comforting thought, but if it were true, surely by now her mother would've given her a sign.

What would Marilyn think of her using reproductive technology to try to become pregnant? Laura grinned. Her mother had accidentally gotten pregnant with her while on the Pill. A third-wave feminist, she was highly suspicious of technology and of men. To Marilyn, IVF would've sounded like science fiction, a futuristic attempt to control and commodify women's bodies, and Laura had to admit that was pretty much how it felt. Relinquishing herself to the doctors and technicians, parcelling life into seven-to-ten-day cycles, using drugs to hyper-stimulate ovulation and drugs to time it, paying to fertilize zygotes and implant embryos. She'd been told in myriad ways that her body was broken and needed fixing. Poor egg quality, incompetent uterus, and those present-day scarlet letters, Advanced Maternal Age. She was just the container for life, not the white coat granting it. Laura set the shoes down and grabbed the dusty pork pie off her keyboard and placed it on her head. Marilyn would've rejected the approach she'd chosen and insisted she take an alternative path. "Sprinkle salt in your pockets," she'd have said, to ward off evil. "Drink Chinese herbs." She'd have had Laura carrying a sprig of white heather in her purse, for good luck.

What about going behind Cat's back and cashing in an RRSP to pay for it? What would her mother say about that? Laura turned to head out of her office and caught sight of Matt on the back patio through the foggy window. He was lit by the porch light, puffing furiously on a cigarette and jumping up and down to keep warm. Behind him, was the unmistakable sight of a little black Scottie rolling around in the snow.

A FLURRY OF activity swept into Eddie's hospital room. A doctor lifted one of her eyelids, then the other, shining a bright light in at her. The nurse with the sharp nails stood at the foot of her bed, while the other nurse, Eddie's favourite, moved between the venti- lator and the monitors, scratching down her vitals on a clipboard. They thought she might be waking from her coma; they were wit- nessing a medical miracle. A rapturous, impatient mood swept over her, as if she were placing the final few pieces of a jigsaw puzzle and couldn't stand the wait any longer. Something remarkable was taking place, but the only miracle her life would ever see had disap- peared long, long ago. Her memories filtered up, keeping it all very much alive.

Eddie was sitting on the divan in her living room, emptying a Somerville box onto the puzzle table. Out fell 460 pieces. She flipped them over onto the green felt while sipping a cup of Earl Grey. Hunched, she scanned for edge pieces. Other than a touch of arthritis in her hands and some "puzzle pain" in her neck and back today, she was feeling well. A ginger tabby leapt onto the table. "Off, you!" she said, swatting at him.

She hadn't named this one, or any of the other mangy visitors who circled her kitchen door looking for a warm spot and to share a tin of sardines. She simply let them in and out as they requested; naming them wouldn't make them any more hers. "I said, off," she repeated, lifting him from the table onto her lap. "You're messing up Venice at Twilight."

These neighbourhood visitors were good company — indepen- dent, quiet, favouring routines. "We've been to all the major cities,

haven't we?" she said, stroking his fur. He began to knead her am-
ple thighs, making a comfortable bed of her lap. "Were you the one
who helped with Big Ben?" she asked, and then answered for him.
"No, that was your cousin."

She thought of the cats as relatives — of each other and of hers
too, family of a sort. Better than real family. The cats didn't judge
or disappoint or come 'round looking for someone she wasn't.
"You know I'm really a dog person," she said, teasing, as the engine
of his purr started under her hand. She arranged knobs and holes,
setting special pieces aside at one end of the table — those with text
or odd shapes or only a bit of colour. Truth was this cat had won
her over with his demanding personality. He'd forced himself upon
her, no doubt from hunger, which was just what needed to happen
if she were to have steady companionship. After a few minutes, she
finished her tea and set in working on a small section of the puzzle.
"Off to Italy we go," she said.

It was Annie who'd suggested they assemble major world cities. "Armchair travel," she'd called it. "Until we can afford a real
trip." They'd been cuddling on the divan. It was so long ago now,
a lifetime and more, and yet the thought of them together, taking in
new sights, still raised in Eddie the spectre of joy. It was a beautiful
afternoon dream she could revisit whenever she wished.

"If you could go anywhere, where would you go?" Annie asked.

"Never gave it much thought," said Eddie. She thought mainly
of paying the bills, building a small, comfortable life.

"But now that I'm asking."

"If there wasn't a war on?"

Annie nodded. Her eyes shone brightly, showing her intelligence.

"And money was no object?"

"Oh, for Pete's sake!"

"Scotland, then."

"Ooh, Edinburgh," said Annie.

"Isle of Arran," Eddie corrected. "I supposed I'd like to see where my ancestors came from."

Annie wrinkled up her nose. "Don't be so sensible all of the time. What about strolling along the Seine in Paris or taking a gondola around the Venice canals?"

Eddie laughed. "If you must know, I'd settle for Sault Sainte Marie. No dictators, and a canal at a fraction of the cost."

"How romantic," Annie drawled, sarcastically.

Eddie shifted on the divan. The cat had fallen asleep in her lap, his full weight — six or seven pounds — cutting off the circulation in her legs. She shifted again. He didn't budge. "These are for the skyline," she whispered, studying the pink pieces on the puzzle table. Starting a new puzzle, even one she'd previously assembled, was a vacation, of sorts, an escape from life. Puzzling suspended time.

The doctor in Eddie's hospital room was calling her name now. "Wake up, Miss Ferguson," he said. "C'mon, open those eyes!"

"Pinch her," said the nurse with the clipboard. "Pain helps them trying to wake."

He reached over. "Nothing." He took hold of her by the shoulders and shook hard, raising his voice this time. Again, Eddie did not stir. Her eyelids had stopped fluttering. She was there, but she was also elsewhere. The doctor let go and stood upright. "False alarm," he said. He sounded baffled, and a little disappointed, as though Eddie was his failure.

"Pity," said the nurse with the sharp nails. Then she turned and yanked the curtains closed on their noisy metal track, shutting out the storm.

LAURA DASHED OUT onto her back porch where Matt was finishing his smoke. "Did you see them?" she said, panting.

"Who?"

"Astrid and her dog. A little black terrier. Didn't you see a puppy?"

Matt's eyes fixed on the pristine blanket of snow covering the yard. "Uh, are you okay?"

"I swear, they were right here. Buddy! Here boy!" Laura whistled sharply, but the dog and Astrid remained elusive. Matt pulled the collar of his puffer jacket up higher around his neck.

"Maybe we should go in, Laura."

Her eyes swept across the property. The dog had been right there a second ago, in the middle of the yard. An inexplicable surge of spirit blew under her skin. Hadn't he? Above, the sky showed subtle gradations of light. Was it snow-blind vision playing tricks on her? A hint of winter light her naked eye failed to detect? Or something more mysterious? Laura's teeth began to chatter. Reluctantly, she followed Matt inside.

A few minutes later, she was handing Isla a glass of cranberry juice. "Here you go. We don't have any soy milk. Sorry again." Her hand was shaking and so was the rest of her, an imperceptible tremor rattling her insides. She was certain she'd seen Buddy in the backyard. Was she hallucinating? Showing early signs of Alzheimer's?

"Thanks. Cool hat." Isla was now sitting on Greg's lap in the wingback.

"It's from a client," Laura said.

"And I really like your necklace. Someone in my prancercise class said the Star of David has magical properties."

Laura glanced at Beth, who rolled her eyes. "I've never heard that," Laura said.

Isla set the drink down on the coffee table and reached into Greg's backpack for a small paper square. She tore the top edge off and tipped it over her glass, sending beige granules into the juice. "Probiotics," she said.

They could've been mistaken for siblings, Laura thought; both were blonde, medium height, with the impossibly slender builds of youth. Isla, with her dreadlocks, was slightly less conventional looking. They reminded her of her mother's friends, flaky New Age versions, for whom counterculture was a religion. Saffron and Ocean and Thom. Betty and Boop. She couldn't wait to see everyone now that she'd made contact again. "You must be disappointed not to be getting home for the holiday," she said.

Isla draped her arms around Greg's shoulders. "We'll go early in the new year." Their easy physical affection was sweet and reminded Laura of how it used to be between Cat and her. Across the room Cat was kneeling in front of the fireplace, tossing a lit twist of newspaper onto kindling and blowing on the logs to grow the flame. Despite the concussion, she looked capable, in charge. Laura felt a twinge of desire for her again.

"One good thing about this storm," Cat said. "It's bringing neighbours together."

"Totally," said Isla.

The faux Tudor-style co-op where Greg and Isla lived was well known in the neighbourhood. Originally Riverdale Courts, it had been designed as part of the Garden City Movement, to deal with working-class overcrowding and unhealthy living conditions. Generations had lived there, Laura knew, families whose men worked in nearby factories, and during the Depression, single women with few other options. Recently designated a heritage site by the city, it remained a long-standing testament to social housing experiments — and a blight, according to many of her snootier clients over the years. Its mixed-income residents, hoarders, and wannabe hippies wafting pot out the windows lowered the property value of the adjacent houses. "How do you find living at the Bain?" she asked.

"Love it," said Greg. "We shared a house with ten other people in Vancouver, so the co-op gives us that sense of community."

Laura smiled politely and lifted an empanada to her lips. Marxists, she thought. Leftist potheads without jobs. She'd spent a lot of time around idealists growing up, people in her mother's circle, those who were young and in love and convinced that capitalism was a false god they could dismantle through multiple orgasms and fair-trade purchasing. Now, here she was numb, a real estate agent, trading in wealth. What must they think of her? What should she think of herself?

"So, home ownership is out then?"

"No offence, it's not our thing," said Greg. "Even if we could afford to buy."

"We're in a three-bedroom," said Isla. "Tons of space. Technically it's against the by-laws, but no one on the internal wait-list wanted it because the neighbours are big partiers. We sublet two rooms to university students."

"Also against the rules," said Greg.

"Rules are for rulers. Isn't that what your mother used to say, Laura? Marilyn was a performance artist," Cat explained.

Suddenly, it struck Laura that along with becoming a realtor, she'd become an agent of convention, pushing the dream of an all-brick, fully detached life onto clients as if it were a drug that would make them happy. It wasn't. It wouldn't. She knew that. The only thing that had ever brought her joy was being attached — deeply attached to people, to love and aspiration. To herself.

When had she last broken a rule, let alone challenged the status quo? Using her last frozen embryo without telling Cat didn't count. The quest for motherhood was about as conventional as it gets. She missed the person she used to be, who'd spearheaded her high school's anti-apartheid group and marched for abortion rights. Where was the person who'd wanted a life working out of doors, digging in the dirt? She dug around inside of other people's closets now, reading a diary or snooping through the mail, but it had been so long since she'd been part of any meaningful action. She couldn't even remember the last time she'd gone to Pride. Stripping the occasional article out of a magazine in her doctor's office, stealing a ring from an old house, these were minor rebellions, sure, evidence that she was uniquely human. Was she fully alive, though, or merely living? *I'm a ghost of my former self*, she thought. She'd let Cat believe they'd stopped trying for a baby, was clinging to the fantasy of a family and to the memory of her mother — to an uncertain future and a definite past. She was not tethered to her world.

"Wait." Greg's face lit. "Not *the* Marilyn, as in, *Marilyn X Will You Marry Me?*"

Laura poured a glass of wine, swirled it around admiring the claret colour, tempting herself to be irresponsible. "That's the one," she said.

"Wow, your mother was so cool! We decided not to get hitched because of her."

Laura had heard this sort of thing before, in the mid-1980s, when the video of her mother's most famous performance piece had first circulated among university students, causing a mini–relationship revolution. "I didn't know that video was still out there," she said.

"What do you mean? It's gone viral," said Isla. "Here." She reached into her bag for her cellphone. "Wanna see?"

"No, that's okay." Laura knew it well. She'd been there for the live show outside City Hall when she was a teenager. Her mother, a masked bride, naked from the waist down, penetrating herself with a bank roll of quarters to make a statement about the patriarchal economic legacy of marriage. Marilyn had been arrested. "You know she changed her mind, right? Later. When we won the right to marry."

"Did she?" asked Cat. "I always thought that was just the Alzheimer's."

PILED AGAINST THE fence in front of Marilyn's tiny one-and-a-half-storey home in Parkdale was someone's yellow-stained mattress, four overfull bags of yard waste, and a wooden chair with a missing leg. Looks junky, Laura thought, knowing the property would appear that way to other realtors too, and potential buyers.

From the driver's seat, she watched through the enclosed porch window as Marilyn searched for her keys. *I can't go through with it*, Laura thought.

She'd been in frequent touch with a nurse and social worker on the Behavioural Support Team at a long-term care home for three years, and on multiple occasions she'd taken Marilyn to meet with them, tried to involve her in decision-making about her future, and every time, Marilyn had refused to consider moving in with Laura. "I won't let this disease ruin your life too," she'd said. "I will not be a burden." She'd had a lawyer draw up papers to that effect. But that last conversation was almost a year ago, and now, after recent events, the doctor had told them there'd been a rapid and noticeable decline in Marilyn's functioning and cognition. The Alzheimer's had progressed to a point where living alone was no longer a safe option.

Marilyn had accidentally left the stove burner on, and a blackened kettle had set off the smoke alarm. Neighbours had called Laura. Marilyn had wandered out alone, become confused, and crossed four lanes of traffic on Lake Shore. She'd been found by police, splashing around in Lake Ontario wearing her medic alert bracelet. Laura gripped the steering wheel. Someone had to make the hard decision. Someone had to be the parent here. Lying to her mother about having tickets to see a fire-eater headline at Harbourfront was the easiest way to get Marilyn into the car without a fight. Some of Marilyn's clothes and small treasures were packed in a suitcase, hidden in the trunk.

Just then, Marilyn bounced out the front door carefree, with a Kent Monkman tote bag slung over one shoulder, and a red felt clown's nose on her face. She started speaking as soon as she was within earshot of Laura's open window.

"No way, I want to take the streetcar. That beast is a major pollutant."

"Just get in."

"Why you can't ride an adult trike, like Thom and I do, is beyond me."

"Let's go, Mom."

"Fine. You need to work on your morals though. Also, you suck at getting into the spirit of things. Don't worry, though." She tapped her red nose. "I've got another one of these in my bag with your name on it."

Laura pulled the car into the road. She consoled herself with the thought that if they turned down this offer of a room at Scaddington Gardens, they wouldn't get another for years. Marilyn would receive top-notch, round-the-clock care and have a community of peers. The place offered all kinds of programming. But in the seat of her stomach Laura knew her mom would be decades younger than anyone else there, and the only artist. She'd hate living in an institution, even though she'd made it impossible for Laura to care for her at her home. Laura felt her gut twist. *Forgive me*, she thought, turning north.

"I don't get fire-eaters?" said Marilyn, struggling with her seat belt. "I mean, tightrope walking and trapeze, that's impressive."

"Hmm." Laura's voice landed in her throat as if it belonged

inside of someone else's body, someone she hadn't met and didn't like. "Do you need help with that? I can pull over?"

"No, I got it."

Laura sped through the next set of lights, instead of turning east on Queen.

"Hey, you missed the turn," said Marilyn.

Laura bit her lip.

"Oh, I see. Picking up roti first?"

Again, Laura didn't respond.

Marilyn fidgeted with her hands. "You're kinda acting strange, kiddo."

"We're not going to the circus, okay?" She tapped the steering wheel with her thumb, then pressed the automatic door locks. "I'm sorry, Mom."

"Sorry for what?"

She could hardly push out the words. There were no words to explain betrayal, even if it was inevitable. "Remember we talked about Scaddington Gardens?"

"Let me out right now!"

Laura veered around a delivery van. "You'll have a private room. With an ensuite."

Marilyn unbuckled her seat belt and lunged for the steering wheel, slapping Laura hard about the arms and head.

"Hey, calm down!" Laura shoved her back into place on the seat.

"How dare you!"

"Stop that. You're gonna cause an accident."

Marilyn began to cry, a stream of tears darkening the edges of her red nose and causing the cheap, dollar store felt to run. She pulled it off. "You promised," she said, catching her breath be-tween sobs. "You promised I could stay in my own home for a few more years." She folded her arms across her chest and seemed to have shrunk to a tiny thing, a spot on the passenger seat, small and insignificant.

"I know," said Laura, shrinking too. She'd grown up seeing the world her mother saw, then her own version. Marilyn, then herself — that was the order, the fabric of their connection, forged through mutual dependence and unconditional love. Alzheimer's had turned everything inside out. "I hate this too," she said. Fate seemed to be hurtling toward them much faster than either of them had expected. She glanced across the seat at her mother, who was rocking back and forth, forward and back, holding herself and trembling. It was hard losing someone in advance, day by day knowing you were being left behind. It was harder being the one doing the leaving. "I'll spare no expense," Laura said, bargaining for forgiveness. "I'll visit every day. I swear." She pulled over to the side of the road because she couldn't see through her own tears. She turned off the car's engine.

"I'm so sorry," said Marilyn.

"It's not your fault, Mom," she said, unbuckling her seat belt and crawling over for a hug. "Please don't blame yourself." But Marilyn had always believed she had more control over life than she had, and with that hubris came self-blame. She believed talismans brought luck and art gave her an edge, that positive affirmations and practising mindfulness would impact her fate by keeping her well. And now this was the destiny she had to accept. She squeezed Laura tightly and held on.

"I don't want to go," she said, and they both knew what she really meant.

IT WAS A brisk October Sunday, nearly five years after Annie had gone missing, and the week before Thanksgiving, when Eddie searched out Annie's mother. She'd been following scraps of information from what Annie had said — and with the aid of the British Women's Emigration Association, she learned that Frances Armstrong had first come to Toronto at the turn of the century. She'd met Annie's father at a dance, where they were introduced by the headmistress of the local women-only immigrant reception home where she had been settled. Eddie had asked questions around town discreetly, visiting taverns that hired evening entertainment, inquiring as to where a single woman who could sing might find work or live. Eventually, she found herself standing on Bain Avenue, outside the Riverdale Courts housing complex.

Eddie meandered onto the property wishing she'd worn a jacket on top of her pullover. The trees had begun to change colour and drop leaves and she felt a certain peace in their decay, the thought that time passes eventually, and all things end and will begin again. The property was vast, designed by a British architect, Eden Smith, to mimic the English Tudor garden style that had been so popular at the turn of the century. There were easily hundreds of apartments. Where to start?

She stepped up to a corner unit and knocked. No answer. Likely at church, she thought. She moved on to the next door and the next, each one identical to the previous, until finally, in the middle courtyard on the north side of Bain, someone answered. A boy of about four or five years, carrying a calico kitten around the waist.

"I'm looking for this woman," Eddie said, holding out the photograph. "Do you know of her?"

The boy shook his head and redoubled his effort to cling to the wiggly kitten now painfully climbing up his shirt.

"Mrs. Frances Armstrong?" Eddie pressed.

Eddie had quit her job at the brick pit just as she and Annie had planned, and she'd tried for the munitions factory, but the war had soon ended, and men had returned from fighting overseas, so that work had dried up. She'd cobbled together odd jobs here and there, keeping a milk goat tied in the backyard and growing and preserving most of what she ate. Over the winter months, she managed by helping her neighbour harvesting and delivering ice. Gone with the years and prosperity was her patience. "Surely you would've noticed an Englishwoman who sings?"

The boy flinched as the kitten's sharp little claws dug into the soft meat of his chest, and then he brightened. "Miss Manchester," he said, pointing across the courtyard to a neighbour's door.

Eddie climbed the short stoop and stood in the archway of the door with a tickle of excitement building behind her ribs — a mix of anticipation, hope, and doubt. All these years she'd wanted to lay eyes on the only other person Annie had loved. She'd wanted to understand why Frances had abandoned Annie, and that time may have come. Eddie knocked and waited, knocked again. A voice finally barked through the open window above. "Leave me in peace!"

Eddie backed up a few paces, craned her neck to see who was speaking from the sunroom window. "I mean no harm," she called up to the second floor.

"There are three of us here," said the woman. "So no funny business. Whatever it is you're selling, we don't want it."

Eddie strained to see the figure in the window, but she'd moved out of view. "Are you Frances Armstrong? I'm a friend of Annie's."

Moments later, Eddie heard footsteps padding down the staircase. The door creaked opened and there she was, all ninety pounds of her, unkempt hair, a few grey strands mixed in with her natural auburn, wrinkled beyond her forty years, and smelling strongly of a cheap perfume that was a vain attempt at sophistication and glamour, but those green eyes …

"What did you say?" Her raspy voice suggested years of cigarette smoking.

"She wanted to find you," said Eddie. "I'm here in her stead." Eddie's palms were sweating, and her stomach was as hard as a rubber ball. "This is all I had to go on." She held the photograph up between two fingers.

Frances squinted to focus on the image, and then her eyes widened at seeing her younger self. A platinotype print from her old life as wife and mother framed by a soft grey mat with a bluish tinge. She stepped back, once again partially concealed behind the door. "Who sent you?" She peered over Eddie's shoulder, eyes darting around the courtyard.

Eddie tucked the photograph into a button-down pocket of her corduroy pants. "I've come on my own steam," she said. "She would've wanted it."

Frances wrapped one of her hands around the door frame, gripping it, should she need to slam the door in haste. "I read the papers," she said. Her knuckles bulged slightly, like knots forming in a tree; Eddie recognized the distorted signs of arthritis starting up because her own mother suffered from it.

"So then you know?" Eddie lowered her voice and tried to come at the sad fact in a gentle, indirect way. "About Annie running out into the blizzard?"

Frances began to tremble, though she seemed unaware of it, as if she'd grown accustomed to fear living inside her body, like a low-level earthquake. "I know he did it," she spat. "He's the one responsible for what happened to my daughter. If she ran, it was to get away from him."

The memory of that cold night was always close, permanently etched into Eddie's mind, and she fought to keep it at a distance and hold on to her composure. She leaned against the door frame, picked at a strip of white paint that was flaking. "I'm sure you're not wrong about that," she said, evenly. "But you've nothing to fear from me. Mr. Armstrong's gone too," she added, in a whisper. "Hasn't been heard from in years."

"Do I look like a fool?" said Frances. Her green eyes pierced Eddie's gaze, as if to say, *I know evil is never far.*

The musky sweet smell of fall — of dying and rotting leaves and plants and trees — surrounded them. "No, you look like a woman who was treated unfairly," said Eddie.

That first visit to Bain Avenue led to other visits, an unburdening, and a consolation. Eddie learned that Frances did indeed live in the apartment with two other women — one who'd also left a bad marriage, and the other, a war widow who danced in a downtown tavern. They shared housing costs and a vegetable garden, and the companionship of those who'd strayed too far from social convention.

Whenever Eddie came by, she brought preserves if she had any, or bread and butter. A puzzle she no longer wanted. Some years, she'd stop along her route and deliver a hunk of ice into the common ice house so Frances and her flatmates might keep a bit of meat and cheese and milk through the summertime.

She understood that Frances was in disrepute, using more than pretty eyes and a lilting voice to make ends meet, though they never discussed that; there were few other prospects for a woman without a husband or family money. Eddie knew it as well as anyone, and she came to believe over time that Frances had stayed away from Annie to protect her only child from the stain of her reputation. It was the one thing she had left to offer as a mother, though a selfless act of love can often appear otherwise to those with the means to judge.

Then, one winter afternoon, Eddie stopped in to visit with a small tube of Old Brown Glue stuffed into her pants pocket, and a copy of the deed to her house hidden under her shirt, tucked into the waist of the pants. After a pot of strong tea and a good, long conversation, Eddie excused herself to use the washroom on the third level — a shared toilet, sink, and a tin washtub to be hand filled for bathing. She climbed the staircase with the document and the glue warming against her body. She and Annie couldn't marry, and they never got the chance at a life together, but this document, signed and notarized, legally acknowledged the love they'd shared. Instead of using the toilet, Eddie slipped into the only other room up there, Frances's tiny bedroom.

Sunlight shone in through the dormer window. The steam radiator was hissing its rusty, leaking pipes that had rotted out a spot on the hardwood floor. The ceiling in the bedroom was slanted. Eddie had to duck at the far end, entering the crawl space she'd seen before, in passing. She knelt and felt around in the dim light, catching her sweaty face on a cobweb. There were stacked crates holding folded off-season clothing, an extra wool blanket, and on the floor, a pair of peep-toe slingbacks.

Creak. Eddie froze. Her heart somersaulted at the sound of heavy footfall on the staircase. *Creak, creak.* Someone was climbing. They were almost outside the door! She held her breath. There was barely enough room for her to turn around. Sweat pooled under her arms and on her brow. *Wait.* The footsteps were coming from the other side of the wall. *Oh*, it was only a neighbour. Eddie quickly resumed palming the wall in search of a flat spot that was out of plain sight. She found one above the entrance to the crawl space.

Below, Frances was running the kitchen tap, singing a tune. Was she rinsing out their teacups or was it the pot? *Hurry*, Eddie told herself. She reached out of the crawl space, knees digging into the floor, and held the tube of glue against the hot radiator. After a few seconds, she turned it and heated it from the other side. When the tube was warm enough, she lifted her shirt and reached for the copy of the deed. Squeezing a line of glue around the outside of the envelope, she pressed the sticky side to the wall where the document would remain unseen and undisturbed, proof that their lives had once been joined. Silly, she knew, to make a symbolic gesture like this, but she and Annie would continue, through the home that should've been theirs. It was enough that she knew, and the best place for a copy of the deed was with Annie's mother. Before heading downstairs, she made sure to flush the toilet.

CATALINA SAT IN the gold chair, feet up on the ottoman, Sourpuss purring on the arm. She appeared pensive, Laura thought, hesitant. The light radiating off the fire had softened the wrinkle in her brow. "Thanks for the fire," she said.

Greg was asking about everyone's bucket list. "Top two for me would definitely have to be riding a mechanical bull," he said, "and being in the *Saturday Night Live* audience."

"The kids should go down soon," Beth told Matt. "Do you want to do it or should I?"

"I'll go. In a minute." He reached for the bowl of roasted hazelnuts on the coffee table and popped a handful into his mouth. "What about you, Isla?"

"Um, I want to manage a GoFundMe campaign for pets who need chemo."

Beth choked on her drink and spit up on herself. "Pets?" she said, reaching for a napkin. "Not people?"

"Animals have souls too," said Isla, defensively.

"Sure, they can't consent though, can they?"

"I want to check out Burning Man," interrupted Matt.

Beth cocked an eyebrow. "You're joking?"

"No, it sounds really cool."

"That's actually where Greg and I met," said Isla.

"See?" Matt gave her a flirty wink. "I'm not alone."

Beth stiffened in her chair. "Well, I've always wanted to try LSD," she said. "But I'm not a child anymore."

Laura hadn't meant to laugh; it wasn't funny. The tension in the room was thick, and she was off-kilter, not herself. Like most long-term couples, her friends had a way of fencing each other in and making it sound reasonable. Maybe Beth *should* leave him, Laura thought. Acts of disloyalty accrete, inevitably spilling over into resentment, and yet part of her envied Matt taking what he wanted from life, everyone else be damned. Had she not had a fearless, occasionally reckless, mother, she too might've been more daring or willing to break the rules. Growing up with a performance artist had been a wild enough ride.

"I did this work exchange thing once," Greg said. "Meals for drugs. Beats my job shelving books at the library. Speaking of." He plopped a clear plastic baggie filled with weed on the coffee table and reached into his jeans pocket for rolling papers. He plucked one from the small box and licked the glue edge.

"Grow your own?" asked Cat.

"Naah, this guy I know gets the best stuff." He rolled a joint then licked the ends to twist them shut. He lit up and took a deep drag. "Sweet," he said, exhaling smoke rings.

"I've never been high," said Cat.

"No shit?" Greg passed her the joint.

"I don't think so. We smoked up with Marilyn the odd time, and of course during university. It never did much for me."

"You have to let it," said Isla.

"Architects dream daringly high," said Laura. "But they prefer to keep their feet planted firmly on the ground."

Cat took an extra-long drag on the joint. "Not always."

What did that mean?

There were dark circles beneath Cat's eyes, wrinkles that hadn't been there the year before. She'd aged, Laura thought, and no wonder. They both had. Along the way they'd lost sight of each other's virtues. Were there things she'd forbidden Cat to do? Things she stopped herself from enjoying? "Name one time you really let go?" she said.

Cat passed the joint to Isla. "What about that New Year's Eve in Montréal when we hopped in my car at midnight and drove to Québec City for hot chocolate and poutine?"

"Oh yeah," said Matt. "Pretty sure I drank a mickey that night."

"See?" said Cat, proudly. "I can be wild."

"Uh, weren't you our designated driver?"

Everyone laughed then, including Cat, though Laura could see she was deflated and she felt badly for teasing Cat. "Does your head still hurt?" she asked, sympathetically.

"Not really," said Cat.

Isla passed the joint to Beth. "I've done E a million times," she said. "Hallucinogens are no big deal."

Beth took three swift puffs, and then held it out to Laura. "Your turn."

She hadn't smoked up in years, not since before her mother died. That was how she measured her life: before and after Mom. Was that how she measured happiness? In the advanced stages of Alzheimer's, her mother's eyes would sail right through her as though she might've been anyone, and as Marilyn became less of herself, she became no one. "I'm good, thanks," she said.

"Who's the stick-in-the-mud now," Cat teased.

"Just not in the mood, I guess."

Greg looked concerned. "Is this okay with you?" he asked. "I should've checked first."

"Go ahead," said Laura. "Enjoy the trip."

"What about you?" Isla asked Cat. "Anything wild on your bucket list?"

"I know," Laura jumped in. "You want to see the Metropol Parasol." She'd heard Cat mention it on several occasions since it had opened in Seville some years ago. The world's largest wooden structure. Another architect they knew had travelled to Spain and said it was spectacular.

"Nope."

"Run the New York City Marathon?"

"Run with the bulls in Pamplona?" said Matt, holding the joint. "Wrestle a gator?"

"Nothing dangerous." Cat laughed.

"Oh, come on." Laura was growing weary of trying to coax conversation.

"Fine," said Cat. She cracked the knuckles on her right hand, then the left. "I've been thinking about what you said yesterday; maybe I should try and get pregnant."

Laura's shoulders stiffened. Her face and neck burned. "What?"

Cat brushed the hair from her face with her hand, as she did whenever she evaluated final designs for a client. "We do still have that one embryo left."

Beth and Laura exchanged glances. "I thought you wanted us to stop trying."

"I knew you'd react this way."

Laura grabbed the joint from Matt and took a long, hard drag. Now how was she going to explain what she'd done? She took a second drag. How dare Cat bring it up in front of all these people! It was so humiliating. Cat avoided her eyes, looking embarrassed. No, caught out.

"It's just the more I think about it, the more I realize I don't want any regrets."

Laura sat rigid on the couch, feeling gutted. Trying for so long to have a baby had been like swimming in molasses, a dark curse that grew more powerful with each negative pregnancy test, each appointment, each invasive procedure or injection. She hadn't been able to stop the longing or the grief and not once, in all those years, had Cat ever been open to carrying. Now she'd done an about-face and ambushed Laura with the possibility. Laura clenched her jaw. "Am I part of this new plan?"

Cat was being cagey, trying to change the subject. "I haven't thought it through, exactly."

There was a moment of excruciating silence, when all the air in the room seemed to have been sucked away, and then Laura burst out laughing again, laughing so hard that she began to cough. It would've been the perfect opportunity to confess that she'd used their last embryo, but if it turned out she were pregnant, that was not how she'd want her child's story to begin. She felt her face flush and didn't know whether to scream or cry. She and Cat had both been dishonest. Their greatest intimacies were no longer with each other, and obviously hadn't been for some time.

"Laura?"

After her last pregnancy, when she was told by the doctor to expect another miscarriage, Cat had dropped her at home and left to deliver renderings to an engineer. She'd lain in bed alone, with her hands crossed over her belly, trying to visualize the heartbeat, her second one. She'd conjured positive words to teach the developing life inside that it was wanted. She'd talked to herself, to the foetus, though she knew it was only the size of her longest eyelash. She'd loved it already.

"I don't know what to say."

Beth leaned over and pinched the joint from between her fingers. She snuffed it against the inside of Matt's wine glass. "We're all getting tired. Let's call it a night."

"Would you want that?" Cat pressed.

Laura reached up and ran the blue feather on the hat between her fingers, where a section of the vane had fallen away, leaving only downy barbs by the shaft. She'd held on to the hope of having children with Cat, clung to that hope like a buoy, and yet until this moment, she hadn't fully realized that love had very little to do with it anymore.

Love. The only reason she'd married Cat. Or had she also married for a sense of stability? Maybe both reasons? Either way, love was a living, breathing thing, she thought, not anything static. Speaking of it aloud diminished its value, cheapened the astonishing fact of it, and made feelings sound commonplace. In the beginning of their relationship, she'd taken months before confessing it to Cat, though she'd known how she'd felt, like an aperture opening onto an ever-widening picture, the space between things filling with light and colour, as more of life rushed in. Now that they were so disconnected, the world had become a sliver, murky and dull, and she'd become a smaller person too. Would she really want Cat to get pregnant now? Laura chewed her lip. Wanting anything meant expecting that more was possible. Did she still believe that? Cat was waiting for her answer, watching, almost daring her to say what she couldn't; somewhere along the line, they'd settled for less and become that too.

"Maybe it is time to pack it in," said Greg.

Just then the house lights flickered, and a low buzzing came from the street outside. By the glow of firelight, they all appeared eerie and insubstantial — Matt, Beth. Cat. Isla's already wan countenance now gave the impression of someone who was hardly there. Laura shivered. All seemed unearthly, the night itself a phantom. The pot began to take effect and for a moment she was frightened and glanced down at her hands to reassure herself of something real. The rose gold band she'd taken from the Condor house was glowing.

The storm had done this, she thought, the storm and the pot and the red wine, loosening their tongues. Making them comfortable with coldness and relaxing them into some dangerous new malaise. "I want a divorce," she heard herself say.

"What?" Cat stood. "What the fuck!"

Once again, the lights flickered, and the low-grade buzzing of a moment ago was replaced by an electric hiss and crackle. "Shit,"

Matt said, under his breath. "You're gonna lose power." Then, with one brief clicking noise, the house went dead.

Laura grabbed the half-finished bottle of wine on the coffee table and marched into the kitchen to collect the rolled-up deed.

"*Adónde diablos vas?!* Laura!"

Racing through the front of the house, she snatched her bag off a wall hook and tipped the bottle. The wine was silky on her tongue and tasted vaguely of fermented plums. She could hear Cat coming after her as she tugged off her wedding band and tossed it into a ceramic dish on the console. She grabbed the flashlight there, threw on her winter clothing, and, heart pounding, slipped barefoot into her boots without lacing them. She was outside in a flash, in the dark, pushing through the whiteout.

FLYING DOWN THE middle of the street, a girl fled into the darkness of December 1944. She could outpace the cold. The frozen night was a wall she could slam into and, with enough force, break through to another side. Her bare feet were stuffed inside unlaced boots and she wore only blue jeans, an oversized plaid shirt, and the golden sheet she'd had time to wrap around her body. She clutched an army surplus bag. A puppy trailed her. Sounds crackled and scratched in her eardrums like a needle on vinyl — fists slamming into bodies, bodies recoiling, the crunching of bone. She turned left at Boultbee, teeth chattering, breath pounding at minus twenty. Nearby, voices rang out, *Adeste Fideles!* The storm would hide her — *laeti triumphantes* — protect her — *venite, venite* — preserve her until it was safe to return.

THE DARK, DESERTED streets were still and silent, otherworldly. Even the stars had abandoned the sky. Laura couldn't say she was sad to have announced she wanted a divorce. Relieved, surprised by her own admission, embarrassed to have made such a public declaration, but not sad, exactly. As she crossed into the Pocket wearing the hat, salt water froze on her cheeks, and her tears were for the losses that had piled up over the years, burying her like unpaid bills — her relationship, her mother, the shell and shadow that Marilyn became at the end. Her own infertility. She cried as she had the day of her last miscarriage.

She'd been at the Gerrard Square mall for more than an hour combing the aisles of the dollar store. On the bottom level of the mall she'd distracted herself from her doctor's warning by looking at appliances and power tools. She'd scanned the sales racks for new handbags. She'd almost made it to that critical twelve-week threshold, she reminded herself. She was almost into her second trimester this time, and doctors didn't know everything, though each approaching minute made her more anxious. Time was no longer an intangible with endless possibilities stretching out ahead, it was something she dreaded, a unit of measurement she wished she could reach out and clasp in her fist, like a firefly, and seal away in a jar. The foetus was almost fully formed, she knew, though tiny.

When she passed the food court she smelled smoked meats and grease, West Indian jerk chicken and Chinese takeout, odours that rendered her nauseous. She'd desperately wanted a can of pop. Instead, she sat on a bench and ate a single scoop of vanilla ice cream, reassured that ice cream counted as one helping of dairy and dairy was good for the baby. When she was done, she stood and pain ripped across her lower abdomen, sharp, like teeth biting down.

In the washroom cubicle, she'd tried not to be alarmed by the blood on her white cotton underwear. After all, spotting during pregnancy wasn't necessarily a sign of miscarriage, and the blood was scant and brown. She would not allow herself to consider the possibility of loss. She would refuse. If she sat motionless, willing the baby to settle, her cramps would cease. Maybe if she prayed, bargained with a God she no longer believed in? If only she could've wished it away. But the longer she sat on that cold porcelain seat — and she couldn't rise anymore because the contractions were severe — the heavier and redder the flow became. Finally, she gasped.

"Excuse me," said a woman in the adjacent stall. "Are you okay in there?"

She stared at the bright red blood in the toilet bowl. "I'm fine. Just having bad cramps."

"Oh, mine are bad too. Take two Advils, that always helps."

After a moment she heard a toilet flush, and the woman moved to run water at the sink, activated the hand dryer, and squished across the tile floor in wet boots. She was by herself again; more alone than she'd ever known was possible.

Later, she'd wish that she could've answered all of Cat's questions accurately, or described what it had felt like, and what she'd witnessed lying in the toilet bowl between her legs. She would've liked to say that she'd thought of Cat because it was their shared experience, a shared loss. But as with her mother's death, this loss was hers alone and she knew it.

What she remembered, she remembered vividly: the blood streaming down between her legs in a pulsing fashion, painting the white bowl in a surprisingly beautiful display. The pregnancy tissue floating, softly as air, each new fold pushing out to the rhythm of the cramps, to the contractions of her cervix.

She'd tried to picture it, the heartbeat, and that was when she'd felt a mass pressing out between her legs, not very big, not solid like a stone, just firm enough and heavy enough to push out of her intact, and to cause a plopping sound when it hit the water. She'd gazed down and there it was: purple, black, and deep, deep red, the membrane, diaphanous as chiffon, waving. She'd tried to discern a shape and found the loose outline of a miniature ghostly figure, more shadow than definition — paddles, head, giant eye sockets. She'd wanted to touch it, feel what she'd made, almost made. She'd forced herself to reach down into the water, afraid of having the sensation it left permanently stuck to her fingertips, and gently poked a flattened plum mass.

Without warning, the automatic toilet bowl flushed, and before she could say goodbye, her baby — or the rudimentary parts that would have been her baby — were swept away. She never got to tell her mother. Just as well, Laura thought; Marilyn's reaction on top of her own would've only made her feel worse, and she shuddered to think how her mother might've turned the experience into a spectacle.

Now, approaching Condor Avenue, her cellphone was ringing. It was Beth. Laura couldn't deal with talking and her phone was running out of battery, so she switched it to low power mode. Then, as if by some cool magic, Astrid and Buddy appeared at her side, the puppy peeking out the front of Astrid's white coat.

"Woof!"

"Where did you two come from?!"

Astrid stroked Buddy between his ears. Snow spun in loose funnels around them.

"Yeah, right," said Laura. "Well, you win. I'm not playing peekaboo anymore."

Astrid set Buddy down to race ahead of them on the icy sidewalk. "It's not a game," she said, plainly.

"Look, I thought I could help you, but you clearly don't want that."

"You're in a snit."

"I just need to be left alone." She wanted away from this strange girl, to run, to escape her own small life. Before she could leave, Astrid reached out to touch her hat.

"That doesn't belong to you." Astrid stroked the faded blue feather on the crown and her touch sparked a charge of electricity that crawled across Laura's forehead and radiated up Astrid's arm, into her body.

For a split second, Laura was winded, as if she'd fallen down a flight of stairs and the air was knocked from her lungs. She was instantly drained of energy; Astrid had somehow stolen it, again. "Get away from me!" Laura recovered and broke into a clumsy jog, crossing Jones Avenue. *Whoever you are.*

Astrid and Buddy gave chase. The sound of the dog's barking was caught by snow on all sides and echoed down the wide road. "Laura, look out!"

The moon's silver light fell on them, and all that ice, mirrors reflecting who they were and who they were meant to be.

"Move! You're in the middle of the road!"

The solid crystalline ice underfoot held her in place. The wind made it impossible to see. The blue lights of a salt truck flashed, *emergency, emergency* as the driver laid on the horn, slammed on his brakes. His back end swerved.

"Out of the road!" said Astrid. She was at Laura's side again quick as lightning, and she shoved her hard, sending her out of harm's way, into a snowbank.

Scrunch, scrunch went the windshield wipers as the truck bar-relled over the spot where she'd just been. Astrid seemed to scatter and reconfigure, like molecules of light.

Laura stared, panted, mouth agape, as white puffs of air clouded from between her lips. "But it should've hit you," she said.

"Horse feathers!"

Laura fumbled for her smart phone. It was still in her pocket, thank God, though it was covered in snow. She brushed it dry with the sleeve of her parka. "I know what I saw," she murmured, and then something in her broke and she began to sob. She wasn't sure of anything anymore. How stoned was she? Were her hormones out of whack? What if she were pregnant? Cat would never forgive her. The silent blue lights of the salt truck carried on in the distance, colouring the snow with a familiar melancholy. A baby wouldn't bring her mother back. She could see that now and it felt as though all the love in the world had disappeared. "This isn't happening," she whispered.

"You can't ditch me yet," said Astrid. "I'm counting on you." She crouched beside Laura and patted her on the back gently, as she might Buddy, her touch so light Laura could barely feel the faint sensation of pins and needles.

Laura lifted her head, and it was as heavy on her shoulders as a bowling ball. Some part of her had believed she would find her mother again through a pregnancy, or at least find Marilyn's vital, radiant vision of life. How absurd. She met Astrid's green eyes. *People dead and gone can't return to us, can they?*

Ice all around them appeared to be solid, transparent too, Laura knew, doubly refracting, blue or green or absorbent black. The snow wasn't white either; melt it in a coffee filter and what was left? Dirt, darkness. Her whole world was a mirage, a deception. What else was a lie? That she was a good daughter? A good person? She'd been willing to turn her back on a homeless kid, like she'd abandoned her marriage, like she'd abandoned her mother to an institution.

"You're the only one who can help us," said Astrid.

A tight twist of terror rushed through her veins. "I can't."

You could if you wanted to.

Laura stood. Losses had built up over time, and each now sat side by side inside of her, like pebbles on a tombstone. Maybe she didn't know what was real anymore because she didn't know how to close out those lost worlds and carve a new one.

"Who are you, Astrid?"

"I think you know," she said. "You're the agent," she added, "who can let me into that house."

"I'd like to keep my job!" said Laura.

The biting wind wrapped around them, hardening Astrid's defences. "Don't flip your wig!" She scooped the puppy into her arms. "Never mind, we don't need an invitation. We'll break in if we have to." She stormed past. "Isn't that right, little Buddy?" Then she and the puppy once more vanished into the darkness.

EDDIE LAY IN her hospital bed, relief washing over her. "White Christmas" was playing from a radio in the nursing station down the hall. Time to go, she thought, visualizing Annie's face, conjuring the sound of Annie's voice. Her heartbeat slowed as she pictured her house on Condor: the way light from the street fell in through the bedroom window, the old coil mattress, feather pillows that needed replacing. From behind the ventilator mask, she focused on the air circling her nostrils almost imperceptibly, and followed her breath — inhaling, exhaling, the ebb and the flow. She was both here and there, there and here, hovering in that liminal space between life and death.

WHEN LAURA WAS in her mid-twenties and about to apply to the Ontario Real Estate Association for the required courses, Marilyn had organized an intervention. Friday after work, Laura had walked into her mother's house expecting the usual shabbat pancake supper, and instead found a semi-circle of their friends crowded around the kitchen table, staring at her. Saffron with purple kohl around her eyes, Ocean wearing a yarmulke. The kitchen was acrid with mentholated cigarette smoke.

"What is this?"

"We have something to say," Marilyn started. "Take a seat."

Thom stood and offered his chair.

"Don't let her do this to me," Laura whispered as she sat down between Betty and Boop. Her mom's pseudo-therapeutic shit was embarrassing.

"Just hear her out," said Thom. He leaned against the kitchen wall, arms loosely crossed and his newsboy cap dangling from one thumb.

Laura crossed her arms too. "Fine. Let's get it over with."

Betty and Boop were dressed in pink power suits with shoulder pads, looking like a mix of Nancy Reagan and Margaret Thatcher, but with more panache. Saffron and Ocean avoided eye contact with Laura. Saffron was chain smoking, the green glass ashtray on the table full of half-smoked butts. Laura had heard she and Ocean had become exclusive now and were talking about having a commitment ceremony.

"You know I believe in destiny," said Marilyn.

"Oh, I know."

"I'm not saying there's a blueprint for our lives, or that they're pre-planned. We're not in God territory here. Still, we do have individual natures, and they bump up against the constraints of our lives. Call it what you will, there are only so many ways that a life can fall out. That's what I mean."

"Like a poem with a particular constraint," said Ocean. She'd given up writing blank verse and was dabbling in Petrarchan sonnets.

"Exactly," said Marilyn. "Like that. Our temperaments and the constraints of our lives are what shape them and give life meaning."

"Okay?" said Laura. She understood the English but not where this was going.

"If you stray too far from yourself, you'll veer off course."

"Got it. Are we done?" She moved to stand and Boop shot out an arm to stop her.

"We think you're lost, Laura." She'd always been the bluntest of the crew. "We think you're floundering like a fish in a boat."

"I'm not," said Laura, taking her seat again. "I've actually given it a lot of thought. As a real estate agent, I'd have a flexible schedule with a lot of control over my time."

Marilyn slid an envelope across the table. "There are more important things than encouraging people to establish equity or save for retirement, hon."

"I like the idea of finding people homes, Mom. I'll be good at it. I'm a people person and I know this city."

"Go back to school and finish your BA," said Marilyn. "Take some archaeology classes again. You might remember yourself. We've all contributed. It's for the tuition."

Laura looked around at the hopeful faces. Saffron puffing anxiously on her Camel cigarette, Ocean and Betty looking stiff, Betty fiddling anxiously with the pendant around her neck. Thom's gentle expression. "Are you serious?" she said. "You realize I could make more money in a year than all of you combined, right?"

Betty and Boop nodded in tandem. They were still years away from leaving sex work and running a trans coming out group at the 519 community centre, but they had a dream of saving to buy adjacent condos in the Distillery District one day, Laura knew. They'd already asked her to help them look if she actually got her licence.

"Listen, archaeology was great," she said. She'd loved it and been sad dropping out, but with her mom's diagnosis she needed to think more practically. She needed a guaranteed way to support herself, and likely Marilyn too. "I only wanted to be out in the field anyway," she said. "Not stuck in a lab analyzing artefacts. Fieldwork will always be seasonal in Ontario."

"Will you be happy with real estate?" Thom asked, uncrossing his arms and shifting weight from one foot to the other. "No, never mind happy. That's superficial. Will you feel alive?"

Laura scanned their faces, full of sincerity and concern. These artists and outcasts were worried about her. *What does that even mean?* she thought. *To be alive?*

"You don't have to pay us back," said Betty.

"Not a moment's thought on that," said Boop.

Marilyn got up to put a kettle on to boil. She snapped on the radio and returned to her seat with Tracy Chapman singing "Give Me One Reason" in the background.

"We've each only got one shot, kiddo. One brief go-around in this life. We just want to make sure you make the most of it."

"Thanks, I guess?" It was such a sweet, if presumptuous, thing to do. How could she not accept? Annoyed by the interference in her life, and the judgement about real estate, she took the envelope anyway, and banked the money the next day. She didn't use a single dollar for almost a decade, until she'd needed it for her mother's care.

THE NIGHT BEFORE Eddie's stroke, she'd made her confession at the dining room table, with a Sheaffer Triumph green stripe fountain pen. Sin was sin, it couldn't be graded, or absolved. Only endured. She was the one left to tell it, so she'd set it down, ink on the page, exactly how it fell out — no hedging, no pulling punches. She'd detail every good and graceful moment they'd had, every little soul, respectable and rotten, they'd encountered. She wasn't any kind of scribbler, but if she set herself to the task, maybe, just maybe, in time someone might come along down the line, read this and see it her way, their way, feel it from the inside out. Then, the meaning of what had happened might shift some.

Armstrong would've killed them, Eddie didn't doubt it, and if he hadn't gone through with it that night, the judge's gavel would've finished them off, bringing the punishing law down upon their heads. So, if she were meticulous, if she told it straight and true, then at least the burden of carrying that cold, blizzarding night would finally be shared. *Whosoever finds this*, she began. *All I've ever known of love is in this story. Now it belongs to you.*

She detailed the murder and Annie's disappearance, describing how she'd concealed the body. She told of her private grief and how after finding Annie's mother she'd returned to the Riverdale Courts apartments every so often, for a cup of tea and some conversation, until the year Frances died in her sleep. Eddie wrote of her family in Hamilton, of how her parents had died without welcoming her home, and of Henry, who'd been softened, not hardened, by the war. He'd periodically made the drive into Toronto to see her until he too died, of sepsis from an abscessed tooth. She wrote of her bowling friends, who'd learned of Annie's tragic death reading the papers. To pay their respects, Evelyn and Dot had planted a Peace rose in Eddie's backyard. She'd outlived them all, including that rosebush. And though there were other pretty girls here and there — met at the alley or in some club at closing time — there never was another made for her.

After Eddie's words had all been spent, she carried the pages into the living room and set them face up in the bottom of her Monopoly game box with the original Deed of Trust beneath the tokens and houses and chance cards. She replaced the lid and left the game on the mantel.

LAURA LET HERSELF into the Condor house nervously, but there were no signs of a break-in, nor of Astrid and Buddy. The house appeared to be empty, and it was remarkably quiet. No wind rattling the windows, no creaking floorboards, not a single sliver of sound.

Using the flashlight, she made her way down the hall into the dining room where she'd left the suitcase full of newspaper clippings. Shivering, she sat at the table in one of the rickety wooden chairs. *Oh!* Her stomach dropped like an elevator. *Had she really been visited by a …* She couldn't finish the thought. She wasn't thinking clearly, that's all, and was stressed out about the IVF cycle and her relationship. Now that she'd stopped moving it all landed on her: Astrid and Buddy, dropping into her life and making her feel things again — how much she was still grieving her mother, her icy marriage. She'd ripped the door to her life right off its hinges. She'd left Cat! Didn't most people make an appraisal first? Leave for someone else? What had *she* left for? Her tongue was dry, and her mouth tasted like dope. If she were finally pregnant, would it still be Cat's child too? In the pitch of night, by the chalky glow of the flashlight, she looked around and the uncertainties didn't matter anymore. The world seemed to have fallen into place. It was all here — the vintage canisters, the old icebox and tea cart with the stained cup, the antique furniture, the sweet little upstairs room that could be made into a home office, the possibility of a fresh start — everything she needed. A house to love.

Marilyn had been bent over in the bay window, rummaging inside the bench seating where she'd stored her costumes, when she'd told Laura about her plans for dealing with the Alzheimer's.

"Where's that darn thing?" Marilyn had said, sounding flummoxed. "The one I found at that place in your neighbourhood." She was tossing blouses and skirts and scarves over her shoulders. "It's in here, somewhere."

"Mom, come sit down." Laura had bought them sushi and udon noodle soup as takeout. "The soup's getting cold."

"They don't make tails like that anymore. You won't see another tux like it."

"I was with you when we bought it. Remember?" She'd been the one to pull it off the rack at Thunder Thighs and the one to pay the curly-haired guy behind the counter. She'd also seen the performance of her mother channelling Marlene Dietrich while tap dancing to *The Muppet Show* soundtrack. The performance was a hit with the art scene crowd, well reviewed in NOW magazine, and the *Globe and Mail* had called it "a provocative commentary on children's sexuality." Laura hadn't understood it.

Marilyn stopped what she was doing. Her shoulders fell almost imperceptibly. Gently, she closed the bench and sat on top of it. "It's getting worse," she said. Her voice wavered, though she was trying to appear stoic. "We need to talk about a plan."

"You're fine. You look fine. Everyone forgets things as they age."

"I've been to see a lawyer, Laura. There will be nothing for you to worry about. I don't have any savings, but I have no debts, either. Sell this place if you want. I don't care. Find a family with young children. Or another artist."

"You love this house. I don't understand what you're saying."

"I'm saying you can't measure love by the square foot. I'm saying soon you'll have to do the remembering for the both of us." Marilyn stood. "Listen, I won't want to, I will fight you on it, but when the time comes that I don't know you anymore, put me someplace nice and walk away."

Bursting into tears, Laura said, "I could never do that. I could never leave you."

In the dark of the Condor dining room, Laura wiped her face dry with the back of her hand. The last few days had been exhausting. Marilyn had ultimately caught pneumonia brought on by a lung infection, but love doesn't end with death. Some relationships continue on, albeit changed. "Oh Mom," she whispered, and then she took a couple of deep, stuttering breaths. She reached into her bag for the Deed of Trust, unrolled it, and pressed it flat. She again read the beneficiary's name: Miss Annie Armstrong. Annie was the girl Laura had seen in the online photograph, and the one the papers had reported dying of exposure during a blizzard. What exactly was her connection to Astrid? And was Astrid really following Laura around thinking she had a claim on this house through a dead relative? Was Laura a stand-in, a surrogate intruding on someone else's meant-to-be? No, she thought. The house had chosen her. Of all the people who could've been asked to sell this property, she was the one sitting here now. It was her job to transform the place.

She tore the document in half. The sound was satisfying so she continued tearing smaller and smaller strips, until she was certain that no one would ever be able to piece it back together. There, she'd made another big decision. Would it be a conflict of interest for her to buy the house? There were no registered claims on the property. It wouldn't be illegal. She reached into the suitcase to lift out a stack of clippings. Out the window there was only the deep, dark, and endless white night. She shone dim light onto the faded print of the articles.

From what Laura could read, the police had interviewed dozens of people searching for leads to the unsolved murder of J.T. Armstrong. They'd spoken to his lodge brothers, and each of his employees at the brickyard. They'd held one former employee in custody, a paraplegic named Dominic Pannito, because they thought he had a motive. He was released once the police confirmed his whereabouts on the night of the murder. Taken together, the newspaper articles painted a picture of Armstrong as a respectable man, one who'd raised his only child himself, after his wife, Frances, had abandoned the family. Laura didn't believe it. Women don't walk away from their children, she thought. Not without a compelling reason. There must be more to it. She riffled through the clippings and pulled out another page, this time an obituary in the *Star Weekly*. It had been circled in pencil:

> ARMSTRONG — (née Hall) Frances Kathleen. Born October 10, 1909, in Manchester, England. Passed away July 5, 1957, of influenza, in Toronto East General Hospital. Predeceased by parents, Wellington and Marie Hall of Manchester, daughter, Annie of Toronto, and Annie's father, J.T. Armstrong. Fondly remembered for her singing voice by friends and neighbours at the Riverdale Courts housing complex. Interment at St. John's Norway Anglican Cemetery, by issue of the Office of the Public Guardian and Trustee.

So that explained how the Deed of Trust had ended up in Isla and Greg's co-op. Frances Armstrong must have lived in the very same apartment! Laura scanned column after column, searching for any scrap of information that might help puzzle out how the coincidences fit together. *Was it the only copy of the deed?* Surely the homeowner would've kept one? Her heart raced. *What if a copy was hidden around here?* She yawned, too tired anymore to play detective.

With the flashlight in hand, she climbed the stairs to the second floor. It was cold in the house, the kind of cold that had come upon her gradually, through a process of accretion, lowering her core temperature and making her feel she'd never get warm. In the master bedroom she threw herself down onto the lumpy mattress, one arm dangling over the side of the bed. The flashlight shone across the floor, and within minutes her eyelids were falling.

Then ... on the other side of the room ... there for anyone to overlook, where you'd least expect it ... She clambered back up onto her feet, chased over, and unzipped the tan bag first. She shone the light around inside. Only two five-pin balls. She unzipped the white bag with red piping. Again, no deed to the house. She slumped down, back against the wall. That would've been too easy.

A moment later, she lifted out one of the old bowling balls and there inside, on the bottom of the case, faded, flaking, barely noticeable except close up with the beam of white light on it, was a smear of blood. She bent over to take a closer look. The stain was small and brown, but it was definitely there. She sniffed it and found it stale and flat and coppery. All at once, the ball scorched her palm and she dropped it with a thud.

"WHERE IS SHE!" bellowed Annie's father. He smashed in the front door window, knocking Eddie's small cedar wreath to the porch floor. Then, he unlocked the house from the inside and charged through the front hall and up the staircase. Before they could finish dressing, he was kicking the bedroom door open. "You goddamned bull dagger thief!" Snow flew from his tweed overcoat and his wet boots puddled the hardwood floor. By candlelight his features were ghoulish. The puppy barked and Eddie struggled into her undershirt and flannel shorts and stood to shield Annie.

"Easy Mr. Armstrong. It ain't what you think."

"What I think, is my safe is empty and my no-good whore of a daughter is in your bed." He swayed in the doorway wagging an Inglis pistol. His peaty, malt whiskey breath filled the room. Annie frantically slipped on Eddie's plaid shirt and buttoned her own denim pants up the sides. She pulled the gold bedsheet around her shoulders.

Eddie tried to think what to do. She flashed on the small pair of scissors in the other bedroom. No way to get there. The window was sealed, and even if it weren't, and they called for help, no one was out there to hear them.

Armstrong stepped forward and the candle on the dresser flickered. "I kept you on when the Italian boys said they didn't like sharing the latrine with a lady. 'She's no lady,' I told them. 'Just cheap labour.'"

"I'm no thief either," said Eddie.

"Stop beating your gums! Where are you hiding it?"

"I told you, I don't have your money."

"Liar!" He lifted his arm, pointed the gun at Eddie's chest. "Hand it over before I drop you!"

"It was me!" shouted Annie. "I took it. Last week, after I made the rounds with the envelopes. I took it out of the safe."

"You little scrag! Just like your mother, gone with the wind and more than happy to clean me out."

"Eddie didn't know anything. I swear."

"She made a run for it too but then she came back begging, sure she did, and so will you when the money runs out."

"Mother came back?"

"Looking to take you with her and crying for a handout, when every man in town knew where to find her and how much it would cost him too. No way in hell my daughter was mixing with the likes of her, and here you are, ruined anyhow."

Eddie eased toward the dresser, where the candle burned, and Armstrong retracted the hammer on his pistol. "I'm warning you!"

"Hurt her and I'll never tell where I put it!"

Eddie was almost within reaching distance now. She licked her index and thumb and ... one more step ... The room fell into darkness. There was breathing and for that brief moment it seemed, to Eddie, as though she'd snuffed the whole ordeal, as though none of it were happening. Then Armstrong's footsteps advanced. "I'll kill you both!" The puppy whimpered. They had only seconds, Eddie knew, before their eyes adjusted to the light.

Armstrong bumped into the chest of drawers and sent the framed picture of Annie's mother crashing to the floor. He stumbled. Tripped on the small area rug. "Sonofabitch!" He went down and the gun fired.

"Annie!?" Eddie's eyes were already taking in light. She squinted. "Are you shot?" She felt around in the dark, came upon the floor lamp. Gripped its iron spine for a weapon. She saw Armstrong on his feet again, lunging and swinging wildly. She ducked.

They could all see each other now, Annie in between them, a foot away from her father. "Thieving whore!" he shouted, and he backhanded her hard across the face. The impact sent her reeling into the dresser. She hit the floor, holding her cheek in both hands. A crimson spill leaked out between her fingers and once again she tasted metal. Her father's lodge ring had cut into her face, a bloody pattern of stars.

She scrambled across the hardwood with the puppy at her side, found the bowling ball case. Unzipped it. Felt inside for a wooden sphere. She gripped the bowling ball tightly in the palm of her hand, stood with the sheet half-hanging off her like a wedding train. She turned.

Eddie was on her knees, shielding her head with her hands. Her father, with his back to her, was towering over Eddie, his sausage fingers gripping the gun, the gun shaking in his unsteady hand. She lifted the wooden ball high with both hands and brought it down as hard and fast as she could. A Headpin Split. Her father's skull cracked open. The gun clunked when it hit the floor. Point value of eight. Annie dropped the bowling ball. It rolled under the bed, trailing blood. Out the window, snow fell in white walls.

Eddie stood with a look of horror on her face. "What have you done?"

Annie, heaving soundlessly, gaped down at her father and at her blood-soaked hands. "Oh my God! Oh my good God! I only wanted to stop him!" She reached out for Eddie, but Eddie flinched. A strike had been played, a deadly strike. Eddie threw herself into the mustard-coloured glider. Annie ran.

LAURA SLID BACK against the bedroom wall. An inky sky churned outside the windowpane as a horrible scene flashed behind her eyes. A drunken man with a gun. Two terrified women. A frightened puppy. The bullet hole was low on the wall, by the floor, near where she'd laid the flashlight. It was about the diameter of a cigarette tip and ragged where the bullet had shot through the wallpaper and plaster. The bowling ball cases had concealed it. She circled the hole with her finger and felt her spine stiffen. The murder had happened in this very room! She spun the rose gold ring on her finger, Annie's ring, and a faint spell of heat, a pulse, radiated up her hand. She turned the ring clockwise, then counter-clockwise, as if unlocking a safe. The story finally clicked.

Annie and Eddie, December 1944.

Laura's heart thundered inside her chest. Of course, the home-owner's name: Edna. How had she not made the connection before? Eddie was Edna. She glanced over one shoulder. Astrid could be there watching. She pushed up onto her feet and stepped over to the window. Astrid could be anywhere …

Snow was falling and it was hard to see out. Laura spread her fingers against the icy windowpane and the sky crackled with electricity. *Ow!* A jolt passed through to her hand and ran up her arm, just as it had each time she and Astrid had touched. Her shoulders tightened to knots. Her limbs went rigid, and then she knew, as surely as she'd known that she wanted to carry a child: there were things about this life that defied reason — invisible, illogical, inexplicable things. Astrid was one of them.

She raced out of the bedroom and navigated the staircase in the dark. Her limbs loosened as she descended, heavy, heavier with each step. Nobody was in the living room or the dining room. *Where was she?* Warmth spread from her abdomen to her forehead, and she knocked into the tea cart. Cups rattled in their saucers, the sound of chattering teeth. She stood in the middle of the living room, bewildered. *What on Earth was going on?* Night peeked in between the gap in the curtains. *What would her mom say?* She'd say, *believe*, thought Laura. Of course, she would; Marilyn had lived in a world of art and imagination; she'd always had faith that a mystery was more important than a certainty.

Laura paced in the dark, synapses firing, and her skin charged and prickling with the mystery unfolding. There could be no sleep now. Should she call Beth, have her come over? Should she call the police? With the bullet hole and the bloodstain, she had new information that could help them close their case. Her phone was dead, and she wasn't going back outside alone, not in this weather. Maybe she didn't want to report what she'd discovered? And there was still the question of whether a copy of the Deed of Trust was hidden in the house. In the morning, when it was light, she could search the property. *For now, what?*

Feeling along the fireplace mantel, she came upon a deck of playing cards and a couple of old board games. She lifted the dusty lid on the first game and rummaged through a nest of small wooden houses and hotels, wads of thin paper money and some other pages. It was only when her fingers touched upon the tiny metal game piece, a Scottish terrier, that she heard barking.

SHIVERING UNCONTROLLABLY, THE girl slumped against the brick remnants of a dilapidated kiln. She'd run to Boultbee with the puppy trailing and the bag of stolen money. She'd ducked through the hole in the fence at the dead end and snuck into what was now Harper's Dump, where neighbourhood boys searched for old blasting caps, and where one of them had blown himself to pieces. She struggled to breathe. The wind picked up and flurries obscured her view.

Her father's was the last pit still in operation, along the west side of Greenwood. The Bell Brothers', the Toronto Brick Company, and the biggest one, the Wagstaff pit, now formed a valley of broken milk bottles and hospital mattresses, a frozen river of litter and tramp waste. Wearing only Eddie's plaid shirt and a pair of blue jeans, the cold was unbearable. All she wanted was sleep. A deep, dark slumber. She cradled the puppy and slunk down the outside of the chimney. She pulled the gold bedsheet around her shoulders, encasing herself in an icy chrysalis. Each time the wind blew, another white wave drifted overtop of her, burying her a little more.

LAURA CRACKED THE door and shone the flashlight outside. She fiddled nervously with the lockbox. "Who's there? Astrid?"

No reply.

She stepped out onto the porch and strained to get a better look. She squinted, could barely make out the girl's silhouette. "I heard your dog."

"Invite us in," said Astrid. Against the dark slate of night, she was a two-toned figure.

"Thought you said you didn't need an invitation."

Astrid lifted the puppy from her coat, as if he were her partner in crime. "I lied."

Laura began to shiver, not from the cold, from a reluctant recognition that she'd known all along it would come to this. She watched Buddy nuzzle Astrid and then lick her face. Could the girl even feel the weight of the puppy in her arms? Or his smooth, warm tongue on her cheek? Did Astrid feel the cold and the ice underfoot, the hard, unyielding loneliness of a premature death? Laura had been feeling it for too long, since she'd lost Marilyn.

"I'm sorry," she said.

"Don't you dare pity me!" said Astrid. "At least I know what I'm missing."

"You're right," said Laura. She'd wasted too much time despairing at loss and scheduling life around her menstrual cycle; *tick, tick, tick*. Hers was a semi-detached existence. She'd forgotten how to live — the hardest thing of all to do.

Astrid gave a weak smile and climbed the first step. "This is Eddie's house," she said.

Laura nodded, wordlessly. Knowing the story was not the same as understanding it. Far in the distance, beyond the house, snow and ice seemed to touch the sky.

"I've been gone a long time," Astrid continued. "A really, really long time."

"And your name," Laura pressed. "Your real name?" The answer was already echoing inside her head, *Annie. Annie Armstrong.*

Astrid took the second step. "I was once the daughter of James and Frances," she said. "Now I'm nobody."

"Don't say that."

"But it's true," said Astrid.

No one ever intends to abandon love and yet it happens. It happens time and again, in homes, in streets, in cities like this one where circumstances collide, and a desperate, driving fear sends a body running.

All of a sudden, the street lights flashed on, illuminating her face and the army surplus bag slung over her shoulder. Behind her, a deep, dark city was buried under ice. "You've been using me," said Laura.

"I didn't mean to, not at first." Astrid stepped closer. "I need your warmth, just for a little longer."

"I'm cold now," said Laura.

"And tired?"

"Dead tired." All day she'd felt she was meant to be somewhere, or was forgetting to do something, fading, blanching. Had it really been less than one week since the storm began? Mere hours since she'd left Cat? It felt like much longer and yet it didn't; time had collapsed together like multiple exposures on a frame of film. She lifted her face to the onyx sky. "Look," she said. "It stopped snowing. That's that, I guess."

Astrid vaulted up the last two steps, landing on the porch. "No, it can't be!" She stood right in front of Laura and yet sounded far away, her voice less defined somehow, and the oversized white coat she wore was softening, becoming uncertain, almost blurry around the edges, its colour blending into the snowy background. Was she vanishing again, right before Laura's eyes? "We're running out of time," she said. "Buddy, come!" The dog leapt onto the porch and stood between them, barking madly.

A melancholy ache pulsed behind Laura's breastbone. They would disappear for good now, she could already feel it, the loss, a bit of beauty going out of the world, like a light.

Astrid stomped her boot. "It's time!" she repeated.

Let me in.

As Astrid faded, another faint spectral figure appeared at the threshold of the doorway, glowing a burnished golden hue, purplish pink around the edges. Riveted, Laura watched in disbelief as the figure beckoned.

"Laura!"

She wanted to believe that nothing really ends, not time or love; love merely changes form, like the weather. Her skin prickled with sensation, a weightless fluttering. No longer caught between who she was and who she wanted to be, she stepped aside. "Welcome home," she said.

Astrid and Buddy rushed into the house, and just like that, something shifted in the air. The temperature rose and Laura began to warm. Minuscule cracks formed in the ice as the storm loosened its grip. Melting snow would soon begin to slide off branches and poles, off rooftops and awnings. People would begin moving around out of doors and the city would again sound slushy and wet. Tomorrow, someone from the Office of the Public Guardian and Trustee would call her brokerage with news that the homeowner had died. For now, there was only this: a cold December night, three people and a dog whose lives had been braided by time and place and circumstance. Laura watched Eddie and Annie receding backwards down the hall, the rose gold light spreading into the house, until they dispersed like vapour.

NOTE TO READERS

Five-pin bowling was invented in Toronto around 1909, by Thomas F. Ryan. In 1940, Tillie Hosken of Toronto became the first woman to bowl a score of 450.

The Rideau Club of this novel was, in fact, located on Gerrard Street East where the Redwood Theatre now stands. The Brickyard Bistro of the opening scene — a casualty of the COVID-19 pandemic — was a beloved neighbourhood hot spot. Its location is a historical marker of the brick pits that once lined what is now Greenwood Avenue. The Flying Pony coffee house Laura frequents with her clients is also now memorialized on these pages. Happily, Maha's Egyptian Brunch survives, and on any weekend, patrons can be found lining up down the street waiting for a table.

Readers may already know that the board game Monopoly, originally called the Landlord's Game, was invented in 1903 by a U.S. woman named Lizzie Magie. She designed the game as a protest against the big real estate monopolists of her time and to promote the theories of land reformer and economist Henry George. The iron, racing car, thimble, shoe, top hat, and battleship were among the original set of game pieces introduced in 1935. The Scottie dog and wheelbarrow were not added until the early 1950s. However, as Astrid's dog is a Scottie, I hope readers will forgive me for taking liberties.

Finally, the Great Snowstorm of December 1944 remains the worst blizzard in Toronto's recorded history.

READERS' GUIDE AVAILABLE AT CORMORANTBOOKS.COM

ACKNOWLEDGEMENTS

Heartfelt thanks to Marc Côté, editor and publisher at Cormorant Books, for ongoing belief in my work, and the entire Cormorant team: Sarah Cooper, Barry Jowett, Sarah Jensen, Marijke Friesen, Luckshika Rajaratnam, Diyasha Sen, Fei Dong. Gratitude beyond measure to my agent, Hilary McMahon of Westwood Creative Artists, a tireless champion. The faith of trusted others can uphold an artist's faith in their own work during challenging times. I thank the Ontario Arts Council, and the various publishers who supported this project through the Recommender Program. Without the assistance of the Writers' Trust of Canada Woodcock Fund this book would not have been completed.

I gratefully recognize: Dionne Brand and Shani Mootoo for offering comments on an early draft. Helen Humphreys who listened with enthusiasm. Kathleen Olmstead for her long-ago alter ego, Astrid — and so much more. Historian Joanne Doucette, for her walking tour of Leslieville, Laura Pettigrew-D'Addario, Sarah Carver, Kate Grossi, Jesse Shiffrin, for answering legal and real estate questions. Sally Cooper, for hand-holding and still being in it with me, and John Miller, for all the years. Jane Byers, Kristyn Dunnion, Christa Couture, Rose Cullis, Brian Francis, Alexandra Shimo, for creating community. Violet Pettigrew-Olliffe, for being my favourite listener, and for giving my protagonist her surname. A mighty thank you to Shannon Olliffe, for the gorgeous cover art on this book, and for sharing a life with me. I am eternally grateful for Linda Dawn Pettigrew, my mother, and for all our adventures — past, present, and future.

For acts of kindness large and small I cannot thank the following enough: Megan Bannon, Juana Berinstein, Helen Berry, Sarah Blackstock, Anuta Bondarenko, Rosanne Brown, Cleo Pettigrew-Brown, Laura Cavanagh, Cheryl Champagne, Sarah, Taya Mae, Rebecca and the late Heather Chernecki, Florencia Choto, Averill Clarke, Erin Rielly Clarke, Sean Conforti, Roewan Crowe, Tara Cubie, Daphne Curtin, Wendy Czaus, Laura Pettigrew D'Addario, Brian Day, Denise Deziel, Emma Donoghue, Samuel Engelking, Paolo Eugenie, Andrea Fabian, Linda Gagatsis. Dr. Ralph George, Anjula Gogia, Rabbi Aviva Goldberg, David Goutor, Lee Gowan, Catherine Graham, Eileen Graham, Tanya Hallman, Dr. Curtis Handford, Dr. Rashida Haq, Janet Harrison, Clive Holden, Jean Jackson, Lorne, Mary Jane and Kristen Johnson, Carina Karain, the late Judy Kondrat, Matti Korhonen, Paul Kowalski, Lynne Kutsukake, Gail Luciano, Pat Magosse, Rabbi Miriam Margles, Janice Martin, Mel McCallum, Derek McCormack, Maria Meindl, Lori Mizen, Jennifer Morrow, Shannon Neufeldt, Isaac Meyer Odell, Lisa Odoni, Anne Parker, Evalyn Parry, Lisa Patterson, Meri Perra, Joanne Pettigrew, Kerry-Lee Powell, Suzanne Robertston, Lori Ross, Chris Roulston, Dana Rudiak, Shelley Savor, Shlomit Segal, Mallory Silver, Jeanne-Mey Sun, Su-Ting Teo, Taylor Thompson, Amy Vreman, Andrea Warnick, Wellspring friends, Alissa York, Bryan Young. Finally, I thank my east end community, and my late pup, Peggy.

We acknowledge the sacred land on which Cormorant Books operates. It has been a site of human activity for 15,000 years. This land is the territory of the Huron-Wendat and Petun First Nations, the Seneca, and most recently, the Mississaugas of the Credit River. The territory was the subject of the Dish With One Spoon Wampum Belt Covenant, an agreement between the Iroquois Confederacy and Confederacy of the Ojibway and allied nations to peaceably share and steward the resources around the Great Lakes. Today, the meeting place of Toronto is still home to many Indigenous people from across Turtle Island. We are grateful to have the opportunity to work in the community, on this territory.

We are also mindful of broken covenants and the need to strive to make right with all our relations.